SECOND TO NONE
Muriel Jensen

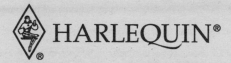

HARLEQUIN®

TORONTO • NEW YORK • LONDON
AMSTERDAM • PARIS • SYDNEY • HAMBURG
STOCKHOLM • ATHENS • TOKYO • MILAN • MADRID
PRAGUE • WARSAW • BUDAPEST • AUCKLAND

ISBN 0-373-70842-4

SECOND TO NONE

Copyright © 1999 by Muriel Jensen.

All rights reserved. Except for use in any review, the reproduction or
utilization of this work in whole or in part in any form by any electronic,
mechanical or other means, now known or hereafter invented, including
xerography, photocopying and recording, or in any information storage
or retrieval system, is forbidden without the written permission of the
publisher, Harlequin Enterprises Limited, 225 Duncan Mill Road,
Don Mills, Ontario, Canada M3B 3K9.

All characters in this book have no existence outside the imagination of
the author and have no relation whatsoever to anyone bearing the same
name or names. They are not even distantly inspired by any individual
known or unknown to the author, and all incidents are pure invention.

This edition published by arrangement with Harlequin Books S.A.

® and TM are trademarks of the publisher. Trademarks indicated with
® are registered in the United States Patent and Trademark Office, the
Canadian Trade Marks Office and in other countries.

Look us up on-line at: http://www.romance.net

Printed in U.S.A.

"I'm here to apologize. I didn't realize that you…"

Veronica looked into Mike's eyes and knew what had brought about his sudden and careful remoteness. Someone had told him about her. She regretted that it placed even more distance between them, and she was determined to put an end to it. "There's no need to keep apologizing. My past is over. If we're going to be crossing paths, you'll have to start thinking of me as a regular person."

If she'd surprised him with her bluntness, it didn't show. She guessed there probably wasn't much that surprised a former cop.

"All right," he said finally. "Get in. I'll close your door."

Veronica couldn't decide if that was courtesy on his part, or an eagerness to get rid of her. In any case, she drove away without a backward glance—except in her rearview mirror where Mike Delancey was perfectly framed, a tall figure standing in front of the beautiful Victorian reproduction.

He was not at all what her nicely developing future needed. Or was he?

Dear Reader,

I'm sitting in front of the computer on a cold and rainy December day, a cat in my lap and my husband at work in his basement studio. I like knowing that when you settle in your chair and open this book it will be a warm and sunny summer day. (Unless you live in Oregon, too.)

What a remarkable medium books are. They put me in touch with you despite time and distance, and allow us to connect as if we sat across from each other over a pot of tea. I also like the notion that if you hold on to your books, thirty years from now your granddaughter, heading off to work on the new international space station, might put one of my titles in her backpack.

Until then, I offer you this second book in the Delancey Brothers trilogy. I have to admit I'm fascinated by wounded people who carry on bravely, despite their pain. I hope you enjoy this look into the lives of Mike Delancey and Veronica Callahan. They live with me still.

Sincerely,

Muriel Jensen

To Diane and Wayne McVey for all the fun!

CHAPTER ONE

MIKE DELANCEY WALKED into the quiet kitchen and made a pot of coffee. He relished the few minutes of solitude the early morning ritual afforded him before his brothers rose, and peace became a distant memory.

Tate, older than Mike by three years, would be sharing ideas for promoting the winery even as he hurried down the stairs. And Shea, Mike's younger brother, would wander down in a semi-comatose state, then come to life the moment he stepped into the kitchen. He would want to make eggs Provençal for breakfast and talk about the opening of the restaurant.

But all Mike wanted was his cup of coffee and a moment to call his own. He loved his brothers, and everyone else who lived on the Delancey Winery compound, but he was still finding the balance in his own life and sometimes needed a brief escape. He poured a cup of steaming French roast and pushed his way out the back door.

The sweet Willamette Valley air was cool and smelled of pine, June wildflowers and the commercial grasses and herbs that grew farther south. Mike stopped at the bottom of the porch steps to take a deep breath.

Tate, who'd come to French River from Boston, was fascinated by the freshness of Oregon air. After twelve years in Dallas, Mike was captivated by the beautiful views in all directions: the rippled hills of the winery, the purple mountains in the distance, the green everywhere, even in the dead of winter.

The compound, bequeathed to him and his brothers by their uncle Jack, was situated at the top of the winery's terraced hill. When he and his brothers had first arrived here in January, there'd been an unobstructed view from here of the long rows of grapes, the road to French River and the farm across the road, which sat at the foot of still more hills with mountains in the background.

Now a Victorian-style house Tate designed stood in the way, and was quite a sight in itself. In another month or so, it would open as the Delancey Bed-and-Breakfast, and Mike, who was responsible for public relations for the winery, would take on additional duty as manager of the B-and-B.

Tate had sold his share in a Boston architectural firm to finance the renovation of the winery. That same boldness had been evident in the commercial buildings he'd designed over the years, so this foray into late-nineteenth-century ornament came as a surprise—to Tate more than anyone.

They'd all endured a long winter of adjustment to their new surroundings, to the rain, to the strange new responsibilities of a vineyard and its motley collection of buildings. But Tate had had the most difficult time. He'd fallen in love.

Colette Palmer, whose father had worked for Uncle Jack, had come to live at the winery two years earlier after her husband had died. Now her wedding to Tate was just two weeks away—but she hadn't been an easy conquest.

Mike took a long pull on his coffee and headed for the broad stairway that led to double front doors. It was a good thing, he thought, that he wasn't vulnerable to a woman's charms. His life was too bizarre already: tough cop turned vintner and hotelier?

He set his cup down on the porch railing, pulled a key out of his pocket, unlocked the big oak doors with their stained-glass windows, and walked into the house.

VERONICA CALLAHAN LOOKED OUT the second-story bedroom window at the hill of leafy grapevines and thought it was the most beautiful sight she'd ever seen. The rich green stretched almost to the road, then took on a lighter, subtler shade in the pasture on the other side. The hills beyond were purple, and the sky above, even in early morning, was already bright blue, with several small, puffy clouds adding charming contrast.

She loved it here. Something about the atmosphere was calming, steadying. Her terrifying and ever-present loneliness—the first emotion she could remember at age four—had been pushed way back in her mind by the beauty and the quiet here.

Here she could learn to be confident and look capable so that parents would feel comfortable leaving their children in her care. And to be fearless enough to deal with those children every day and not be swamped by the demands of their intelligence and their neediness.

She remembered the friends she'd left behind in Los Angeles, and then in Portland, Oregon, and felt homesick for the people, if not the places. But then she reminded herself that she had a friend in French River.

She'd met Colette Palmer on a tour of the winery a couple of weeks earlier. Since then, they'd talked on the phone and had met several times in Portland for lunch when Colette had gone to the city to shop. Colette had invited her here to talk about opening a day care center in the winery's empty barn.

Step One of her five-point plan—finding a location for her business—would soon be realized. She drew a calming breath and looked at her watch. Almost seven.

She took another moment to survey the empty room, drywalled but unpainted, and thought it was too bad it wasn't finished yet. Living at the B-and-B while she got the day care center in order would be preferable to driving back to town every night.

But that was a small problem. Her new apartment was convenient to everything and probably far less expensive than this room would be.

She shouldered her purse as she walked down the hallway's bare floor. Here, too, the walls were drywalled, but not painted or papered. She'd use a soft colored wallpaper with a small print and a bright border above the oak picture rails.

Imagine living here, she thought fancifully, *with an adoring husband and half a dozen children, and cats all over the place.*

The notion made her exuberant. *And I know what I would do, if they were out, and I was alone in the house.*

At the top of the stairs, she didn't stop to think, but just swung a leg over the thick, straight banister and started down with a little squeal of excitement.

MIKE HEARD THE SOFT CRY as he walked toward the parlor, and stopped. That had been a woman's voice. Long conditioning put every nerve ending on alert.

An instant later he saw her, and, conditioning or not, he was stunned. A young woman was sliding down the banister toward him, canvas tennis shoes coming at him soles first, slender legs in jeans held out for balance in a inverted V, arms over her head, a smile on her lips, short, dark hair flying around her face.

Then she spotted him. Her laughter turned to openmouthed surprise and she seemed to forget that she was about to run out of banister.

Mike braced himself, opened his arms, and prepared for impact. The next moment he was flat on his back with a woman who smelled of flowers sprawled on top of him.

He lay there one protracted moment, the wind knocked out of him. Then he finally drew a breath and moved sufficiently to realize that nothing was broken. But he became quickly aware of other problems: soft curves pressed against his chest, something round and also soft in his hand, a leg riding up his as she groaned.

Because of the length of time since he'd last experienced such an intimate embrace, his body reacted automatically.

She pushed against his shoulders suddenly, her cheeks pink, her brown eyes wide and horrified. She opened her mouth to speak, but no sound came out.

Then she scrambled to her feet and proffered her hand to help him up.

Ignoring it, he stood, feeling as though he'd crossed into another dimension. He was in the right house—but *where* had this woman come from?

"Hi," she said. Her voice was breathy. "I'm... Are you Tate?"

"I'm Mike," he replied, suspicions beginning to surface. "Who are you? What are you doing here?"

"Colette invited me," she replied. "You're Tate's brother, aren't you?"

He resisted the distraction of her easy smile. She was an intruder.

"She invited you to an empty house?" he asked doubtfully.

"We were going to have tea." She pointed over his shoulder toward the kitchen. "In there somewhere. She told me...to go straight through."

"Really? Then why were you upstairs?"

She closed her eyes a moment—to strengthen her resolve, he supposed. He noticed that her lashes were thick and dark. "I know I shouldn't have done that," she admitted, opening her eyes again and giving him a guilty look. "I wanted to see the view."

"You get a clearer view from *outside*."

Her eyes narrowed as if she finally understood the reasons behind his questions. "You think I'm a thief?" She spread her arms to indicate the empty room. "There's nothing here to steal."

He studied her levelly, trying to determine her sincerity. He used to be good at it in his old life.

"You didn't necessarily know that when you came in. How *did* you get in, anyway?"

"Colette left the back door open," she replied mildly, then added, "Are you this suspicious of everyone?"

"I don't believe Colette would leave the back door open. And why would she invite you for tea at 7:00 a.m.?"

Veronica felt flustered and naive, hardly the image she'd intended to present the owners of the Delancey Vineyard, her potential landlords.

She cleared her throat. "I'm here to talk business," she said with a dignity she knew was laughable under the circumstances.

"And you usually prepare for business discussions by sliding down a banister?" he asked.

She had to admit she had that coming. She smiled ruefully. "It was something I always wanted to do. And when I was given the opportunity, I couldn't resist. Hasn't that ever happened to you?" She looked into his chocolate-brown eyes, trying to assess his thoughts, but she couldn't see beyond the cool suspicion. So she answered her own question.

"No, I guess not. And that makes it hard to explain—"

"Explain what?" Colette walked into the house, a small, lidless box balanced on the flat of her hand. She looked from one to the other with a smile. "All *right*. I'm glad you've met. What's hard to explain?"

A pleat formed on Mike's forehead. He glanced at Veronica. "What she was doing sliding down the banister in a locked house on private property at 7:00 a.m."

Colette hesitated a moment, raised an eyebrow at Veronica, then laughed lightly. "I don't know the reason for the banister, but I can tell you I invited Vee here for a meeting. I have a full day that's starting early, and she's used to being up with the birds." She glanced from one to the other again. "Did you mistake her for an intruder?"

He seemed to have come to the conclusion that he wasn't going to escape this situation without embarrassment, and apparently decided not to try. He looked wryly into Veronica's eyes, then turned his attention to Colette. "In the future, you might let me know what you're up to." He drew in a deep breath and turned back to Veronica. "I apologize, Miss...?"

"Callahan," she said, offering her hand again, and resisting the impulse to appear righteously indignant. "Veronica. I'm sorry, too. I should not have been upstairs." She cast Colette an apologetic glance. "I was admiring the view."

"That's all right," Colette assured her quickly. "Vee, this is Mike Delancey, Tate's brother. He used to be a cop." She grinned and added facetiously, "And you have such a suspicious face."

Mike acknowledged the jab with a self-deprecating nod. In actuality, Veronica Callahan had a very open and innocent face—wide-eyed, pink-lipped and apple-cheeked. But he'd once arrested a woman who'd looked that innocent after having shot her boyfriend and their landlady's daughter because they'd spoken to each other on the apartment stairs.

"I apologized," he reminded Colette.

She laughed and gave his arm a squeeze. "So you did." She angled her head toward the kitchen. "Want to join us? We're going to talk about setting up her day care center in the barn. This was the best place to meet, since the house and the winery are both so busy. I unlocked the back door for her when I went to pick up the pastries." She smiled coaxingly. "You can share my coffee."

He shook his head. The day care center. He'd hoped Tate and Shea would change their minds about that. "No, thanks. I've got lots to do."

"Oh, come on," Colette wheedled. "If you listen to Veronica's plans, it might put some of your fears to rest."

"Fears?" Veronica asked. She took a step toward Mike as he started to leave. "About what?"

He really didn't want to go through this again. He'd argued with his brothers until he was hoarse about the incompatibility of a day care center with a winery. But they didn't see the problem, and he'd finally given up in exasperation.

"This is a winery," he said simply. "How smart is it to have children here?"

"You mean legally? I checked. As long as we don't give the children wine, we're all right. And, of course, I don't intend to do that. Apart from that, I think children would love this setting. It's so beautiful—"

"We're several miles out of town. Who's going to bring their children here?"

"All the people," she replied, "on their way to work in Portland." She pointed in the direction of the road at the bottom of the hill. "It's a perfect location. Lots of outdoor space, and Rachel's animals." When he expressed surprise that she knew about Aunt Rachel's menagerie, she added a little defensively, "Colette and I have met in Portland a couple of times. She's been telling me all about the compound."

Mike knew it was futile to argue with two women allied in a common cause. He smiled politely at Veronica Callahan, then at Colette, and excused himself.

He walked to the winery at the opposite end of the compound. On the first level, Armand Beauchamp, Colette's father, was seated at an old desk near the door. He looked up from a supplies catalog to wave at Mike.

"Good morning, Armand," Mike called as he ran up the stairs.

Two-thirds of the winery's second level was a storage area that would one day be used for bottles and labels, but which now stood empty. The other third was an office with movable partitions that allowed space for individual or group projects.

Tate sat at a desk in the corner, the wall beside him decorated with framed photographs his teenage daughters had sent from Paris. Interspersed were photos of Colette and her little girls.

Mike grabbed the back of his own chair and pulled it over beside Tate's. He sat down and began without preamble. "You still think a day care in the barn is a good idea?"

Tate concentrated one extra moment on the letter he was reading, then focused on Mike, an eyebrow raised. "Yeah. You said you were okay with it."

"No." He was surprised Tate had distilled his protest down to that. "You just wouldn't see it my way, so I told you to do whatever you wanted. But this is a *winery,* Tate. We make booze, for God's sake. Who's going to bring their children to a day care where they make booze?"

Tate gazed at Mike in silence, then shook his head. "You know, for the person in charge of public relations, you have a scary concept of what we do here. We don't make 'booze,' we make fine table wine— or we will, as soon as we get a harvest—and this is a beautiful place to which tourists bring their children every afternoon to walk the grounds and pet Rachel's animals. Why wouldn't other children be safe and happy here?"

"Those kids are visiting. When this Callahan woman brings kids here, they'll be around all day, every day. It just seems like an awkward blend of enterprises to me."

Tate leaned back in his chair as though something had just become obvious to him. "*She'll* be responsible for the children. You don't have to be concerned with them. She has credentials as long as your arm."

Mike frowned at him. "Come on, Tate. When kids are underfoot, every adult in the vicinity is concerned with them. And in a couple of weeks you and Colette and the girls are leaving for your honeymoon, so who's going to be responsible for what happens around here? *I* am."

Tate was wearing the expression that meant he was going to get paternal on him. The only thing that drove Mike insane about this man—for whom he'd die in minute—was that even now, when they were in their thirties, Tate could turn into the Big Brother.

"Well, I'd like to be able to promise you you'll never have to be responsible for another child's safety again, but you've got to know that isn't realistic."

Mike shot him a severe look. "I'm not talking about that. I'm talking—"

Tate, however, had taught him the look and gave as good as he got. "Yes, you are," he interrupted. "You've learned to live around it, but it still affects every decision you make about your future. Because you're a conscientious and sensitive individual, you're holding yourself responsible for that woman and those kids, and that's self-destructive. Not to mention completely unnecessary."

Mike opened his mouth to dispute the analysis, but Tate raised a hand to stop him. "I know," he said.

"You explained to me it's not really that you're assuming the blame, but that when something so awful happens, the survivors feel responsible anyway. The department shrink told you the situation was already hopeless when they called you in."

"Nothing's ever hopeless," Mike insisted moodily. "Otherwise, what's the point of trying to negotiate a hostage situation in the first place?"

Tate nodded. "But when somebody's drugged out, the whole equation's distorted. You're trying to bring reason to a situation when you're operating on a different plane of reality. As hopeful as you want to be, I'm sure sometimes you know it's just not going to happen."

God. Mike had always thought memories lived in your head, but this one had taken root right in the middle of his chest. Every breath he drew had to go around it. Every emotion he experienced had to elbow the memory aside.

"Look," Mike said reasonably. "I got into this winery thing with you and Shea because I was ready to take my life in a new direction. But having a day care in the middle of our—"

"Won't be at all like a hostage situation," Tate finished for him. "Come on, Mike. You've got to confront this. You can start fresh, but not by hiding from what you left behind."

Mike ran a hand over his face. "Yeah, well, for the moment at least, I'd like to try it. That barn's going to take six men a month to make habitable."

"The crew is going to power-wash it and give it a quick white spray. According to Colette, Veronica thinks the barn's the perfect size because she can bring playground equipment inside in the winter. The guys'll put up a few walls inside and install a furnace, but she's doing all the painting and decorating. In return, she has two months rent-free. Every building on this place has to pay its way. I'm just trying to protect your investment.''

Mike sat up in his chair. "Well, then you'd better double-check and triple-check all her references, because she seems a little flaky to me. She was sliding down the banister when I walked into the B-and-B.''

Tate laughed as he handed him a sheet of paper. "You're kidding!''

"I'm not.'' Mike perused the résumé. Besides Veronica Callahan's name, address and phone number, there was a long list of schools where she'd been educated, and then five separate schools at which she'd taught kindergarten through the second grade. All of them were private schools. She'd also counseled at a teen center.

He looked at Tate in concern. "Don't you think she moves around a lot? She's been all over the place. She's taught at five schools and she's only— what?—'' he checked her birth date and calculated "—thirty? Either she moved every other year, or she was asked to leave—or was being chased.''

Tate shook his head, grinning in a way that made Mike suspicious. "She wasn't asked to leave, she was transferred.''

"Schools don't transfer teachers around.''

"They do if they're nuns.''

Mike stared at him, the shock of his brother's announcement clashing in his mind with the memory of Veronica Callahan lying on top of him, all soft and fragrant. He remembered for a moment, then refocused.

"A nun," he said flatly. "A nun came flying at me off the banister."

"An ex-nun," Tate corrected. "Now she's just a woman."

Kids *and* a nun—a woman. *Great.* His life was right on track—backward.

"I'm sure you'll like her once you get over this bad start. From what Colette says, she seems very genuine and not at all sanctimonious."

Mike stood to leave. "I guess we'll see."

Tate got to his feet and put an arm around Mike's shoulders. "You have a suit for my wedding?"

"No. I don't think I've even worn one since Mom's and Dad's funeral, and you lent me that one."

"I can lend you one again."

Mike headed for the stairs. Tate followed. "No, I should buy one. There are a couple of events coming up that call for something other than my jeans and boots— You got the ring?"

"Yeah. We're all set."

They stopped at the top of the stairs. It occurred to Mike that when they'd started this venture, he and his brothers had been without women in their lives. Tate's ex had remarried a diplomat and taken his daughters to Paris to live, and Shea had clearly left his heart in San Francisco with a woman he'd refused to discuss.

Tate's first marriage had changed their relationship, of course, but they hadn't actually been as close then as they were now. They'd had big plans in their youth, and a belief in their invincibility. But they'd since lost their parents in an accident, and individual calamities had befallen each of them.

Then their uncle Jack had been legally declared dead in January after an absence of seven years, leaving the winery and all its properties to be shared equally among Tate, Mike and Shea. Jack's disappearance remained a mystery, though Mike and his brothers were making an effort to find answers. In the meantime, bringing the winery back to life was teaching them each other's strenghts and weaknesses and deepening their relationships.

No bond, Mike thought, was quite as strong as the one forged by shared grief and adversity. It made the gift of a brother or a friend invaluable.

He clapped Tate on the shoulder. "I wish you happiness. It's too bad your girls can't come."

Tate nodded. "We talked it over, and they decided they'd rather be here for Christmas. Susan and Sarah are taking special language classes this summer, and that's important if they're going to be living in France."

"But you're still going to have two kids with you on your honeymoon. You're sure about that?"

"Yeah." Megan and Katie, Colette's two daughters, were seven and eight. "They're pretty excited about getting a father. I'd hate for my first official act as their dad to be to leave them behind to take off with their mother. You guys still okay with Armand taking over my old room when we come back from Banff?''

"Of course. Shea and I both like Armand."

"Good. I didn't want him to move, but he insisted."

"Don't worry about him. He'll be fine with us. Anything else?"

"Yeah." Tate grew serious. "You willing to live with the day care thing?"

No, he wasn't. It was going to prey on his mind until the children showed up, and then would probably cause him sleepless nights. But Tate had given up so much to get the winery going—and not just as an investment in his own future, but in Mike's and Shea's as well. Right now Mike didn't want Tate to worry about anything.

"Sure. I'll adjust. And I should probably start by apologizing to Sister Mary Trouble."

"I really think this is a good idea."

"Sure." Mike said the word with convincing sincerity as he started down the stairs. But in his heart, he knew there wasn't a chance of that happening. Veronica Callahan represented the two things he'd sworn he'd never be involved with again: women and children.

CHAPTER TWO

VERONICA BIT INTO a buttery cream cheese pastry and moaned her approval.

Colette put down her coffee cup and indicated the few crumbs on her paper plate. "I know. Isn't it wonderful? I've probably gained ten pounds since Shea started testing recipes for the tasting room and the restaurant."

Veronica chewed and swallowed, thinking that no one could look better at 7:00 a.m. than Colette did—and there was no evidence of an extra ten pounds on her. She had bright, curly red hair that framed a fine-featured face and lively gray eyes. Her warmth had appealed to Veronica the moment they'd first met, and had gone a long way toward diminishing her loneliness. During their several lunches in Portland, a friendship had been born.

"You must burn it all off working on the vineyard. Is Shea going to cook for the B-and-B, too?"

"No, Rachel's going to do that. Shea's swamped with last-minute preparations. The restaurant opens when Tate and I—and the girls—get back from our honeymoon."

"There's so much happening here."

Colette smiled thoughtfully. "When Tate and his

brothers first inherited the winery, I knew everything was going to be different. The Delancey brothers have so much energy and enthusiasm, and I expected to hate seeing things changed and tourists swarming the place.'' Veronica could sense the moment when Colette's thoughts began to focus on Tate, because she heaved a deep sigh that was all contentment and anticipation. ''But now I feel as though my life's been recharged. As though…'' She paused, presumably to grope for words, then apparently decided the thought was too big for them. She smiled at Veronica. ''Anyway, it's wonderful here. I know you'll be happy. And don't worry about Mike. He's really a wonderful man.''

Veronica wasn't so sure about that. ''I understand why he was suspicious of me,'' she said, reaching for her coffee. ''But I hope he's not going to act that way around the kids.''

''He's good with children,'' Colette assured her. ''My girls love him. I think his reluctance to have a day care center here has something to do with his days as a cop.''

Veronica waited, interested.

Colette looked grim. ''He was a hostage negotiator. I don't know all the details, but this druggie killed his wife and children while Mike was trying to talk him out of it. Mike knows it wasn't his fault, but he still blames himself.''

Veronica could only imagine the horror of that experience. Watching children suffer when you couldn't do anything to help them must be unbearable. "How awful," she said.

"Yeah." Colette pushed away from the table. "He's trying hard to move forward, but it's got to be difficult. Come on. Let's go look at the barn again."

THE BARN WAS HUGE but somehow friendly. Veronica loved knowing that it had been built more than a hundred years ago, that animals had been cared for here, that someone had sat here on frosty mornings and milked a cow, or groomed a horse. Her own life had been a very urban experience, but a part of her had always longed for life in the country.

She smiled. Almost every little girl wanted to own a horse or play in a barn, but she guessed few had embraced those dreams for the same reasons she had. At least, she hoped not.

"I told Tate about the partitioning you'd like in here, and he's sketching out a plan." Colette walked across the concrete floor, looking up at the loft. "If you approve it, the work can probably be done by the wedding."

"You did explain that I'm coming to this with extremely little capital?" Veronica tore her mind from the dreams she had for the space and back to reality. "I can't afford architects from Boston."

Colette dismissed that with a curve of her lips. "He wanted to use the barn for something, and I think he's happy to have another project." She walked to the right side of the building and stretched her arms out to indicate the area. "I told him you wanted to be able to bring the playground equipment inside during the winter."

Veronica followed her. "Right." Then she pointed to the other side. "And a big room for general play, then two smaller rooms for naps."

"Right."

Colette gestured toward the loft. "I wondered if you might want to turn that into an apartment for yourself? Then if parents run late or want to come in early, you won't have to worry about the commute. I know you just got your apartment, and it's not far—but fifteen minutes is fifteen minutes. What do you think?"

No travel and being able to look at the view of the vineyard anytime she wanted? Veronica was touched by Colette's thoughtfulness. "I'd love it, of course," she said, "but you don't think everyone else will think I'm…intruding?"

Colette laughed lightly. "We're all 'intruders.' Rachel lives here because her husband was a friend of Jack's. He invited her to stay after her husband died and left her broke. I came when my husband passed away so my father could help me with the girls, and I could work with the grapes. And Tate and his brothers are here because Jack disappeared and they finally inherited the place." She paused. "The crew can do your apartment first so you can be here to watch over the rest of it."

"I'd love that," Veronica admitted unashamedly.

"Great. And we'll carpet for you, too. Something

tweedy that won't show every little spot but will be easy to clean and still protect the little darlings when they fall.''

Veronica eyed the floor. "That'll cost a bundle.''

"Tate has connections. You still want to do the painting yourself?''

"Absolutely.''

"Okay.''

The arrangement was far better than okay. She gave Colette a big hug. "I don't know how I blundered into such good deal, but I'm so grateful. I had a feeling the day I met you that you were going to become an important part of my life.''

Colette held her in the hug a moment longer. "So was I. I didn't know then that you'd left the convent so recently, but I thought I recognized a kindred spirit. I've had to start over against difficult odds, but I had my girls and my father. You're all alone.''

Veronica drew back and smiled. "I don't feel all alone anymore. Thanks for caring so much.''

Colette looped an arm through hers and started toward the door. "Actually, I have a ulterior motive. I need a favor from you.''

"Anything.''

"Will you stand up for me at my wedding?''

Veronica stopped several yards from the door. Sun beamed in on them from grimy windows. "Are you teasing?''

"Of course not.'' Colette shrugged as she prepared to explain. "I moved here two and half years ago, but for most of that time, I've worked long hours.

I've made acquaintances in town, but no real friends. I feel as though I know you as well as anyone. Will you? We're getting married on July third.''

Veronica felt joy bubbling through her. She was getting a life! ''Of course. I'd be honored to.''

''Good. Do you have plans for this afternoon?''

''Nothing critical. I was just going to get paint and wallpaper samples.''

''How about if the girls and I meet you in town for lunch and we go dress shopping? No taffeta or chiffon, but something practical we can all wear again.''

Dress shopping with other women. That was something she'd never gotten to do in the convent. Or before. She agreed calmly as they walked out into the compound, knowing Colette probably wouldn't understand a leap into the air and a click of her heels. The simple pleasure of shopping would be no big deal to anyone else.

''Where's your car?'' Colette asked.

Veronica pointed to the B-and-B. ''I parked on the other side. I guess that's why Mike didn't see it when he went into the house.''

Colette put an arm around her shoulders. ''That was good for him. Men are so sure of what they know. I think they need to be shocked every once in a while. I've got to get to work. See you this afternoon.''

Veronica walked across the sunny compound with a spring in her step. She did a full circuit of the fountain that stood in the middle surrounded by col-

orful pansies, then continued on her way, excited by
ideas for the day care center. This was what she'd
wanted for so long. She couldn't believe it was actually happening.

Then, before she could feel too secure about her
future, she spotted a tall, lean man propped against
the trunk of her old, light blue compact, arms folded,
ankles crossed. *Mike.*

She resumed her purposeful stride, unwilling to let
him see he made her anxious. First, he was a man,
and as a nun she'd had very little experience with
them. She'd known priests, of course, as well as fathers of students and repairmen, but she hadn't
known men on an equal footing. Her veil had placed
her on an untouchable level. Still, she'd experienced
an attraction to him that was unlike anything she'd
felt before. She'd found it both exciting and unset-
tling.

Second, she knew he didn't want her here, and that
was a major threat to her burgeoning self-confidence.
And to the new life she was trying to establish for
herself. The life that might one day—if she was really lucky and determined—banish the loneliness forever.

He straightened away from the car as she approached, and she noticed things about him that her
previous life had conditioned her to ignore. Broad
shoulders stretching his Dallas Cowboys sweatshirt,
formidable biceps, long, strong legs in old jeans. She
remembered in vivid detail what it had felt like to be

sprawled on top of him. Despite her inexperience, she hadn't felt endangered—at least not physically.

"Hi," she said. "I thought you were out of the business of giving parking tickets."

He met her gaze, but didn't smile. "I am," he said finally. "I'm here to apologize."

"That isn't necessary. Your suspicions were understandable."

He agreed with one perfunctory nod. "But I didn't realize that you…"

She looked into his eyes and knew what had brought about this sudden and careful remoteness. Someone had told him about her. Though his apology was chivalrous, she regretted that it placed even more distance between them.

She went past him to put her key in the lock. "Well, it was either let me land on you or let me fall on my backside. I'm glad you chose the former."

He held the door for her while she tossed her purse in. "I'm sorry I was rude."

She was determined to put an end to this now. "There's no need to keep apologizing. I was a nun, but I'm not that delicate." She spread her arms, forcing him to look at her. "I've survived. If we're going to be crossing paths, you'll have to stop envisioning me in a black dress and a veil. All right?"

If she'd surprised him, it didn't show. She guessed there probably wasn't much that surprised a former cop.

"All right," he said finally. "When does your day care open?"

"In about a month. Tate's going to have some partitions put up, and the floor carpeted. Colette thought they'd be finished with that by the wedding. Then I have to paint and paper and move in some furniture."

"You know, with Tate gone, I'll be too busy to help you. Will you be able to manage on your own?"

She gave him smile that had nothing to do with mirth. "That's my specialty. Anything else?"

"Get in," he said. "I'll close your door."

Veronica couldn't decide if that was courtesy on his part, or an eagerness to get rid of her. In any case, she reversed expertly into the compound, then drove away without a backward glance.

Except one in her rearview mirror, where Mike Delancey was nicely framed, a tall figure standing in front of the beautiful Victorian-style home.

He was not at all what her nicely developing future needed.

"TUXEDOS?" MIKE LOOKED at the sign above the rental shop as Tate, Shea and Armand walked in. "I thought we were wearing suits."

Tate beckoned him inside. "Changed my mind. Colette was talking about her, Veronica, Rachel and the girls getting dresses they could wear again, and I decided we were being too casual about this. A wedding should be special—particularly a second one, where you get to apply all the lessons you learned during the first. So the ceremony should be bigger, better."

Shea frowned over a pink cummerbund on a mannequin torso placed on a glass counter. "But there were eight hundred people at your first wedding. This is little country church."

Tate gave Shea an impatient look.

"He means bigger and better in spirit," Armand explained, paternally cuffing his shoulder. "In the approach to it." Then he grinned at Tate. "A man after my own heart. It's good to astonish women with your sensitivity once in a while. It prevents them from thinking they have the upper hand."

Shea raised an eyebrow at Mike, as though asking if *he* understood what Armand was talking about. But Mike returned his attention to something else Tate had said. "Colette talked about her and *Veronica* getting dresses?"

Tate leaned over the counter, looking at the ties and ascots displayed inside. "Yeah," he said absently. "Veronica's her maid of honor."

As Tate's best man, Mike was less than delighted with that news. There seemed to be no escape from the woman he was certain would be a problem.

"I didn't realize she knew her that well."

"They've become good friends in a short time. She's moving into the loft in the barn."

Before Mike could comment, a small round man with a tape measure around his neck appeared from behind a curtain at the back of the shop. He eyed the four of them in a clinical way. "No pink or lavender accessories, and no ruffles, am I right?"

''You're right,'' Tate said, shaking his hand. ''We're after morning coats.''

''Fashionable choice. Let me get some measurements.''

Forty-five minutes later, the four men walked across French River's main street.

''Now where?'' Shea asked.

''We're meeting the girls for coffee. We're supposed to pick them up at the dress shop by the bank.''

''Don't call them 'girls,''' Shea advised him. ''They don't like that.''

''Megan and Katie are girls,'' Tate disputed.

''Yeah, but don't lump the women in with the girls. It gets you in trouble every time.''

Tate and Mike stopped short. Shea's observation was clearly a commentary on the woman in San Francisco he consistently refused to talk about. ''And how do you know this?'' Tate asked.

''Experience.''

''With whom?''

''Doesn't matter, just trust me.''

Tate met Mike's eyes with a grin. ''Thought I had him that time.''

Mike slapped Shea on the shoulder. ''Someday she's going to come looking for him, and we'll see her for ourselves.''

Shea laughed scornfully. ''Her last words to me consigned me to hell. I don't think she'll be dropping by any time soon.''

VERONICA STARED at her reflection in astonishment. She could hear giggles and playful banter as Colette helped her daughters into matching yellow organdy dresses in one dressing room. In another, Rachel, who'd been declared mother-of-the-bride for the occasion, was trying on a soft green chiffon with pleats.

But in this narrow cubicle with a mirror and an empty hanger dangling on a hook, Veronica looked at a total stranger—herself.

For twelve years, she'd worn the simple blue jumper, white shirt and blue veil of the Sisters of Faith and Charity. Then in the six months she'd been out of the convent, she'd taught an English-as-a-second-language class in two very plain suits, both navy blue, that had been given to her by the St. Vincent de Paul Society. When she'd moved to French River, she'd bought a few functional clothes at the thrift shop.

It was exciting to see herself in yellow. The dress was the chiffon Colette had insisted they didn't want, until Tate had changed her mind for her. It had a simple round neck, a short, flirty, three-layered sleeve, a nipped-in waist emphasized by appliqued flowers with seed-pearl centers and a full tea-length skirt.

The style flattered her tall, slender figure. And the color lent an apricot glow to her complexion and a sparkle to her brown eyes.

But something had to be done about her hair. She tugged at the short do that skimmed her eyebrows and her earlobes, then lay in a simple, masculine cut in the back. Under a veil it had never mattered, but now she thought it shattered her fragile aura of femininity.

She heard Colette and the girls leave the dressing room and go into the shop to look in the big mirrors.

"How're you doing, Rachel?" Colette called.

"I'm coming," Rachel replied. "Looking like a very large grape leaf, but I'm coming."

Veronica continued to stare at herself. It wasn't vanity, but a sort of fascination. Not that she'd be wearing yellow chiffon every day, but this was the woman she could be when the occasion warranted. It amazed her.

"Vee?" Colette again.

"Coming," she called back, fluffing her skirt and combing her fingers through her hair in a vain attempt to give it a little height.

The first people she noticed when she walked into the shop were Colette's daughters, standing together in front of the large mirror, looking like an Anne Geddes photograph. Their flat little torsos emerged from bouffant yellow skirts like the pistils in a lily. Megan, the eight-year-old, had rumpled braids, and Katie, seven, had a disheveled ponytail, though Veronica had been there half an hour ago when Colette had brushed it.

Veronica rushed forward to wrap her arms around them. Even when she'd finally realized she'd entered the convent for all the wrong reasons, she'd stayed because of the children constantly crowded around her.

"You are so beautiful!" she told the girls. "Oh, and you, too, Aunt Rachel." Rachel stood to the side, fussing with the sash at her hips. She looked lovely, the dropped waist concealing her slight plumpness.

"But look at Mommy!" Megan said, pointing to the other side, where Colette stood.

She'd chosen a simple, fitted dress with a straight skirt of ecru lace. It was set off by a veiled pillbox hat perched atop her red hair, which was coiled into an elegant twist.

"You look like a magazine cover!" Veronica said.

"Well, look at *you!*" Colette exclaimed, then said to someone behind Veronica, "Isn't this color perfect for her?"

Veronica turned, expecting to see the clerk who'd helped them make their selections. Instead she faced four watchful males, studying her with varying levels of interest.

Armand smiled at her with fatherly indulgence. "The bride will have competition for everyone's attention," he said with Old World gallantry.

Tate's expression was fraternal as he moved across the room to put an arm around Colette. "If I didn't have eyes only for this woman, I'd find out what you were doing after the wedding."

The other man, who must be Shea, seemed stricken. "I know a woman who wore that color all the time." He sighed, then seemed to pull himself together. "It looks even more wonderful on a brunette."

Mike heard Tate say, "Aha! Now we know you're

carrying that torch for a blonde or a redhead.'' But he was too distracted to join in the banter that followed.

The only thing on his mind was how much more difficult his life was going to be with Veronica around. She was beautiful. And though he'd briefly held that trim body in his arms, he hadn't realized just how perfect it was.

Feelings he'd thought long dead weren't dead at all. They were asleep. And waking up.

It wasn't simply lust. That would be easy enough to deal with. This was interest…longing. Lust with depth and complications. He wanted to touch her, but he wanted to know her, too. What had sent her into a convent? What had brought her out again?

She'd been a nun. He'd seen things she probably couldn't even imagine in her worst nightmares.

No. If he got to know her, she'd get to know him, and that might not be a good experience. It had certainly sent Lita, the last woman in his life, running in the opposite direction.

Anyway, he didn't want anyone that close right now. He wasn't ready. He might never be ready.

Katie came to take his hand, and smiled up at him, all freckles and sparkle. ''Don't you think she's pretty, Uncle Mike?''

He couldn't lie to a child or to a former woman of the cloth. ''I think she's beautiful, Katie,'' he admitted, smoothing her hair.

The men decided to wait outside while the women

changed. Mike couldn't remember ever being so desperate for a breath of fresh air.

THE WEDDING PARTY FILLED the small coffee bar with laughter and loud conversation. Veronica sat in the midst of the din and thought how wonderful it was to be surrounded by such joyful noise.

Katie sat in Tate's lap, Megan talked nonstop to Mike, and Shea, his moroseness banished, was having a serious discussion with Rachel about breakfast menus for the B-and-B.

Colette grinned at Veronica. "Those three are always charming the men," she said with a jut of her chin in the direction of her daughters and Rachel. "We don't stand a chance of getting any real attention."

That was fine with Veronica. She just enjoyed watching the happy group.

She noticed the rapt attention Mike paid to Megan, and the little girl's complete confidence that she had his interest. He might not want other children around the compound, but he certainly seemed to treasure Colette's daughters.

"We're starting on your loft tomorrow, Veronica," Tate said from the far end of the table. He pulled a sheet of paper out of his shirt pocket. "This is what I had in mind to make best use of the space. Will that work for you?"

Colette leaned toward Veronica as she unfolded the sheet and studied the rough blueprint for her new home. A bath and bedroom were side by side at the far end of the oblong space, a U-shaped kitchen took up the middle and a breakfast bar separated it from the living room at the front.

She noticed a narrow space that ran along the very edge of the loft. "What's that?" she asked, holding up the sheet and pointing to the strip.

"It's the gallery," Katie answered. "For keeping books and plants and things. And it's gonna have windows so you can see down into the day care."

Colette looked startled. "You didn't even tell *me* that," she complained to Tate.

He shrugged. "You weren't sitting in my lap when I did it."

Colette poked a playful finger at her daughter. "That's because someone else is always in it."

Katie giggled and leaned back into Tate's chest, apparently not feeling repentant.

"I think it's wonderful!" Veronica folded the sheet and handed it back. "I appreciate all the trouble you're going to for me."

"We're happy to have someone in the space. It'll make the compound completely operational."

"I can help you with a nutritional menu for the kids' snacks and meals," Shea offered. "And we can order your food with ours to make it more economical."

"Shea's the sweet one," Colette said to Veronica in a stage whisper.

Shea pretended modesty.

There was simultaneous grousing from Tate and Mike.

"She plays up to him for his white-chocolate-macadamia-nut brownies," Tate accused. "*I'm* the sweet one."

"No, you're the orderly one," Shea corrected. "The detail-obsessed slave driver who never gives any of us a moment's peace."

Tate opened his mouth to dispute the point.

"Save it," Mike advised before Tate could speak. "That was more on target than a smart bomb."

"I think Mike's the sweet one." Rachel, seated between Mike and Shea, patted Mike's arm. "He takes me shopping once week, and he even had a step installed on the Blazer to make it easier for me to get in."

Mike spread his hands wide—the seated equivalent of taking a bow.

Then Rachel added with a taunting grin, "You just don't think of him as sweet because he always looks as though he's going to arrest you." She elbowed him affectionately. "You do have to lighten up, dear."

Veronica watched Mike take the resultant laughter and ribbing with good-natured aplomb. This man was not at all what she expected.

CHAPTER THREE

VERONICA WATCHED THE CREW at work and wondered if this was what an old-fashioned barn raising looked like. Except that in this case, the barn had been put up a hundred years ago and now its innards were being renovated.

Half a dozen men swarmed over the barn, cutting holes for large, modern windows, and building walls both downstairs and up in the loft, according to Tate's specifications. A full kitchen was installed in the day care, as well as a small, efficient one in her apartment.

Then the carpet came, a mottled hunter green that was vibrant and patterned to conceal dust and spills. Veronica walked across it one evening when the workmen had gone and found it wonderfully springy underfoot.

She sat down in the middle of it, drew up her knees and looked around. Except for light fixtures, which would be installed tomorrow, the structural work was done. Now it was her turn to paint and paper—and get ready for business.

She blessed the impulse that had made her come to Delancey vineyards for a tour three weeks ago. When she'd left the convent, a relative of one of the sisters had gotten her the ESL job in Portland. While she'd been grateful for it, she'd known immediately that she didn't want to stay there. The small parks throughout the city were beautiful, and Portland was a wonderful city, but for the first time she was able to *choose* where she would make her home, and she wanted to live in the country.

She'd wanted it since she'd been a girl. From the moment she'd become aware of the ugly world surrounding the filthy tenement rooms that were all they could afford after her mother had spent her welfare checks on drugs and alcohol, Veronica had dreamed of living where there were grass and trees, and animals that didn't come out of the walls at night to fight you for your food.

Once, when her mother had been in rehab, Veronica had stayed in a foster home with a TV. She'd watched reruns of *Green Acres* and enjoyed the antics of the characters. But mostly she'd thought the setting marvelous. She'd decided that when she grew up, she'd live in the country where there'd be no neighbors screaming on the other side of the wall, no dark alleys...no loneliness. Country people always looked so well-fed and cheerful—and they always stuck together.

Veronica lay back on the carpet, closed her eyes and said a prayer of gratitude. Tomorrow, Tate and his brothers were moving unneeded furniture from their house into her loft. She would bring her few possessions from the apartment and stay overnight for the first time.

She had accomplished so much more than she'd expected to—and so quickly. Good. Step Two of the plan—finding an apartment convenient to her business—almost completed.

MIKE'S GAZE FELL to the newly laid carpet as he pushed on the half-open door of the barn. He was here with a message for Veronica from Colette, but he forgot it temporarily as he admired the renovations.

The walls looked neat and sound, and the upstairs had been completed, though not yet painted, windows looking down on the playroom below.

And it was as his eyes swept the rest of the area that he saw Veronica lying on the floor. His heart lurched. What had she fallen from? Or had she just collapsed? Earlier he'd watched her helping the workmen put up wallboard, then roll out the carpet padding. She'd probably overdone it—

He was halfway toward her, his concern mounting, when she sat up, looking perfectly sound, and blinked at him in bemusement. He stopped in his tracks, relieved and exasperated. He drew a steadying breath. "If you're going to take a nap," he said, "don't sprawl out on the floor that way. I'm liable to draw a chalk outline around you."

He almost expected her to be annoyed with him, but she laughed instead.

"Sorry." She got lightly to her feet. "As you can see, there's nothing to lie on but the carpet. I was just relaxing. Did you need something?"

She wore a pair of baggy, dark blue sweats, splattered with paint. The pants hung on her, yet failed to detract from whatever there was about her that he always noticed.

She smoothed the sweats self-consciously, probably thinking he'd been studying her with criticism rather than admiration. "I got my wardrobe," she said, "from the St. Vincent de Paul Society and the thrift shop when I left the convent. You won't find it at Bloomingdale's."

He looked down at his own winery "uniform" of jeans and sweatshirt. "I, on the other hand, am outfitted by JCPenney's..." He indicated his jeans, then plucked at his sweatshirt with its Dallas Boys' Club logo. "And the fund-raising efforts of a friend of mine."

"You worked with a boys' club?"

"No. My old partner did, and I often got roped into helping out. The shirt sale was to raise money for gym equipment..." That was all he wanted her to know right now. It wasn't like him to talk about himself, even in a general way. But she'd looked embarrassed about her clothes.... "Colette wondered if you needed the winery's truck to move your things."

"I've ridden in that beast with Colette. It's pretty temperamental, and I can't drive a stick. But tell her thanks. I'll just make a couple of trips in my car."

"Actually, she was offering you the truck and an assistant with stick experience."

She raised an eyebrow warily. "You?"

He tried not to be annoyed by her obvious reluctance. "Me. Tate's picking up some friends who are coming out for the wedding. And Shea's busy cooking for the reception."

"It's not that I'd prefer someone else's help." She seemed impatient that he thought so. "It's just you've made it clear you don't want me here, so I'm sure there are things you'd rather be doing."

That was frank. He responded with equal honesty. "That's not entirely accurate. I don't think the day care center should be here. It has nothing to do with you personally."

"You're sure?" She smiled suddenly. "You're convinced I'm not a B-and-E artist, but you always look as though I worry you. Are you afraid I'll force you to pray or light candles or something?"

He didn't think he'd ever known a woman who'd kept him so off balance—and he'd known a few who had loved to try. But this one didn't seem to be playing at anything, and that was somehow harder to deal with.

"B-and-E artist?" he asked, trying to unsettle *her*. "You talk more like a cop than an ex-nun."

She shrugged and folded her arms, her stance becoming just a little aggressive. "My mother did time in every prison east of the Mississippi, several times for breaking and entering. But mostly for drugs and prostitution."

He had to concede that round. He was pitched a little further off balance, while she seemed to root herself in place, as if she'd taught herself to stand firm under the assault of childhood memories.

"I'm sorry," he said with quiet sincerity, his earlier annoyance with her evaporating.

She shrugged again. "Everybody has something ugly to live with. But that's beside the point. I can move my things over tomorrow, a little bit at a time. Thanks, though, for the offer."

He knew it was chauvinistic of him, but he'd never be the kind of man who could happily let a woman tell him what to do. He'd be the first one to admit they were equally intelligent and capable, but upbringing and instinct made him feel responsible.

A policeman protected the small and the weak and anyone else who asked for help, and although he was off the force, at the core, he'd always be a cop.

"I'll be at your apartment at nine," he said, ignoring her attempt to interrupt him. "It'd help if you had boxes packed already. We have the wedding rehearsal early in the evening."

She followed him to the door, still objecting, but he turned only to remind her, "9:00 a.m.," then walked away.

EVERYTHING VERONICA OWNED was in the bed of the truck in less than an hour.

Mike looked at the dozen or so boxes, and the clothing on plastic-wrapped hangers held together by a rubber band, and asked in surprise, "This is it?"

She nodded. "Yeah."

"No furniture?"

"No." She reached into the truck to secure the flaps on a box. "I took a vow of poverty, remember?"

He frowned and closed the tailgate, then walked around to open the passenger door for her. "I guess I didn't realize that was meant literally."

She dropped her purse on the floor and climbed in. "It was a promise," she said as he handed her the end of her seat belt. "You took all your oaths as a cop literally, didn't you?"

"Of course I did. But they didn't require that I face the world with only twelve cardboard boxes."

"They required you to risk your life." It amused her that he was less horrified by that. "Poverty's easier."

Mike looked uncomfortable, and shifted the conversation.

"We scrounged you a table and chair and a couple of other things from the house, but you have no bed, no sofa, no television." His message of doom delivered, he closed her door and walked around to climb in beside her. "You're going to have to spend your life standing up."

"I'll sleep in the bathtub."

"People only do that in the movies."

She shook her head as he backed the truck out of the driveway. "That isn't true. I slept in a bathtub in New York for several months when I was about nine. I even had to keep the plug in so nothing climbed out of the drain."

He stopped before joining the mid-morning traffic to focus on her. "You're kidding."

"No. It was quite comfortable." Veronica always made references to her past with a smile. It masked the ache the memory brought. "So, don't worry because I don't have a sofa. I've dealt with worse deprivation. And if I'm in the tub, you won't be tempted to draw a chalk outline around me."

He waited for a mail truck to pass, then drove half a block and stopped at a red light. He turned toward her, as though trying to see how she really felt.

"Your mother was in or out of jail at the time?"

"Out. She…you know…worked in the bed."

He said something under his breath that was seldom heard in a convent. "Where the hell was Children's Services? You must have been in foster care when she went to jail. Didn't anybody notice it was happening a lot?"

Veronica wondered why she'd made the tub remark. She had only talked about her past to a couple of priests, and once to another nun. It would have been much easier to let his casual remark about her lack of a bed lie unchallenged.

She didn't think she *needed* to talk about it. She'd made her peace with the past long ago—the day she walked into the motherhouse of the Sisters of Faith and Charity and offered them her future.

But she'd reneged on that offer twelve years later because she knew she didn't have a true calling. Did that mean she hadn't adjusted, after all? It was a sobering thought.

"I was finally taken away when I was twelve and went to live with the Porters, an older couple in Philadelphia who took in foster kids. My mother ODed in prison, and I stayed with them until I graduated from high school and joined the convent."

He studied her face for a moment, the said with a conviction that was unexpected, "You've made it your life's work not to be angry about your childhood, haven't you?"

"I'm not angry." She looked out at the sunlight gleaming off store windows and windshields and chrome. "My foster parents were loving and protective and taught me that your life is your life. You take what you get. And if you're in a bad situation, you do your best to make something good out of it."

"Are they still around?"

"No. They died within months of each other shortly after I went into the convent."

"Is that why you joined?"

She turned to him. "What do you mean?"

Another red light. He stopped the truck, then faced her again, his eyes gentle. "To make something good out of your situation? To atone for your mother? Or for yourself? For all the horrors you saw and endured and couldn't do anything about?"

It was an astute observation, but not quite on target. At least, she didn't think so. "I entered because I was lonely. I wanted people in my life who would be there, who would be dependable. My mother obviously wasn't that. She always wanted me back when she got out of jail, but I was never sure why.

And in the foster homes, kids came and went—nothing ever stayed the same. Val and Henry—my foster parents—tried, but they had other foster children, too. I never dated until my senior year. My past was so different from everybody else's, I didn't know what to talk about. And I didn't want anyone to know.''

She rolled down her window and breathed deeply. ''I'd been in the convent a couple of years, though, before I realized that. I started to wonder why I still wasn't happy, I examined my motives and decided I'd been looking for a big family, not necessarily for God.''

''Tate said you were part of the order for twelve years.''

''Yes. I'd started helping in the classrooms while I went to school myself, and I was enjoying the children so much, I couldn't leave.''

''But you could have taught outside the convent.''

''I didn't have my degree yet, and I couldn't afford to go to school and set up an apartment, buy a car and all the things working people need. And I was still somewhat confused, so I stayed in. And the longer I was there, the harder it got to think about leaving. I wasn't happy, but I was…safe.''

''Safe.'' He repeated her word as though considering what it meant. ''From what you went through as a child?''

''Yes, definitely that.'' They left French River and followed the winding, tree-lined road to the winery. ''About eight months ago, I went on a retreat. I did some serious soul-searching and realized I was using the convent not only to protect me from the past, but as a buffer against the future. Convent walls were a fortress between me and what might be expected of me on the outside. I was hiding.''

"What brought you to French River?"

She explained about teaching in Portland but longing for the country, and the sudden impulse to take the winery tour. "I was standing behind the B-and-B, admiring the view, and Colette approached me. We got talking…and we've been friends ever since. Then a parishioner I used to help in Portland heard about my wanting to open a day care and sent me a generous check for supplies. So I called Colette and asked if I could rent the barn." She hesitated a moment, then added, "I am sorry you disapprove, but I promise the children won't get in your way."

"Children get in the way anywhere. It's how they learn," he replied matter-of-factly.

Mike helped her carry her belongings to the loft, then looked around at the still considerable emptiness.

"What are you going to sleep on tonight?" he asked. "And please don't tell me you're curling up in the bathtub."

She pointed to the stack of boxes. "I have a sleeping bag in one of those. I'll be fine."

He didn't seem to think that was possible. "I'll bring the table and chair over right away, so you can at least sit down."

"Thank you. That would be nice."

As he loped down the stairs, Veronica put her meager groceries into the cupboards she'd washed and lined with paper yesterday. She had oatmeal, mesh bags of onions and potatoes, a string of garlic, a can of chili, a small bottle of olive oil, pasta, herbs and spices, a box of tea and a shaker of Parmesan cheese.

She would have to go shopping at the first opportunity. But tonight was the rehearsal, and tomorrow was the wedding.

She put two towels and two facecloths in the small cupboard under the bathroom sink, a hairbrush in the drawer and a bottle of aspirin in the medicine cabinet.

Then she hung her clothes in a closet with sliding doors, stopping to admire the shelf that ran along the top and the pigeonhole divisions on the bottom for shoes. She smiled wryly because she had very little to put into it.

She'd put two boxes of school and art supplies in the center, leaving one final box to unpack. She unrolled her sleeping bag and placed a thin pillow on top, then leaned a crucifix against the window.

Mike returned with a rocking chair, a battered coffee table, and gray metal shelving. "I know this is really ugly," he said as he put it, under her direction, against the living room wall, "but it might be useful until you can get something better. In the truck I've also got two small file cabinets. With a board or a door across them, you'll have a desk."

He brought those up, one by one, then gave her a

picnic basket. "Shea sent you some lunch and a few things for the kitchen."

"Oh!" Veronica delved into it excitedly, finding two sandwiches, a small casserole bowl of pasta salad, two apples, and two cans of pop. She smiled at Mike, warming to the idea of sharing her lunch with him. "It looks as if I'm supposed to invite you to join me."

He didn't even take time to think about it. "Thanks, but I've got a million things to do."

She nodded and moved to put the sandwiches and salad in the small refrigerator so he wouldn't see her disappointment. When she turned back to him, she had a bright smile in place and a hand extended.

"Thank you for your help." He took her hand in his, and she noticed its considerable size and strength. And its warmth. She drew hers away and folded her arms as she walked him down the stairs. "I appreciate your giving up your morning to help me."

"Sure."

The situation had become awkward, a circumstance fairly foreign to Veronica. She was good with people, and they usually warmed to her. But dealing with single men her own age was different. She felt awkward because he'd turned down her invitation, but he seemed equally uncomfortable. Because he'd rejected her? she wondered. But she was doing her best to pretend it didn't matter.

Either she wasn't as good an actress as she'd thought, or she still had a lot to learn as a woman.

"Do you need a ride to rehearsal?" he asked when they reached his truck.

She stood aside as he opened his door. "No, thanks. Colette and I are going to town to pick up my car this afternoon."

"All right. See you in church, then."

That, at least, was comfortable territory.

AFTER THE REHEARSAL, Veronica met Bill Markham and Gina Free, Tate's former partners in the architectural firm he'd left to come to French River. Their two-year-old, Jacob, was passed from lap to lap and fussed over particularly by Megan and Katie.

The couple had also brought with them Tate's former secretary, Cece Phips. The girl was blond with a buzz cut, an eccentric taste in clothes and a sweet, extremely enthusiastic nature.

Over appetizers at the Chinese restaurant where they'd all convened after leaving the church, Cece couldn't stop talking about Oregon.

"I didn't expect it to be so beautiful, you know?" She dipped fried wonton in duck sauce. "I mean, all everybody talks about is how green it is because it rains so much, but, I mean, there must be a *million* shades of green, and those yellow flowers along the road—what do you call them?"

Veronica knew the answer because she'd noticed them, too, and had asked Colette. "Scotch broom," she replied. "A real problem, I've been told, if you have allergies."

"I'm strong as an elephant," Cece boasted after a

bite of the crispy appetizer. "Had all the childhood diseases, but now I never catch anything. No allergies, no sensitivity to food." She smiled wryly. "A few phobias, though. And sometimes I go at things too anxiously and I screw up. I *want* to do it perfectly, but I sort of go into overdrive." The smile became rueful. "Guys don't like that. You either have to be helpless or totally together. But if you're sort of competent, but not entirely, then they're tempted to get involved but don't like it that you mess up, so they kind of come and go—you know what I mean?"

Veronica was tempted to explain that she'd just come out of the convent and really didn't know at all. But it seemed like the wrong time to get started on that. So she ignored it altogether. "Maybe you're just meeting the wrong men."

Cece nodded as though that was a possibility. "I go to school part-time. I'm a Psych major. College guys are either party, party, or they're totally intense! And the clients at Markham, Free, and McCann are so into their building plans, they don't even see me."

"That could change tomorrow." Veronica passed her the mustard for the barbecue pork. "Some wonderful man who's looking for all the qualities you possess could walk right into your office, or your lecture hall, and you'll be the first one he notices because he's ready to find you, and you're watching for him."

Cece considered her words wistfully. "You think?"

"Sure."

"Are you married?"

"No." Veronica saw Cece's faith in her prediction shrivel, forcing her to explain anyway. "But I've been a nun since I graduated from high school. I just left the convent a couple of months ago."

Cece's eyes widened. "A nun! How cool! So you must, like, understand everything. Life, purpose…"

"Actually, no. We struggle along the way everybody else does. We simply have more time to pray about it."

"Wow."

Tate interrupted, pushing a tall, lanky young man into the chair on the other side of Cece. "Cece, I'd like you to meet Tony Fiorentino. Tony, Cece Phips with Markham, Free, and McCann. She came for the wedding. Tony's spending the summer out here and is working with the crew that's doing the renovations around the winery. I spotted him in the lounge and knew you had to meet him."

Tony had a gold hoop earring, curly dark hair, a beautiful beaky nose, and a smile that was all for Cece.

"You'll never believe where Tony goes to school," Tate teased.

"Where?"

Tony was obviously pleased to tell her. "I'm a Psych major at Southern Massachusetts University."

"You're kidding!" Cece squealed.

Veronica turned away discreetly as the conversation between Tony and Cece took off. Mike had slipped into the chair on her other side, and she felt an instant resurgence of that uncomfortable feeling she'd experienced when he'd turned down her invitation to lunch.

She decided to fight it. "Did you get your million things done?" she asked with a smile, then tacked on, as if the answer didn't matter, "Did you get some of this pork? It's wonderful."

"Only 999 thousand of them," he said, helping himself to a piece. "The rest will have to wait until after the wedding. Did you eat both sandwiches and both apples?"

"Yes," she lied, "and all the salad. I did save you a pop for another time, though."

She was sure he knew she was teasing, just as he was teasing her. It seemed to be a way to skate over the strangeness of their relationship. Or their acquaintanceship, she mentally corrected—it could hardly be called a relationship. And she liked being able to challenge him about his rejection of her invitation by telling him there was nothing of significance left anyway.

He acknowledged her comment with a small nod. Then he reached into the pocket of his chambray shirt and handed her a business card. "Got you two candidates for your day care center."

She blinked as she took the card. "You did?"

"I ran into someone I know from the Rotary Club—Tate and Shea and I each belong to a service organization so we'll be involved in the community. Anyway, this guy has a girl and a boy, five-year-old twins. His wife's a teacher, and he happened to mention that she's taken a group of high school kids to Europe for the summer. Right now his twins are at their grandparents' until the middle of July, but he was wondering what to do with them when they come back. So I suggested you.''

''Well—'' Gratitude warred with guilt over teasing him. ''Thank you. But, why? I thought you didn't want a day care here.''

Mike didn't actually know why. Some do-gooder need to make peace for having opposed her presence after she'd had such difficult odds to fight? He didn't necessarily understand her, but he could relate to her uphill climb.

He smiled self-deprecatingly. ''Everything doesn't always have to make sense, does it? Like sliding down a banister.''

She giggled. The sound was ingenuous and surprising, and warmed him deep inside.

''You're right,'' she said. She touched his arm, and he felt it in his fingertips. ''I can't tell you how much I appreciate it.''

''Sure. You can reach him at that number from 9:00 to 5:30, then at the number he wrote on the back in the evenings.''

Veronica read the information on the card: Bob Burgess Furniture and Appliances. The address was on Front Street in French River.

''He doesn't mind driving out here?''

Mike shook his head. ''He lives a mile beyond us. It'll be convenient for him.''

She grinned with the excitement of having her first two clients. "Told ya," she said.

He grinned, too, but shook his head at her. "Nice of you not to gloat."

She touched him again. "Thank you, Mike. Honestly."

He moved, intending to cover her hand with his, then caught a fried shrimp with it instead. "You're welcome," he replied, then excused himself to resume his place farther down the table, just as a team of waitresses wheeled in carts loaded with food. He could take Veronica's touch only in small doses.

Tony Fiorentino had apparently also excused himself because Cece claimed Veronica's attention, her cheeks flushed, her eyes bright.

"What was that you were saying about the right guy walking into my life at any moment?" As she piled food onto her plate, she went on to report everything she'd learned about Tony.

VERONICA LET HERSELF into the building, which was now outfitted with a dead bolt, and flipped on the light. She stood in the middle of the large space, admiring the beginnings of Green Acres Day Care.

It wasn't much now, but in a few weeks it would be the brightest, most cheerful place for miles. It was going to require a lot of work and energy, and she looked forward to every moment of it.

She went up to the loft, turning on more lights as she went through the living room and the kitchen.

What she was most anxious to be rid of, she

thought as she placed her purse on the counter and put on the kettle, was the silence. When it closed in on her—as it did now after a busy day filled with people—it reminded her of how alone she was.

When this place is filled with children all day, she told herself, *you'll be very grateful for this silence.*

But that was little comfort. Silence after a day spent with children was very different from the silence that lived with you day after day when you had no one else. And the few hours spent in the noisy company of the Delanceys brought that home sharply.

She should be grateful she hadn't had a sibling who'd had to endure what she'd been through as a child. But selfishly, she'd often wished she'd had the company. It would be nice, now that she could come and go as she pleased, to have someone to visit, to make plans and talk over problems with.

She'd had good friends within the order, but she'd left that life behind. She corresponded with some of them, but it wasn't the same as having them nearby. And Colette, her first friend in French River, would leave tomorrow night for several weeks in Canada.

She grabbed one of her two mugs, found a tea bag and waited for the water to boil. She went to the window that looked down on the slope behind the barn, and saw herself reflected back.

She told herself she would be fine. She'd been alone in one way or another for much of her thirty years, and she'd survived. She just didn't *like* it. But life was about learning to cope with what you got, not about getting what you wanted. And pretty soon her life was going to be filled with children. Step Three—friends—was accomplished, and she'd only been in French River a couple of weeks. What more could she want?

She smiled at her reflection, but chose not to think about it. She didn't want to be greedy.

The kettle whistled, and she filled the waiting mug with hot water. Then she turned off the light, walked into the bedroom—and stopped in the doorway.

Someone had tossed her sleeping bag and pillow onto a double bed already covered with a pink-and-green flowered bedspread. It was a four-poster with large, rounded knobs in a light finish—pine, she guessed.

She approached it slowly, shocked, wondering where it had come from. Colette? But why? She'd done so much for Veronica already.

And then a memory from earlier in the evening struck her like a sledgehammer, and she delved into her pocket for the business card Mike had given her.

"Bob Burgess Furniture and Appliances," she read aloud into the ringing silence.

After staring at the bed another moment, she climbed into the middle of it and sat down. The mattress was soft and cupped her body. With a sigh of pleasure, she let her head fall back against equally soft pillows.

Every muscle in her body seemed to loosen. But every nerve ending fluttered in confusion.

Mike Delancey had bought her...a bed?

CHAPTER FOUR

IN THE VESTIBULE of the church, Veronica adjusted Colette's hat to a jaunty angle and stepped back to study the effect. "What do you think?" she asked Megan and Katie, who pressed close, little baskets of daisies and ivy in hand.

"I think she's the prettiest mother in the whole world," Katie said.

"I must agree with that." Armand came from the men's dressing room, fussing with the unfamiliar tie. His wiry gray hair was combed into order, and the morning coat gave him a handsome elegance.

Colette handed Veronica her bouquet of roses and orchids and reached up to adjust his tie for him.

Katie and Megan trembled with excitement, taking every opportunity to swish the long skirts of their yellow dresses and to look for their reflections in the glass doors of the church. Their beautifully curled and upswept hair made them look like an ad for a children's shampoo.

Colette wrapped her arms around them, then urged them into position as Shea arrived to walk Rachel up the aisle.

"You ready?" Colette whispered to Veronica. She looked absolutely beautiful and remarkably serene, considering she was about to make a life-altering vow.

"Yes." Veronica moved to stand behind Megan.

She put a hand to her fluttering stomach, thinking she was probably more nervous than Colette. Being in a church was certainly familiar and comfortable, but she'd never worn a dress like this to a house of worship before.

She felt as though something life-altering was about to happen to *her*.

She turned to Colette, who was now behind her, her arm tucked into Armand's. "Did you give me a bed?" she asked quietly.

Colette looked at her through her chin-length veil. "Pardon me?"

"A bed." Veronica kept her eye on the front of the church, where Shea was just seating Rachel in the first pew. Then she glanced quickly at Colette. "When I got home last night, there was a bed in my bedroom."

Armand raised an eyebrow. "And that is odd?"

Colette nodded. "Yes, Dad. She didn't have one." Then to Veronica, she replied, "No, I didn't give you a bed. You mean, a new one?"

"Yes. The mattress and box spring are still wrapped in plastic, and there was a bedspread thrown over them."

Colette giggled. "Did you pray for one? With your connections—"

The opening bars of the wedding processional began with loud, commanding drama, effectively putting an end to conversation. Colette shrugged, then winked.

Veronica faced forward as Katie, well coached on when to start, set off at a stately pace. Megan followed, the length of seven pews left between her and Katie.

Veronica counted pews and decided she was not going to walk up the aisle thinking about the bed. This was her friend's wedding and it required her full attention.

When Megan reached the seventh pew, Veronica followed, focusing on the front of the church where the minister and the Delancey brothers waited.

Despite her promise to herself, she was temporarily distracted by the handsome picture the brothers made, shoulder to shoulder, family resemblance evident though three distinct personalities were also visible—elegant Tate, tough Mike, witty Shea.

"Tough Mike" who'd helped her move, found her first two clients and bought her a bed.

Veronica returned the smiles of the small group of wedding guests as she continued walking toward the altar, wondering if they could detect her scattered thoughts.

Mike was watching her, a frown line on his forehead that made him look as if he regretted everything he'd done for her.

She didn't care. There'd been a time in her life when kindnesses had been few and far between, and she'd learned to be grateful for any she received.

She'd also learned to return them.

If anyone deserved kindness, it was a man trapped in a cage of self-imposed guilt and painful memories.

Veronica smiled to herself as she realized that her previous career as a soul-saver made it impossible for her to do what others would probably do in these circumstances—let him work out his problems by himself and keep an understanding distance.

But she couldn't believe that a man who bemoaned her presence, yet continued to do things for her, didn't want, deep down, to be her friend.

As she reached the minister, she couldn't help giving Mike a meaningful glance before turning to take her place beside Megan.

MIKE STOOD BESIDE Tate as he repeated his vows, then handed him the ring that would seal this ancient ritual. This time, he wanted Tate to get back from the marriage all he gave. He'd always thought his brother remarkable in that respect. Even personally beset with problems, Tate could find something to give to someone who needed him.

Mike had seen that firsthand when he'd been placed on leave after the fatal hostage incident. He hadn't know it then, but when Tate had flown to Dallas to spend time with Mike, his marriage had already ended.

They hadn't done much—sat around, drank coffee, talked about other things. Then Mike had fallen asleep on the sofa one afternoon, and dreamed the entire incident in detail, except that in his dream he'd been in the room with the victims when it all went bad, instead of outside watching. He'd awakened screaming—and Tate had been there to wrap a blanket around him and hold him while he wept with impotent rage.

That debt was hard to pay back. The small financial stake he'd been able to contribute to the winery hadn't meant much in view of what Tate had given. For now, the best Mike could do was see to it that everything went smoothly while Tate was honeymooning with Colette and the girls.

Mike was beginning to wonder if he was going to have to send Veronica Callahan away, too, so that he'd be able to concentrate. He'd thought about her half the night, and now he was going to have to live with the image of her floating up the aisle in that sunbeam of a dress.

He'd always thought he preferred women like Lita—curvy women with flowing hair. But this slender little reed with hair not much longer than his was beginning to haunt his thoughts.

He knew what the problem was: he'd been too long without a woman. He looked around surreptitiously as the ceremony continued, half expecting to be struck by ecclesiastical lightning. Thoughts of sex were probably not appropriate for church. Particularly when those thoughts involved an ex-nun.

It didn't help that when they paired up to leave the church, Veronica gave him a sweet smile and squeezed his arm.

She stood on tiptoe as they reached the vestibule door and whispered in his ear, "Thank you."

He gave her his best What-are-you-talking-about? expression. It had worked during hostage situations when he'd been accused of slowing proceedings to allow other cops to get in position, and on convicted felons who'd tried to tell him someone else had promised them a deal.

But it didn't work on Veronica. "You gave me a bed," she said as they took their places beside Tate and Colette in a line on the church porch.

"Maybe Colette—"

"No. I asked her. *You* gave me the bed. And you have to let me thank you properly."

Her dark eyes were so frank that it seemed futile to pretend. "Okay. But stop saying that." He'd begun to regret having given her such a gift, concerned about how it might look to someone else, or how she might misunderstand his intentions. He—a single man—had given her—an ex-nun—a bed.

Though he did think about her a lot, sex had been far from his mind when he'd walked into the furniture store.

He couldn't imagine her doing all the work required to get the day care center ready, then getting into a sleeping bag set on a wooden floor—or in a bathtub. He'd seen her possessions. He knew how little she had. He'd had to do something.

She rolled her eyes, apparently never giving a second thought to his intentions.

"Don't pretend you had evil motives," she scoffed lightly, smiling and shaking hands with the owners of another local winery as they offered cheerful greetings. "You were probably the kind of cop who gave homeless people shoes, and lost children ice cream."

He frowned at her. Every cop spent time developing a stern, hard attitude. It irritated him that she could peel it away with a few words.

"Tate thinks we should furnish your apartment as we get things for other parts of the compound. That's all that was."

He was grateful to see Felicia Ferryman approaching—probably the first time he'd felt that way since he'd met her. French River's mayor wore a short, silky dress in a pale shade of lavender that accentuated her delicate features. Her blond hair had been swept up under a broad-brimmed hat that matched the dress.

Mike watched Veronica offer her hand with a warm smile. Felicia took it, her smile more predatory than friendly. When he and his brothers had first moved to the winery, Felicia had set her cap for Tate. When Tate had proposed to Colette, Mike became the object of Felicia's machinations. He usually dodged her whenever possible. But now he was happy to have an excuse to stop talking about the bed.

"And who are you?" Felicia asked Veronica, shaking her hand. She'd come with Henry Warren, a city councilman who owned a sporting goods store.

"I'm Veronica Callahan," replied Veronica, innocent and unsuspecting. "I've just arrived at the winery."

Felicia looked her up and down and reacted as she usually did to competition. She stiffened visibly. "Really. In what capacity?"

Mike saw an easy and instant solution to the problem of Felicia. He didn't stop to think about it twice. "She's the love of my life," he said, putting an arm around her shoulders and leaning closer. "Veronica, this is Felicia Ferryman, our mayor."

Veronica gazed at him for several seconds, clearly trying to figure out what he was doing. He waited for her to denounce him as a liar.

She turned to Felicia instead. "Hello," she said mercifully. "It's, uh, so nice to meet you."

Felicia intently scanned Mike's face, then Veronica's. "You hardly ever leave the winery," she challenged suspiciously. "Where on earth did you meet?"

"We—met before he came here," Veronica said, turning to him for corroboration, a flicker of panic in her dark eyes. "I'm from…Los Angeles and… around there." Her voice fell a little as she named the city, as though afraid it wouldn't work into whatever Felicia already knew about him.

Felicia pounced. "I thought you came here from Dallas."

Mike nodded. "I did. We met when she was visiting a friend." That, at least, was true. She'd been in the B-and-B to have tea with Colette. If Felicia presumed that friend had been in Dallas, that wasn't his fault.…

Felicia looked hurt, but he'd have bet his stake in

Delancey Vineyards that it was disappointment rather than pain. She took Veronica's hand and tapped her naked third finger. "No diamond," she commented. Then she freed Veronica's hand and focused on her eyes. "So, you followed him here?"

Mike braced himself. This was going to be embarrassing. Certainly Veronica hadn't abandoned her past so completely that she would actually lie for him.

But she seemed to have borrowed his creative approach to the truth. "I just sort of...*flew* into his life," she said with a nervous little laugh. "Then, he caught me and wouldn't let go." Veronica turned to Mike with a loving smile for Felicia's benefit, but he saw the humor sparkling in her eyes.

"Felicia, for God's sake," Warren said, reaching around her with an apologetic smile to shake Veronica's hand. "It's a wedding, not a council hearing. They're in love. You don't need the details."

Felicia remained unconvinced. "I just think it's strange that, despite all the times I've run into him, he's never mentioned her."

"Maybe you just didn't give him a chance." Warren put his hands on her shoulders and gently pushed her forward. "And we're holding up the line. Maybe there will be an opportunity for further questions at the reception."

As the Ledbetters from the neighboring property greeted Veronica then moved on to Mike, he heard Felicia's pouty voice congratulate Tate and Colette.

Then she added casually, "So Mike's in love, is he?"

Mike managed to catch Tate's eye over Colette's head. A long history of covering for each other allowed his brother to read the unspoken message.

"I guess Colette and I are contagious," Tate said without hesitation, squeezing his bride to him when she would have spoken—probably to ask him what he was talking about.

"Why did he never mention her?"

"Well, you know how private Mike is."

Henry urged Felicia on to Shea, who stood with Megan and Katie. Shea, unfortunately, was too far away to warn. And the girls would never understand the subtle deception. Mike was about to be unmasked as a liar—and after such a brief career.

Then Warren reached around Felicia to shake hands with Shea, as she frowned back toward Mike. "You'll have to excuse her," Warren said. "Mike's romance with Miss Callahan has come as a shock. I think Felicia had designs on him. You're probably next."

"Henry!" Felicia stalked off, and he followed with an apologetic shake of his head.

"Really?" Mrs. Ledbetter asked. "Well, how serious is it? Have you set a date?"

Mike opened his mouth to reply, thinking fast, but Veronica said quickly, "No, not yet. We're still at the staring-into-each-other's-eyes stage."

The woman nodded. "And that's very wise. Young people get trapped in the tide of sentiment, then the first quarrel comes along and they divorce because they never talked about the important things, much less thought about them. You give yourselves plenty of time.''

''On the other hand,'' her husband put in, ''if you have a good thing going, you'll learn how to work together. Do you want the same things?'' He looked from one to the other.

Veronica clearly didn't know how to respond to that.

''I don't know. What do you want?'' Mike prompted her.

''Um, love.'' She tilted her head in thought. ''Laughs. Little ones.''

Mike might have agreed once, back when he'd thought he would marry one day. He smiled at the Ledbetters. ''Guess that's a good starting point for our discussion.''

The Ledbetters laughed and wished them luck, then moved on.

Before Veronica could comment on the little comic opera Mike had just put her through, the photographer assembled the group for pictures in front of the church. First, he posed the whole wedding party, followed by the bride and groom, then the pair with the girls, then the girls and Shea, then Mike and Veronica.

''Are you insane?'' she whispered to him as they stood together on the top step.

''Apparently,'' he replied. ''But Felicia's been after me—I'm sorry, but putting it more modestly just wouldn't cut it—ever since she realized Tate was a lost cause. I'm desperate to convince her that I'm not available.''

''You lied!''

''You helped me.''

A laugh bubbled out of her, and the photographer shouted his approval. ''Good, good!'' he called as he moved several feet to the right and took another picture. ''You two were looking awfully serious there.''

''It's a little upsetting,'' she said, ''to see how quickly I was able to lie while saying nothing that was technically untrue.''

''Welcome to the outside world, Sister.''

''I suppose simply saying a firm 'no' to her hasn't occurred to you?''

The photographer finished and told them he'd meet them at the reception.

''I've done that several times.'' Mike took Veronica's hand to help her down the steps. ''She doesn't notice what she doesn't want to see or hear. Either you play along with me, or I'm going to have to have her bumped off. Do you want that on your conscience?''

''How did someone who doesn't listen to people get to be mayor?''

''Burgess says her father owned lot of property around here and was a pretty good man. I guess everybody hoped she'd be like him.''

''But she isn't?''

''According to Colette, she's done a few good things. She just seems to get opinion on her side on the council and the various committees by…'' He hesitated.

Veronica understood. "I see."

"Look." He turned her to him at the bottom of the stairs. "You said you'd have to pay me back for the bed."

"I said," she corrected with disapproval, "I wanted to thank you properly. I expected you to do the gracious thing."

He pretended to look regretful. "You can never count on me for that."

"Oh, *that's* right. You're big and bad. I keep forgetting. So what do I have to do?"

"Just pretend I'm the man of your dreams during the reception, and whenever Felicia happens along." He spread his arms to show her how easy it would be. "That's all."

"But now the Ledbetters think we're in love. And if we behave that way, so will everyone else."

He shook his head, denying that was a problem. "The important thing is that Felicia believes it."

"What thrilling news!" Colette swatted Mike's shoulder playfully with her bouquet. "I understand the two of you are wild for each other." Mike started to explain, and she laughed. "I know. It was lie or be carried off by Felicia. She gave Tate a few bad moments, too."

"If she starts on me," Shea warned, coming to put an arm around his new sister-in-law, "I'm ratting you out. So, we're supposed to pretend you two are an item? How long is this going to go on? Felicia's not likely to leave town in the near future.''

''I think Henry Warren has feelings for her,'' Colette said. ''Maybe she'll turn to him and the whole problem will disappear. And speaking of disappearing—'' Colette frowned ''—what happened to Tate and the girls?''

''They're getting the car,'' Shea replied, just as Tate pulled up to the curb in the roomy van he'd bought for the honeymoon. He honked and everyone piled in.

The reception was held in the finished but undecorated B-and-B, with a buffet Shea had prepared. The young woman Mike had hired to work for him part-time helped serve. Shea shed his morning coat to don an apron, as guests sampled the buffet set up at the table and on the counter in the kitchen, then moved to rented tables and chairs set out in the great room.

Their plates were laden with boiled shrimp, salmon canapés, onion tarts, crab-stuffed mushrooms, prosciutto and cheese roll ups, and a variety of molded salads. Several tangy dips were served with crostini cut into triangles.

The atmosphere was lively and festive. When everyone had finished eating, the tables were folded away and the chairs moved to the edges of the room to clear the middle for dancing.

Tate and Colette started when a small local band played ''It Had to Be You.'' Then Armand and Rachel joined them. After a few moments, Megan and

Katie ran to the dance floor and squeezed between Colette and Tate.

Veronica felt her throat tighten and her eyes burn. That was what a childhood should be filled with. She knew the girls had had a difficult time when their father died—Katie particularly. But they'd always been loved. Someone had always been there to offer comfort and lend support. And they'd always had each other.

Veronica looked around at all the cheerful faces, resisting the loneliness threatening to overwhelm her. She hated that the past still had this much control over her, that it could find her in a room filled with celebration and laughter, and make her feel as though she was all alone.

That's because you are, a bedeviling inner voice told her. *These people don't belong to you or you to them. You're just an acquaintance—*

"Do you dance, Veronica?" Mike appeared at her side, one hand held out.

She sighed wistfully. "Actually, I don't. Except for the Funky Chicken, and the Charleston."

He laughed. "An eclectic repertoire."

"I know. I learned them for a school play written by a parishioner. Needless to say, it never left the rounds of community theater to make it on Broadway." She tried to shoo him toward the dance floor. "But you can ask someone else. I'll be an understanding lover—though I must say, you haven't been very attentive."

"I apologize," he said. "I was going over a few

details with the landscaper—'' he pointed ''—he's the one in the gray suit. Come on.''

She resisted his efforts to pull her toward the floor. ''I wasn't kidding,'' she said. ''I really can't dance. I was a wallflower in high school, and once I entered the convent, it never came up.''

''Come on.'' He closed his hand over hers. ''We'll find a quiet corner, and I'll teach you.''

''But—I'm not very graceful.''

''Cops are flat-footed. We'll be a good match.''

''Oh, you are not.'' She let herself follow him, but reluctantly. ''You move as though every muscle in your body hears music. I've watched you.''

She didn't realize what she'd said until he turned to her, one eyebrow arched, and put his arms around her.

She covered her eyes. ''That wasn't cool, was it?''

''I like it.'' He pulled her hands down, then drew her a little closer. ''I didn't know you'd been watching me.''

''Well, you know…'' She struggled to regain her composure. But she knew her cheeks were pink. ''Proximity to men is a new experience for me, and you're…'' She sighed. There was no way out of this without further embarrassment. ''I find you attractive,'' she went on in rush. ''Not only because you're good-looking but because you're kind. There.'' She sucked in a breath and made herself look at him. ''But don't worry. I'm not really after you, like Felicia. I'm just—denying that you're flat-footed.''

MIKE COULD NOT FORM one coherent thought. He didn't know whether to grin in satisfaction, or run as far away from her as he could get.

His self-image had suffered greatly since the hostage incident, and his confidence had hit bottom when Lita had walked away. She'd shared his love for motorcycles and camping, and often his bed, but had been unable to deal with his depression.

It fed his ego to hear Veronica's estimation of him: good-looking, graceful, attractive, kind.

But, he reminded himself, she'd come sailing at him off a banister. She was a little nuts. Beautiful and captivating, but a little nuts.

"Okay, dancing's pretty simple." He held her firmly to him in the classic ballroom dance pose, turning his attention to the music. "You know the box step? Side, together. Back, together. Side, together. Front, together."

"Yeah." She followed him easily as he slowly executed it. "Why do we hold our hands out, anyway?" She wriggled the fingers she was talking about.

"I've no idea." He shook their clasped hands to reclaim her attention. "It's the feet we're concentrating on now."

"Sorry. Okay. I know the box step, but I don't understand what happens once you start moving around. It's not a box anymore, it's a—"

"It's still a box," he insisted, going through it with her one more time. "It just becomes a box you can take with you." He turned and laughed at her little groan as she double-stepped to keep up. "Nothing's changed," he said. "Still the same steps. You're moving your body in a different direction, but the steps remain and in the same order."

"I don't get it."

"But, you're doing it."

"I am?" She looked down at her feet in surprise—and collided with him.

He grinned and repositioned her again. "Don't watch your feet. Watch me." He did the basic step again, helping her get her bearings.

"Why?" she asked. "Is that a rule?"

"I don't think so, but that's what dancers usually do. I guess it helps the radar work."

"Radar?"

"The body's radar. It works really well when you're dancing. Even if you're not touching, you can second-guess each other's every move."

"Maybe because many couples dancing are married, or in love."

"Maybe sharing the same dream moves them in the same direction. Or maybe it's just instinctive and would work with anyone. Want to try it?"

"Mike, I don't even have this down when we're holding on."

He dropped his hands to his sides. She tucked hers behind her back with an anxious little sigh. "If it is a common dream thing, we're going to fall flat on our faces."

"But if it's instinctive, we'll be all right. Come on, just do what I do."

And she did. Her dark eyes looked into his, at first as though actually searching for a meter that would indicate his every move. There was a subtle change, and he felt as if she could not only read him but knew him—better than anyone else ever had. He looked away, trying to break the spell.

But he couldn't.

What was it about her? In her eyes, he saw warmth, sadness, serenity, and…desire?

He stopped abruptly. She stopped, too, the instant he did, so close to him that her full yellow skirt swirled around his legs.

His hands were at his sides, hers behind her back, their bodies one breath from touching.

Desire? No. He couldn't allow that, didn't want that. Kindness was one thing…

"So, what have we proven?" she asked a little breathlessly. "That it's instinctive, or that we share the same dream?"

He remembered her answer to his question earlier in front of the church, when he'd asked her what she wanted. "Love, laughs, little ones."

That was what he'd once wanted, but not anymore.

He made himself pull free of her snare. "Experiment's inconclusive," he said. "Oh, looks like Tate and Colette and the girls are making their getaway. Got your birdseed bundle?"

She seemed to need a minute to pull herself together. Then she glanced around a little distractedly. She pointed to a chair across the room where her basket of daisies and ivy rested. "I left it there."

They hurried toward it as people streamed out the door in the wake of the bride and groom. "Am I wrong?" she asked as she scooped up the small mesh bag. "Or didn't people used to throw rice at weddings and not birdseed?"

"It's an ecological thing," he replied, holding the door open for her. "The birds will eat the seed, but not the rice, so the rice just becomes litter. This way, no one has to clean and the birds are happy."

"But does birdseed promise fertility?"

Mike looked exasperated. "I don't know. Do you have a profound question for every situation?"

"I simply thought—"

"Will you just throw your birdseed before they get in the car?"

Veronica yanked on the little yellow bow that held the mesh bag closed, let the seed fall into her free hand and tossed it.

Megan and Katie screamed with laughter and got into the back of the car. Tate shielded Colette from the barrage with his shoulder, as she turned her back on their guests and prepared to toss her bouquet.

Veronica lost her enthusiasm for the ritual. She knew her friends were coming back eventually, but they were still leaving. She would miss Colette's laughter and encouragement, and Megan's and Katie's cheerful giggles.

Veronica had a lot to keep her busy, but she guessed it would still be an endless couple of weeks. She longed for the solace of the view at the back of the B-and-B and slipped away from the small crowd of guests, heading off in that direction.

"Come on, throw it!" she heard Cece Phips yell. "Over here!"

She heard other calls and applause, a sudden, breathless silence, then Mike shouting, "Veronica!"

As she reached the side of the house, she turned, hoping he didn't want to dance again.

"Wha—?" She caught a mouthful of the bride's rose-and-orchid bouquet as it struck her in the face.

"Head's up," Mike warned—a little too late.

CHAPTER FIVE

DELANCEY VINEYARDS BUSTLED with tourists over the Fourth of July weekend. Before he left, Tate had cordoned off the buildings still under construction so that tourists could visit the winery and Rachel's petting zoo safely. He'd also erected a large rendering of the completed compound.

On the other side of the barricade, workmen painted and papered the inside of the B-and-B, put a new roof on the restaurant, and power-washed and painted Mike's and Shea's house.

After the weekend, everyone was busy. Armand walked the vineyard every day to check for fruit-set—the transition from flower to grape berry. He'd told Veronica that only about a third of the flowers were usually fertilized, but that could vary from none to two-thirds. He hoped half would bear fruit.

Rachel helped Shea in the tasting room and also baked for it. Veronica volunteered to stay with the animals while Rachel worked, and learned the brief spiel Rachel had prepared to tell the children about them.

The job was great fun, and she loved being with children. She also enjoyed the animals. Her old life hadn't allowed her to have pets, though one of the convents had had a Saint Bernard. The mother superior always joked that the dog was canonized and therefore a member of the church.

The rest of the time Veronica spent painting the day care center in flower colors—rose, daffodil, lavender—and the trim around the doors and windows in bright white. With the green carpet, it looked like an indoor garden.

She found a wallpaper border designed with whimsical insects in those same colors and used it in the big playroom and the room where the older children would rest. For the younger children's room, she found a border with teddy bears wearing dresses and bow ties.

She worked from morning till night for a week, stopping only to eat and sleep. Rachel, who dropped by to bring her cookies one afternoon, remarked that she looked tired.

Veronica dismissed that with a wave of her pink-tipped paintbrush. "I'm pushing to get the painting finished, so I'll have time to apply finishing touches, and shop for just the right things."

Rachel pulled up a sawhorse left by the construction crew, and took a thermos out of her bag. "Well, you're having a break whether you want one or not. Put that brush down, and come and sit with me."

Rachel, Veronica had discovered, could be something of a bully. Veronica laid her brush across the mouth of the can of paint, wiped her hands off with a rag, and went to occupy the other end of the sawhorse.

"Hazelnut shortbread," Rachel said, holding the open tin out to her. "Hazelnuts from the tree in my backyard. Mike been over to help you?"

Veronica selected a star-shaped cookie and shook her head as she took a bite. She chewed and swallowed. "This is my project and I want to do it myself."

Rachel poured coffee into two pottery mugs and handed Veronica one. "So you don't have to share the credit?"

Veronica wasn't sure if Rachel was teasing or not. "No. Because I know everyone has a lot to do, and I don't want you all to feel as though you have to help me."

"Why not? The world is all about people helping people. And one of the good things that comes with progress is that men and women can deal more freely with each other. If you want help, you can ask for it."

Veronica smiled into Rachel's carefully neutral expression. She was sure the woman had matchmaking on her mind.

"I know," Veronica said. "But in the convent there were a lot of times when there wasn't a man available to help us, so we learned to cope. And I'm just painting. That's pretty easy work."

"Not when you do it after putting in a fairly long day. I've seen your light on far into the night."

Veronica popped the last bite of cookie into her mouth and tried not to react to that observation. It wouldn't serve to have everyone know her weaknesses. The very beautiful surroundings Veronica had been so anxious to live in also brought the silence she hated.

"It's so quiet up here. It takes a little getting used to." She took another cookie, hoping to distract her guest. "Rachel, these are wonderful! Do you have grandchildren? They must love your cookies."

She could see instantly that Rachel was on to her. This must be what it was like, she guessed, to have a mother who read your mind. Her own had hardly remembered she existed.

"Is life on your own a little more difficult than you'd imagined?" Rachel asked gently. "You can be honest with me. I've been on my own for a while."

Veronica patted Rachel's hand. "I have, too, Rachel. Longer than I've been physically alone. I just have moments when—" She couldn't describe what happened exactly. But every now and then she craved what she didn't have. And in the middle of a dark and quiet night, it was harder to talk herself out of those moods. So she worked.

"When the night seems interminable?" Rachel finished.

It was more complicated than that, but... "Yes," she replied. "So I keep working. But that's no cause for worry. As soon as the children are running around here, I'll probably have trouble staying awake through dinner."

Rachel poured the last of the coffee into the two cups. "I think the nights get long for Mike, too," she said, capping the thermos and replacing it in her bag. "I've seen his light on. Seems silly for the two of you to be coping with insomnia separately."

Veronica looked her in the eye and said gently but firmly, "I know what you're doing, Rachel, but Mike and I *are* separate." If the older woman had seen his eagerness to stop dancing with her at the reception, she would have known that. "He's one of my landlords, that's all. And we happened to be in a wedding party together. Each of us has too much to deal with to have time for romance—not that he'd want it if he *did* have time."

Rachel heaved a deep sigh, downed the last of her coffee, and placed the cup in her bag. "Young people! The world finally comes around to making it easy for you to be friends before you have to be lovers, and here you are—still at opposite ends of the room. Or, in this case, the compound. You don't think his introducing you as the love of his life was entirely for Felicia's benefit, do you?"

"Yes, I do. Besides, I've just come out of the convent," Veronica said reasonably. "I'm not ready to—"

"Ready." Rachel said the word as though it were distasteful, and got to her feet. "Who is ever ready for what a relationship does to you? No one! But life is about stepping in, mixing it up, taking part. By the time you're 'ready,' the fates will have moved on to someone else and there you'll be—painting rooms alone at two in the morning."

Veronica followed her to the door. "I appreciate

that you care, Rachel,'' she said, giving her a hug. ''But, you know, I've noticed you're in that cottage all alone despite two handsome gentlemen showering you with their attentions. Armand and Mr. Reynolds, the attorney.''

Rachel's eyes widened, then she looked down to pay sudden and close attention to rearranging the cup in the bag she carried. ''They're just friends,'' she said in a tone considerably quieter than her usually kind but bossy one. ''And I'm an old woman.''

''Hmm.'' Veronica leaned a shoulder in the doorway as Rachel played with the bag's straps. ''Then that directive about stepping in, mixing it up and taking part—that no longer applies after a certain age?''

Rachel finally stopped fiddling and scolded Veronica with a shake of her index finger. ''It isn't nice to throw people's words back at them.''

Veronica grinned. ''I just thought we were expected to practice what we preach.''

''You're a little smartie, aren't you?''

''It's required when you work with children. Thanks for the cookies. And the philosophy. I promise to give it some thought—if you will.''

''Harrumph.'' Rachel walked away, but she was smiling.

''THE VINEYARD RESTAURANT?'' Shea looked up from a sheet of paper in front of him to gauge Mike's reaction. They sat on stools facing each other in the restaurant's kitchen. The laughter and conversation of a pair of workers putting a wallpaper border around the dining room provided a soft background to their search for a name for Shea's restaurant. "Too ordinary?"

Mike considered that. "I don't know. It's appropriate. But there are a lot of vineyards in the area."

"That's true." Shea drew a line through the name. "The Delancey Vineyard Restaurant? Too long?"

"Maybe. Let's keep it as a possible."

"How about just Delancey's?"

"Not bad. You've given up on the western theme?"

Shea nodded. "I think so. I was going to play with the idea that this used to be a bunkhouse. But the more I thought about it, the less it sounded like someplace you'd want to eat at. Or if you did, you'd expect charbroiled steaks, or something."

"What did Tate think about Delancey's?"

"He said he was leaving it up to you and me. I can't wait any longer. I have to make a decision, get menus printed, do some advertising. So do you like it?"

"Yeah. And I like that blue-gray color in the dining room."

Shea laughed lightly and leaned an elbow on the chopping block beside their stools. "It has a calming effect. Good digestion means repeat customers. Tablecloths'll be brighter blue for lunch, silver-white for dinner, and anything we decorate the walls with should look good against it."

"What about the wait staff?"

"They'll wear modified tuxes for lunch and dinner."

"Women, too?"

"Yeah. It looks best on women." Shea grinned. It reminded Mike of the first time they'd discussed women together when he'd been fourteen and Shea ten. "Sexy women look as if they might break out of them at any moment, and dignified women look even more so. For the male customer, it's a win-win situation."

"Did the woman you don't want to talk about work for you?"

Shea tensed visibly, but he shook his head. "No, she didn't."

"Was she a customer?"

"She was the woman I don't want to talk about," Shea said pointedly. "Remember?"

"I know, but Tate's gone," Mike went on unreservedly. "There's no one here who'll try to fix it for you. I know how you hate that. All I'll do is listen."

"Yeah, right." Shea made a production of folding his sheet of names for the restaurant. "You always say that, then you try to help me."

"Helping's different from fixing."

"I'm not your little brother anymore," Shea insisted, though more patiently than Mike had expected. "I'm just your brother who happens to be a couple of years younger. The woman—*the one I don't want to talk about*—is out of my life, so all the things you and Tate are curious about don't really matter.''

Mike made what he considered a safe guess. ''She hurt you,'' he said.

Shea stared at him in silence for a moment, and Mike braced himself for the explosion that meant he'd pushed too hard. Then Shea dropped his pencil on the block and pocketed the note. ''No, *I* hurt *her*. You want to get out of here so I can get some things done?''

''I'm wagering,'' Mike said as he stood, ''that it was your unwillingness to share that got to her.''

Shea fixed him with a look that said he was ready to lose it. ''Pardon me, but isn't that the same problem you had with Lita?''

''Yeah.'' Mike started for the door. ''That's why I'd have understood. See you.''

''Armand's coming for dinner,'' Shea said. ''You going to be home?''

''Yeah.''

''Good. Rachel has other plans, and Veronica says she's going to bed early. So, since it's just us, I'm going German. Sauerbraten and the fixings.''

''Great.''

''We can show him his room. He's going to move in next week and hire someone to clean the house before Tate, Colette and the girls come home.''

''Fine. Seven o'clock for dinner?''

''Yeah.''

''See you then.''

Mike spent the afternoon in the winery office,

planning an ad campaign that would feature the compound and all the services it offered as a whole, then highlight each of its various entities separately.

He could see the barn from his window, and wondered what Veronica was doing. He'd made a point of dropping in once a day to make sure she had what she needed, but she was never more than pithily polite, so he never stayed.

Which was fine. He had lot to do, and he didn't want to have to worry about her. He'd warned her that she'd be on her own fixing up the center, so if she was cool because he was true to his word, so be it.

But it worried him a little that he'd even noticed she was cool.

It worried him a *lot* that he cared.

MIKE, SHEA, AND ARMAND sat in the living room drinking Valley Winery Pinot Noir, which had been bottled when Uncle Jack was still alive. Coupled with the big meal, it brought on a mellow exchange of confidences.

The three kittens that had been a gift to the Delanceys from Megan and Katie—Joe Boxer, Tate's tuxedo cat, Bonnie, Mike's calico, and Sterling, Shea's pale gray tabby—lay in a pile in the middle of the room like some weird soft sculpture: black-and-white leg, orange-and-white face turned upside down, striped gray tail.

"I need advice," Armand said without preamble.

He was slumped in his chair, his gaze unusually distant.

"From us?" Shea asked in astonishment.

Armand frowned. "I am thinking a younger man might understand."

Mike shifted in his chair, hoping the question wasn't too taxing. He was sluggish from too much sauerbraten, red cabbage and hot German potato salad. "Understand what?"

"Women," Armand replied.

Shea groaned. "I can't help you, Armand. All I understand about women is that they defy understanding. Mike, on the other hand—" he gestured lazily toward Mike at the opposite end of the sofa "—is trained to understand everyone. Maybe he'll have some insight."

"No, no," Mike denied quickly. "I was trained to understand the *criminal* mind."

"Well, essentially they're the same." Shea reached for the wineglass on the end table beside him. "I've always thought a woman's mind worked in a devious and secretive way. That's criminal, isn't it?"

"Maybe the problem is mine," Armand went on, apparently determined to share, whether or not either of his companions was qualified to help. "Perhaps I am invisible." He plucked at the sleeve of his chambray shirt. "I see myself, but perhaps I am invisible to everyone else. Lloyd Reynolds, however, does not suffer from the same affliction."

"What does Reynolds have to do with it?" Shea asked.

Armand shrugged moodily. "She's aware of him," he said. "In fact, she's out with him tonight."

"Who is?"

"Rachel."

"Ohhh." Shea drew the sound out, then sat up a little straighter. "She does notice you. I see the two of you talking together all the time."

Armand sighed. "We talk about the vineyard, about her animals, about the renovations. Always business or impersonal subjects. If I try to tell her I value her friendship, or ask her if she'll join me for dinner, she always has something else to attend to or somewhere else she has to be. Like tonight." He turned hopefully to Mike. "What shall I do? I've loved her for a long time, but all I am to her is the old winemaker."

"I'm not the one to ask, Armand." Mike took a sip of wine, then placed his glass on the coffee table. "I don't *want* a woman in my life, so while on some level I might understand how their minds work, I wouldn't know how to begin to get one interested in me."

Armand looked surprised. "But Veronica is interested in you."

Mike didn't want to hear that—couldn't believe it. "No, I helped her out a few times," he explained offhandedly. "What you see is her gratitude, not—interest."

Armand shook his head at Mike, his expression

amusedly pitying. "Do not tell me what I see in her eyes. She sparkles when she looks at you. She may not have much experience with men, but I believe she's found one she would like to know much better."

"If you read women that clearly, why are you coming to *us* for help?"

Armand slouched despondently in his chair. "Because it is so much easier to understand someone else's life—or someone else's woman." He groaned a little as he stretched out a leg. "It must have been simpler in the Middle Ages, when a man could kidnap a woman he loved and hide her away until she, too, was convinced she should be his."

Mike stared into space, letting his mind conjure up just such a solution. It had everything: simplicity, expediency, uncomplicated purpose.

"Unfortunately," Mike said, "that's not acceptable today. It would probably end up with her slapping a lawsuit on you."

Armand nodded wearily. "Modern life has such complicated courtship."

"For all of us," Shea said. "Young or—older."

"That's true." Mike agreed. "I'd say, follow your instincts, Armand, and do whatever you think is right where Rachel is concerned. Neither one of us has a better idea."

"We are a sorry lot," Armand concluded.

Shea raised his glass. "I'll drink to that."

Mike reached for the bottle and stood to refill everyone's glasses. He suddenly felt older than Armand. Though in his early seventies and plagued by arthritis, Armand was working on a tactic to bring a woman into his life, when all Mike wanted to do was avoid them at all costs.

What kept hope alive like that? Character? An adventurous spirit? Belief in the future?

He hadn't lost those things, had he?

"Baseball's getting interesting," Shea said. "Let's talk about that. Less depressing."

Mike laughed dryly as he sat down again. "Unless, of course, you think about getting to first base. Then women and how to reach them are the issue all over again."

They did talk about baseball, speculated on what sights Tate and Colette and the girls were seeing, planned the grand opening for the restaurant.

Armand went home just before midnight. Shea had fallen asleep on the sofa, and Mike tossed a throw over him, then went to the kitchen to make sure the stove was turned off and that there was cat food in the bowls. Bonnie rubbed on his leg and sat down in front of her food.

He stroked her, put a little milk in a saucer, then went back to the living room to turn off the porch light. Joe Boxer and Sterling had moved onto the sofa—one of them on Shea's chest, the other on his legs. Mike knew from experience that in an hour or so Shea would wake up paralyzed by the weight of those small bodies.

Smiling, Mike went up to bed.

He was awakened with a start some time later by the ring of the telephone. The clock read 2:27.

His first thought was for Tate, Colette and the girls.

"Delancey's!"

Rachel's voice said, "Mike?"

Rachel. "What is it?" he asked anxiously. "Are you all right?"

She was a dear old woman, and he and his brothers felt she and Armand sort of filled the space left by the deaths of their parents. Ironic, he thought, in view of what Armand had told them tonight.

"What is it?" he asked anxiously when she didn't answer him.

"I'm fine," she said, "but I noticed that Veronica's light was on even later than usual, so I called. She answered the phone, but she could hardly talk for being sick. I tried to go help her, but the barn door's locked. Would you check on her? You have the key, don't you?"

He was now wide-awake. "Rachel, I can't just let myself in to her place."

"Mike, we're all she has. I'll come with you."

"All right," he said finally. With Tate gone, everything on the compound was his responsibility. "I'll meet you there."

"Bless you, Mike."

He pulled on jeans and reached for the sweatshirt he'd tossed on the chair earlier, but Bonnie was curled up on it. He pulled out a fresh one and ran down the squeaky stairs.

Shea was still asleep on the sofa; one cat now slept in the curve of his head and shoulder, and the other was sprawled lengthwise across his waist.

Mike took the flashlight hanging by the back door and let himself out of the house. Once he went down the slope to the compound, he could see the light on in the barn—the windows forming six bright squares in the darkness.

The night was cool and fragrant as he strode toward the barn, lighting his steps with the flashlight. Rachel's llama, Victoria, whickered at him as he passed, and from inside Rachel's house, he heard the dogs bark. Rachel herself came out to fall into step beside him.

He went to the door of the barn and listened. Silence. No radio, no TV.

He rapped lightly on the door. Still nothing.

He knocked a little harder, knowing that if she was upstairs, she probably wouldn't be able to hear him.

No answer.

"Open it!" Rachel insisted.

Mike dug the compound keys out of his pocket, found the one for the barn and opened the door.

The main room was brightly lit, the smell of fresh paint thick in the air. The walled-off rooms stood open, each a different color. A ladder stood in the middle of the room, but there was no painter in sight.

Rachel coughed. "She's been breathing this for days. No wonder she's ill. You go up. There're too many steps for me."

Mike ran up the steps to the apartment. The lights

were on in the living room and kitchen, which were now the same shade of yellow that he'd seen downstairs.

The bedroom door was open, but there was no one in it. The bed had been moved to one corner and was covered with a tarp. One and a half walls had been painted the soft blue from downstairs; a roller leaned against a still unpainted stretch of wallboard.

Mike stared at the room in confusion and consternation. If Veronica wasn't here, where was she? Her car had been parked outside.

Then he remembered the bathroom, and went forward cautiously. He found Veronica hunched in the middle of the vinyl floor.

She was green. And she hadn't been painted that color, either.

CHAPTER SIX

"WHAT HAPPENED?" Mike demanded as he kneeled in front of Veronica.

She looked at him miserably, her eyes wide and soupy.

He put hand to her forehead, then her cheek. Her skin felt clammy.

"I've been...sick," she said, then a sudden urgency in her eyes and an attempt to get up onto her knees told him it was about to happen again.

He reached down to help her, but she tried to push him away. "Go...'way," she ordered feebly.

He ignored her and got her onto her knees just in time. He wet a washcloth and found a towel.

She flushed the toilet and sat back on her heels, breathing heavily.

Mike wiped her cheeks and her mouth. "What'd you have for lunch?" he asked, rinsing out the cloth.

She thought. "Uh, cookies."

"That's it?"

"I was...busy." She moaned and he held the cool cloth to her eyes.

"What'd you have for breakfast?"

"I, um, M&M's, I think."

"That's nutritious," he teased gently.

"They were the peanut kind."

"How long have you been working?" he asked. He removed the cloth and was relieved to see that she was no longer green. But she was now white enough to bury.

"Since six."

He swept her bangs back with the cloth. Eight hours since six p.m. would have been bad enough, but he had a feeling it had been since six *a.m.*

"What are you doing…here?" she asked, trying to sit up. Halfway, she changed her mind and collapsed against him with a *thunk.*

"Rachel was worried about you," he said. "She's waiting downstairs."

"Oh, yeah." This time she used the rim of the sink to pull herself upright. "She called. I think I…hung up on her. But I'm fine. I'm sorry she woke you." She swallowed and appeared to be making a supreme effort to look capable and well. But she was losing. "And I'm sorry you had to see…such a spectacle. You can go now."

He grinned. There was something touching about her embarrassment and her attempt at self-sufficiency. "When you've hauled in as many drunks as I have, this is nothing new. Or horrifying."

She leaned heavily on the sink. "I'll be all right now."

"Yes, you will," he said, lifting her into his arms. "Because I'm taking you home."

She tried to resist, but she was too weak. Her voice, however, still worked.

"You are not taking me anywhere." She tried to sound firm, but failed.

"Yes, I am. The paint fumes are probably getting to you."

"I'll open the windows."

"I think it'd be better if you just gave the place a day or two to air."

"But I'm not finished!"

"You're finished for now."

"Mike." Up to now, she'd been lying limply in his arms, but she wrapped an arm around his neck and held on as he went down the stairs with her. "How will that look? I'm going to be taking care of children. I can't stay overnight in a house with two men."

"There'll be no one here to see," he said. "And I won't tell anyone, if you don't."

Rachel was waiting at the bottom of the stairs. "What happened?" she asked worriedly. "Was it the paint fumes?"

"Paint fumes and cookies," Mike replied. "Can you turn off the light and pull the door closed, please?"

"Of course." Rachel did as he asked, then followed him out into the night. "*My* cookies? Veronica, did my cookies make you sick?"

"I think the fact that she ate nothing else but M&M's and cookies, while working since six o'clock this—or rather, yesterday morning, is what made her sick." He started toward the house with

Veronica, Rachel hurrying to keep up. "I think a day of rest and some real food will help a lot."

"Rachel." Veronica reached a hand toward her. "Maybe I could stay with you."

Rachel shook her head regretfully. "I only have one bedroom, sweetie," she said. "And animals all over the place. No, I think you'll do better at the house. Good night. Mike, thank you for checking on her."

Rachel turned toward her cottage, and Mike thought there was a curiously cheerful air about her, given Veronica's misery.

Mike got into the house and kicked the door closed without waking Shea. Sterling raised his head and looked mildly interested, then, realizing there was no food involved in whatever was going on, lay down again and closed his eyes.

"I'm going to disrupt everything," Veronica whispered as Mike started up the stairs.

"Not if you're quiet and cooperative."

"I have too much work to do to—"

"And how much work are you getting done now that you've made yourself ill? How did you expect to feel after painting for twenty hours?"

She sighed wearily and dropped her head to his shoulder. "I hadn't really paid attention to the time. I never sleep that well, so as long as I was up, I just kept working. I didn't notice the fumes."

"A good night's sleep and a day off," Mike said, reaching the top of the stairs, "and you should be in good shape again. I understand your excitement, but you have to use some common sense.''

"Common sense flies,'' she said, as he carried her into Tate's old room, "when you're finally where you've always wanted to be, doing what you've always wanted to do. Or haven't you ever felt like that?''

He put her down in the middle of the bed and leaned over her for moment, thinking about her question. "No, I guess not. After I graduated from the police academy, there was a job in Dallas, so I interviewed and got it. I liked it there. I like it here. I guess I just haven't had the passion to be anywhere in particular.''

"That's so sane.'' She sighed as he drew the bedspread over her. "A sort of bloom-where-you're-planted mentality. That's probably because you've never been deprived of something basic.''

He went to the foot of the bed to make sure her feet were covered. "You're right. It was sort of a Beaver Cleaver childhood, even though we moved around lot. Except for a year or two when my parents weren't getting along very well, but they never took it out on us, and we got to spend a whole summer here with Jack.''

She gave him a frail but warm smile. He was a little surprised by it, in view of how much she'd complained about his bringing her here. "That sounds really nice. And it must have been wonderful to have brothers.''

He had to laugh. "Wonderful and awful. I was

always competing with Tate, but he wouldn't give an inch. And we were both always trying to escape from Shea, but he was the most determined little kid. He always found us. How's your stomach? Do you want tea or anything?''

She wrinkled her nose and shook her head. ''No, thanks. I think I'll be fine as long as I don't put anything in it.''

''Okay. I'll find you something to sleep in. Be right back.''

VERONICA WATCHED MIKE walk away, and felt a flutter in the pit of her stomach that had nothing to do with a need to be sick.

Dear God. She wondered what the rung above sexual attraction was called. She'd admitted to Mike at the reception that she found him appealing, but she was beginning to feel something even deeper and stronger.

About half an hour ago, when she'd felt so ill that she'd simply sat on the bathroom floor, certain it wasn't sensible to leave the room, she'd missed the comfort of the convent. Though she'd known for many years it was not the life for her, it'd had a lot to recommend it. One of the pluses was other women around to help you when you were ill. Sister Clement would have tucked her in to bed, and Sister Jeanne would have sent for Mother Helen, who would have come running, brandy bottle in hand. Mother Helen cured everything with brandy....

Then Mike Delancey was in her doorway, big and

solid and frowning in concern, and she'd thought that
there was no one she'd rather be with. Although she
did regret that he'd seen her in such a state.

He was back in a moment with a pair of long
underwear and a matching shirt.

"Best I could do," he said, putting them on the
edge of the bed beside her. "Can you manage all
right?"

"Yes, I think so." She tossed the coverlet back
and sat up, feeling a little better already.

"Okay. I'm going to leave your door open a little.
I'm right next door. If you need me, holler. The bathroom's across the hall."

She smiled. "Thanks. Good night."

He turned the light off as he left the room, and
she changed in the cool darkness. The clean smell of
laundry detergent clung to the shirt as she pulled it
over her head. It was soft and cool, and she liked the
notion that it had once touched Mike's skin. It was
a shameless thought, but she couldn't help it. She
was taking to the world, big time.

She rolled up the sleeves a couple of times, then
slipped into the bottoms. The ribbed ankles prevented
the legs from puddling over her feet, but all the extra
fabric gathered below her knees. She folded the waist
over twice, then climbed back into bed.

This mattress wasn't new and firm like the one
Mike had bought her. It was a little lumpy, and
sagged in the middle, but it was still comfortable.

She felt reassured, knowing Mike was just a few
feet away. She heard him moving around his room

and remembered how she'd craved that in her childhood. The sounds she'd heard at night in the cheap apartments or the shelters were usually loud and angry or filled with distress.

Soon the sounds quieted. She listened for the squeak of a bedspring or the bump of a hand connecting with a lamp or a clock. But the house was silent.

"Mike?" she called suddenly. She hated that her voice held an urgent note.

"Yeah?" he replied instantly, clearly.

Everything inside her relaxed. "Good night," she said.

"Good night, Vee."

Vee. She liked that. She closed her eyes and went to sleep.

MIKE AWOKE in the dryer on Spin.

At least that was what he thought when his dream about towers and maidens and dragons was interrupted by Shea's violent shaking. He had the front of Mike's T-shirt in one hand and a silencing finger over his mouth.

"There's somebody in Tate's bed," Shea whispered. "At least, I think it's human. All I can see is a foot."

Mike's brain began to work. Someone in Tate's bed. Yes. "What do you mean, you *think* it's human?"

"Come and look."

Mike pulled on his jeans and followed Shea. The

door was open halfway, and Shea stepped back so that Mike could lean in.

A slender foot protruded from the covers. But it was the only thing that could be distinguished from the mound of blankets and bedding. She had burrowed under the pillow so that her head wasn't even visible.

So this was the result of all the tossing and turning he'd heard during the night. She was a very restless sleeper.

He pushed Shea out the door.

"It's Veronica," he said quietly when they were in the hallway again. He told his brother about Rachel's call and what he'd found when he got to the barn. "She was pretty sick. Paint fumes, I think. That, and working for twenty hours with nothing but candy for breakfast and cookies for lunch."

Shea winced. "Not good. Cheese omelettes for breakfast when she wakes up. You ready for one yet?"

"Sounds great."

"I'll get right on it."

The crews were already hard at work when Mike went out into the compound after breakfast. He checked on the progress at the B-and-B and the restaurant, then headed for the office to make a few phone calls. But Rachel intercepted him.

"How is she this morning?" she asked. She was smiling widely for someone who was supposed to be concerned.

"She was still asleep, but that's probably good.

Shea's going to fix her an omelette when she wakes up.''

Rachel hugged him. ''That young woman really needs a hero. Colette told me a little about her childhood, and you can see in her eyes how haunted she is. I think it's hard to envision a bright future when your past is so dark. But she's trying so hard.''

Mike didn't know how to respond. ''You're welcome to go over and eat with her,'' he said finally. ''I'm sure Shea would love to cook for you, too.''

She shook her head. ''Thanks. But I think *you* should eat with her. It'd be good for both of you.''

He began to wonder about the look in her eyes. ''You're not matchmaking, are you? Because neither one of us is—''

She smiled and patted his chest. ''I think the match has already been made. You just have to let it happen. Trust me on this. I'm old and I know things.''

''Really?'' He folded his arms and shifted his weight. ''Maybe you don't know as much as you think you do. For instance, did you know you have an admirer?''

She nodded with a superior smile. ''He took me out to dinner last night.''

Mike shook his head. ''I'm not talking about him.''

She frowned suddenly and looked away. ''Armand,'' she said.

He was confused by her reaction. Armand was kind, interesting and the youngest ''older'' man he'd ever met. ''Yes. Armand. What's the frown for?''

"Well." She put her hands in the pockets of her coveralls. "He's an old-fashioned man. And I promised myself I'd never get involved with another one. I loved my husband, but he controlled our finances, didn't want me to work, and left me out of every major decision. He didn't even tell me he was dying. He let me find out the hard way—when he finally did."

"But none of that sounds at all like Armand."

"He's always trying to do everything for me!"

"Probably because he's concerned about you. Or because he wants to help you."

"I won't live my life for another man again."

"I can't imagine he'd ever ask that of you."

She tossed him a scornful look that gave him a glimpse of what she might have been like as a young woman.

"That's because you're a man, too," she said.

"But you just said Veronica needed a hero. You called me to check on her because you were worried about her."

"But Veronica isn't me."

"I don't understand."

She sighed and raised both hands in defeat. "Neither do I. And you can just tell Armand not to talk about me, because I'm not Mrs. Beauchamp material. See you later."

Mike made his phone calls, then went back to the house around ten. Veronica was up, still wearing his shirt over her own sweatpants. She sat in a corner of the nook, drinking something with a tall mound of whipped cream on it. Shea stood at the stove, gently prodding an omelette with a spatula.

Veronica raised her head from the mug. There was a dot of cream on the tip of her nose.

Mike took a napkin from the middle of the table and dabbed it off as he sat beside her.

THINGS WERE GETTING out of control. When Mike had dabbed at her nose, her heart had lurched against her ribs. Dealing with her feelings was going to be harder on her than the paint fumes.

Was it a sign of girlish inexperience to idolize a man who offered a simple helping hand? She couldn't decide. And some instinct told her the helping hand hadn't been all that simple. He'd been doing his best to keep his distance from her, and she'd been trying to accommodate him, but the effort seemed to be getting more difficult for both of them.

She wanted to know more about him, to understand him, to find a way through or over that protective wall to the man inside.

She would be able to connect with him; she had no doubt.

Shea brought her a perfect omelette oozing cheese, and two pieces of whole wheat toast. Several orange rounds, a strawberry, and a pitted cherry were speared through with a decorative pick.

He brought the coffeepot, and a mug for Mike.

"Thank you," Veronica said. "I usually don't eat this much for breakfast. I appreciate your cooking for me."

"My pleasure. You can't live on candy and cookies."

She made a face at Mike. "You had to tell everyone."

Mike shrugged. "I had to explain why there was someone sleeping in Tate's bed."

She smiled ruefully. "I suppose you did."

"Oh, Dorset Linens just called," Shea said to Mike, replacing the coffeepot on the warmer. "Everything's finished for the B-and-B."

"Good. I'll pick it up today. You need anything from Longview?"

"No, thanks. I checked, but the restaurant linens aren't ready. Tablecloths are in, but not the napkins. I was hoping we wouldn't have to make another trip, but them's the breaks. You want something with your coffee?"

"I'm fine, thanks."

"All right, then I'm off to the restaurant. Veronica, do you have everything you need?"

"More than I need. Thanks again, Shea."

Shea dismissed her gratitude with a wave and walked out of the kitchen.

Mike passed Veronica the salt and pepper, and a little pottery bowl of blackberry jam. "Why don't you come with me?" he asked her abruptly.

Caught off guard, she stammered. "I—I…" The spoonful of jam she'd intended to drop on her toast landed on her omelette instead. She scooped it off and onto the toast. "I should be…working."

"No, you're supposed to be resting. It's about an

eighty-mile drive, so you can kick back and relax. There's a toy store there, too. You can look at things for the day care.''

She hadn't needed convincing, had just been trying not to look so eager to accept that she'd frighten him.

''Okay,'' she said, pretending he'd changed her mind. ''I'd like to.''

''Good. I have to do a couple of things first. Can you be ready to leave about eleven?''

''Yes. I'm showered, but I'd like to change into something more respectable.''

He plucked at the sleeve of the waffle-knit shirt. ''It's very respectable. Saw me through a lot of cold winters.''

She got that image again of the fabric against his skin. ''It's wonderfully comfortable. I hate to give it back.''

''Consider it a gift.''

She should have demurred, but she wanted it, and she didn't care to examine why. She put jam on another toast point and handed it to him.

''Thank you,'' she said. ''This is the best I can do as a return gift.''

''A return gift isn't necessary.''

''Well, this isn't technically a gift anyway. It's just sharing. A different concept altogether.''

''Thanks.'' He took a bite, then chewed and swallowed. She thought she noticed him withdraw slightly. ''That's something I'm not always very good at.''

She instantly recognized the meaning behind his statement, but chose to ignore it. "But you just gave me the shirt off your back. Literally."

He studied her a moment, the look in his eyes suggesting he knew what she was doing. "It was more like out of my drawer," he corrected. Then, apparently deciding that she couldn't be allowed to ignore his message, he added bluntly, "I'm not the kind of man who'd fit in to your plans, Veronica."

She smiled innocently. "Not a problem. I haven't gotten to that step yet, anyway."

He finished the rest of his toast while frowning at her. He swallowed and asked, "What step?"

"Number four of my five-step life plan." She cut a bite of omelette and stopped all conversation as she concentrated on it. Shea had grated several different kinds of cheese into it and added seasonings. The result was delicious. "Would you like a bite?"

He shook his head. "I had one before you got up. But I'd like to hear more about the plan."

"Okay." She put her fork down and ticked off on her fingers. "Step One was finding a location for my day care."

"Very logical."

"Two was finding a nice place to live nearby."

"And Three?"

"Making friends. I thought you might be a problem there, but you've turned out to be a major part."

"And Step Four would be…?"

She hesitated. Revealing a plan to someone who

might oppose it was tricky—especially when that someone might become part of the plan.

"The man."

"What man?"

"The man I'll spend my life with. The man who'll be in agreement with all the other steps."

CHAPTER SEVEN

HIS YEARS AS A COP had taught Mike that the only way to face a problem was head-on. "You have someone in mind?" he asked.

"No, just a few of the details."

"What are those?"

"As I said, mostly that he has to be in agreement with all the other steps."

"But doesn't he have to be in agreement with *that* step, too?" he challenged reasonably. "I mean, it also involves him."

She gave that some thought over a bite of toast. "Ideally, of course. But I understand many men resist the thought of marriage. So there's always the possibility he'd have to be convinced."

"Bad move," he cautioned. "A guy hates it when a woman tries to change him."

"I wouldn't want to change *him*," she said. "Just the way he feels about me, or marriage. Because first impressions can be wrong, you know. The day we met I thought you were suspicious and hard-nosed, and really you're very sweet."

He groaned and took a sip of coffee. "Guys," he told her, "also don't like to be called 'sweet.'"

"Nice, then."

"That's a little insipid, too."

She pushed her plate away and picked up her cup. "Then how do men like to be described?"

He laughed lightly. "Handsome and heroic, if the truth be told. But tough enough never to be considered sweet."

"Well, I'm sorry, but I'm staying with my initial observation."

It was only then that he realized they were straying from his original concern. He was going to have to be candid. "Tell me I'm not Step Four, Veronica."

"I told you," she said with that same evasive innocence she'd used before. "I'm still on Step Three."

"Then, what's five?"

"Children," she replied. "Of my own. Three or four."

"I'm never having children," he said frankly, wanting to make sure she understood his position. "So while I might have helped with the other steps, I'm not your man for four and five."

"I understand."

"You're sure?"

"I'm sure."

"All right. The I'll pick you up at the barn in—" he glanced at his watch "—forty-five minutes."

"I'll be ready."

THE DRIVE TO LONGVIEW was not very scenic. It was mostly freeway with a lot of traffic and industry in Portland obscuring the green hills. About a third of the way through the journey, they crossed into Washington; the traffic remained heavy, but the view softened, with hills and trees on the right and the Columbia River on their left.

"I take it you fell in love with the winery's location," Mike said after a while, "because you've spent most of your life in big cities?"

She was a good traveling companion. She didn't talk his ear off, but she noticed things he also found interesting.

"We spent a lot of time in New York when I was small," she said, her voice quiet as she stretched in her seat to see over him to the busy little port of Kalama. "Then we were all over New England as my mother tried to find new drug sources. I remember living in seedy hotels and overcrowded shelters filled with people who scared me."

"I'm sorry," he said, wishing he'd thought twice before raising the subject. "You'd probably rather talk about something else."

"I can talk about it," she said with a sigh. "It's just not very pleasant. But, yes, that is why I fell in love with the vineyard. It reminded me of *Green Acres*. Not literally, of course, but it gave me the same feeling I used to get when I watched the show as a child."

"*Green Acres?*" He cast her a sidelong grin. "Us?"

She laughed. "Not the people, but the place. The Eddie Albert character dreamed of a life in the country, and so did I. It made me feel hopeful, I guess,

because he found it. There was comfort in the knowledge that life like that existed somewhere beyond the
ugliness I knew.''

"But it wasn't real.''

She shrugged that off. "It didn't matter. I turned
my life around so that my past was fiction, and a
future in the country was reality.''

"But you entered the convent.''

"You know how you are at eighteen. I was very
idealistic, and I guess I misinterpreted my need to
escape my old life as a need to be in God's service.
Mind you, it was a wonderful place to learn about
who you are—which is what I did. That's how I
came to realize I'd entered to hide rather than to
find.'' She turned toward him. "Why did you become a cop?''

Sometimes he couldn't remember back that far.
The hostage incident had had such a monumental
effect on him it seemed as though the twenty-four-
year-old Michael Delancey existed in another lifetime.

But for some reason it came right back to him
when she asked the question. "I loved the world I
lived in then. I was strong and healthy with a wonderful family and good friends, and I thought the best
thing I could do with my life was put it to some kind
of service.'' He cast her another grin. "I have to tell
you, though, that the priesthood never occurred to
me.''

"I imagine celibacy doesn't have much appeal to
a robust young man,'' she teased.

"No, it doesn't," he agreed heartily. Then he grew serious again. "It turned out to be a sound decision on my part. I was good at the work. As a kid, I could talk my friends into trouble or out of trouble—whatever the situation called for. Six years ago, I happened to be called to the scene of a domestic dispute where a distraught wife was holding her neighbor—who happened to be the police commissioner—and her husband at gunpoint."

"Distraught over what?"

"She'd just lost a pregnancy, her medications were conflicting, and a friend had told her she'd seen her husband with another woman."

"Poor woman."

"Yeah. That's what I thought, too, until she shot me." He grinned again. "It's become one of those stories that's funny now, but hurt like hell and scared me spitless then."

Veronica gasped. "She shot you?"

"Want to see my scar?"

She hesitated. "Where is it?"

He laughed aloud. "I thought I was part of Step Three and you considered me a friend."

She laughed with him. "But you were weaseling out of having anything to do with Step Four, so I think I have a right to know where it is first."

Her honesty always surprised him—and somehow relaxed him. He put his left hand to his right biceps. "Right here."

She surprised him again by putting her fingertips

to his arm and rubbing it. A glance told him the gesture had been completely unconscious.

"Are you leading up to telling me this is how you became a hostage negotiator?"

"I am. Why? Is it getting boring?"

"No. But if you got shot," she said, as though hating to bring up that detail, "it means, well, you weren't very good, doesn't it?"

He scolded her with a frown. "No. Because even though I was bleeding and in excruciating pain, I still managed to talk her out of the gun."

Veronica made a self-deprecating face. "Sorry. So the commissioner was impressed. He probably thought he was next."

"He did. Afterward I went into special training, and for a couple of years I was quite a hotshot."

Silence fell. He checked his rearview mirror to pass a large, slow camper, then settled into the right lane again.

"You don't want to talk about what happened next?" she asked.

"No," he replied, resisting the cloud that always tried to engulf him whenever the subject came up. It was just too nice a day. "Like your story, it's rather grim."

"Fair enough. But since I'm interrogating you—" she gave an apologetic laugh "—do you mind talking about your uncle? Colette said he was missing and that's how the three of you inherited the winery."

He nodded, his eyes on the road. "That I don't

mind talking about. Unfortunately, some important details are missing. We know he left the compound about seven-and-a-half years ago and never came home.''

"Where was he going?''

"We're not sure. Rachel was away at the time. Anyway, my father and Tate flew out to try to help the police figure out what had happened, but Uncle Jack just seems to have fallen off the face of the earth. There was no sign of him or his car, a big old yellow Cadillac. You'd think it would be hard to lose one of those.''

"You have no clues to go on?''

"A couple. Tate found a letter and a photograph that suggested Jack might have been going to see a woman he'd been involved with. Apparently, she'd been married and met Jack during a brief period when she'd left her husband. But her husband had severe diabetes and he went blind, so she went back to him. But when Tate and Shea and I tried to check her out, we discovered the woman had died in a train wreck before Jack disappeared. So we wondered if he might have been going to...end it all.''

"Does that fit what you know about him? Did you know him very well?''

"Pretty well. Tate and Shea and I spent time with him every summer, and it honestly doesn't seem like something he'd do, but love can make you pretty desperate, I guess. And there was a child involved, too. When she went back to her husband, she was pregnant with Jack's child, so he had a son he couldn't claim. Rough stuff."

"How sad. Do you know what happened to the child? And the husband?"

Mike shrugged. "We don't know. I have a detective friend looking into it for me. Here's our turn-off." He pointed to the huddle of commercial roof-tops right off the freeway. "I suggest we have lunch first. There's a seafood place, or Mexican."

"Oh, Mexican!" she said with enthusiasm. "The cheese omelette whetted my appetite, and I feel as if I could eat a lot!"

"All right. Mexican it is."

AFTER LUNCH, Mike took Veronica to the toy store.

"But, don't you want to pick up the linens first?" she asked. "To make sure everything's all right?"

He pointed across the street to an Italianate build-ing. A sign on the second floor identified it as Dorset Linens. "I thought I'd leave you to look around while I go and pick up the stuff. Will you be all right?"

"Of course."

"I shouldn't be more than an hour. And there'll be a little room left in the back of the Blazer if you don't buy anything too big."

"Okay. Go on. I'll be fine."

Veronica wandered into the colorful store, looked around at the enormous stuffed animals, games of every description and an entire wall of books, and decided this must be a child's concept of heaven.

If Mike Delancey was in the middle of it, it would be pretty close to hers, too. She shook off the thought, knowing their relationship was nowhere near the point where she could give it serious consideration.

She concentrated on the books and small toys, and bought a wide selection for children aged five and older. She found teddy bears at a reasonable price and bought half a dozen of those as well as several small dolls.

She bought three riding toys, a large, brightly colored playhouse and two doll carriages, all of which she arranged to have delivered.

Then her attention was completely captured by a dollhouse. It wasn't fancy, just a simple plastic two-story, track-style home with rugs painted on the floors, pictures and kitchen cupboards painted on the walls, and tiny plastic furniture. A plastic woman with jointed arms and legs, wearing a red dress and a white apron, stood in the middle of the kitchen. A little boy and girl and a yellow dog sat on the floor in a corner where a board game was also painted on the floor.

A plastic man in a suit sat in the living room on a gray sofa, facing a tiny television.

Someone else might have considered the scene a misguided representation of family life in the fifties, complete with a mother's overburdened role, but to Veronica, it was the perfect home.

Annie Holloway, her foster parents' daughter, had had a similar dollhouse, and she and Veronica had spent hours rearranging furniture and creating domestic scenes. Sometimes, when Veronica had it all to herself, her imagination would take flight and create the perfect husband and six beautiful children to bring the house alive.

This dollhouse had been placed on a display table. Veronica knelt and ran her hands lovingly over it. There were three upstairs bedrooms, with an en suite bathroom off the master bedroom and a smaller one between the other two.

The downstairs included a large kitchen and pantry, a dining room, living room, and a room at the back that seemed to be a combination exercise room and office.

She smiled at that very contemporary amenity. In Annie Holloway's dollhouse, that room had been a laundry-mudroom.

Veronica decided she had to have the dollhouse, but she hated the thought of waiting for it to be delivered.

"How long will that take?" she asked the clerk.

"About a week," he said.

Seven days. Silly to feel this way, but the house represented everything she wanted from life—Steps Four and Five of her plan.

MIKE FOUND VERONICA on her knees in front of a dollhouse, a clerk leaning over her in concern. The urgent look in her eyes erased from his mind the question he'd come to put to her.

"We have to send to our store in Seattle for the

fire truck and police car," the clerk said. "Those won't get here until Tuesday. It's just not possible to make two separate deliveries."

"Of course," she agreed, pushing to her feet. She caressed the roof, then reached to trace the line of the chimney.

Mike saw the need in the gesture; he was reminded of their conversation about her dream of a perfect life in the country, and wondered if this was connected to it.

She smiled at the clerk. "I understand. I just don't want to wait that long to play with it." Then she laughed, clearly trying to convince the clerk she was kidding.

He fell for it.

Mike didn't.

"Can't we just take it with us?" Mike asked the clerk.

Veronica started and turned to him. "Oh, hi. Well, you can see it's pretty big. You won't have that much room, will you?"

Mike consulted the clerk again. "Does it come disassembled?"

"Yes. In a box about a foot-and-a-half high and three feet wide."

"That'll fit," Mike said.

"And still leave room for books and bears?" she asked hopefully.

He loved the light in her eyes. "Depends," he teased. "Black bears, maybe. Grizzlies, not a chance."

She laughed, wrapped her arms around his waist and hugged him.

He thought his heart might stop. He held her to him, not sure what this meant—part of him wishing he did understand, part of him glad he didn't. Ignorance excused him from an appropriate response, didn't it?

Then she looked at him and he knew without a doubt that excuse would never work for him again. Much as he'd tried to resist it, he and Veronica were attracted to one another. He'd understood her need to take the dollhouse with her, and that meant a lot to her—more than the simple gesture should.

He refused to think it through.

She gave him another breath-stealing squeeze, then dropped her arms and proceeded to direct the removal of a tall stack of books, six loose teddy bears, several dolls, and the boxed dollhouse into the back of the Blazer.

When that was finished she checked over the list of things to be delivered, then shook hands with the grateful clerk.

As they walked back to the Blazer, she looked through the closed hatch to the colorful stacks of sheets and bedspreads. "Those are so pretty. Is there anything else we have to do?"

"Sort of."

"Sort of?"

He leaned against the back of the Blazer. "Remember this morning, when Shea said he checked with Dorset about the restaurant linens and was told the napkins hadn't come?''

She nodded.

''Well, they told me they'll be in tomorrow's shipment.''

She continued to watch him, apparently missing the point he was afraid might offend her. He was about to explain, when he saw it dawn on her.

''Oh,'' she said calmly. ''You mean—it would be easier to stay the night rather than come back tomorrow.''

''If you have a problem with the idea,'' he assured her quickly, ''I can take you home. I have an appointment with the newspaper tomorrow afternoon, but I can certainly come back later in the week.''

''Of course not.'' She squared her shoulders and her sudden smile seemed genuinely amused. ''This isn't going to turn into one of those situations where there's a convention in town and all we'll be able to find is one room with a double bed that we'll have to share?''

He didn't understand why her scenario had such appeal.

''I doubt that very much,'' he replied. ''It's July. Everyone's probably on vacation somewhere else. We should have no trouble getting rooms. We'll have an early dinner, you can go through all the books you bought, and I'll get some much-needed sleep.''

She looked regretful. ''I apologize again that Rachel woke you last night.''

''That's not why I need sleep.'' She was why he

needed sleep, but not because of last night. He just found himself thinking about her a lot lately, sometimes in his dreams, but often while he was wide-awake. "Tate's a tough act to follow. I don't want him to find anything to complain about when he comes home. I find myself worrying about it during the night."

She walked around to the passenger door and pulled it open. Her manner was deliberately nonchalant. "Then let's find someplace to stay and put your plan into practice. I'm dying to look through my books."

Within the hour, they found adjoining rooms at the first hotel they tried, a short distance from Dorset Linens. It was old and elegant with an attentive staff and a large clientele of businesspeople—always the sign of a good house.

They showered, then went to the mall across the street, where Mike bought a shirt and Veronica found a cotton sweater in a luscious shade of fuschia.

She held it in front of her and turned to Mike. "What do you think?"

But Mike picked up the same sweater in a buttery yellow and handed it to her. "This is more your color." He stood back to study the effect and nodded emphatically. "Yeah. I'd say the yellow one."

With that recommendation, she was tempted to buy three.

They had dinner at an Italian restaurant in the mall, then got her books out of the back of the Blazer.

"Would you mind carrying up the dollhouse,

too?'' she asked. ''Just so I can read the directions and look at the figures.''

''You don't think I believe this is for the children to play with, do you?'' He pulled the large box out, balanced it on his knee while he locked the door again, then hefted it under his arm.

''Of course it is,'' she said, smiling into his eyes, then looking away so he wouldn't see she lied. ''I just want to play with it first.''

They went back to the hotel. Mike carried the dollhouse into her room, then unlocked the door that adjoined their rooms. ''I left my side open earlier so if you have a problem, or need anything, you can just knock on the door. Unless you'd prefer to leave yours locked.''

She leaned against the wall. ''After you've made it so clear that you couldn't possibly be interested in me, it's hard for me to consider you a threat.''

He opened her door, then looked at her with a seriousness that stole her breath. His dark eyes roved her face with an interest she hadn't expected to see there. ''I can't make a lifelong commitment to anyone,'' he corrected softly. ''But you're annoyingly attractive.''

It took her a moment to recover from his admission, then she asked doubtfully, ''How can something annoy you and still be attractive?''

He shrugged, a slight smile pulling at the corner of his mouth. ''I don't know. But you manage it all the time. Good night.'' He walked into his room and shut his door.

Veronica stared at the expanse of wood and wondered if she'd been complimented or insulted. Then she decided it didn't matter. Mike found her *attractive*.

Was that a move toward Step Four? She couldn't be sure. The man was stubborn and unpredictable.

Leaving thoughts of him for morning, when she was bound to be more refreshed, Veronica reached for her stack of books, then changed her mind and pulled the heavy dollhouse into the middle of the floor.

She loosened the heavy staples that secured the box with the Swiss army knife in her purse. It had been given to her by the mother of a student who'd collected wildflowers with her for a class project and who had been horrified that they'd had to cut them with convent-issue nail scissors.

Veronica pulled piece after piece from the box, smiling over the painted rugs and pictures, then carefully read the instructions. It was soon clear they'd been written by someone for whom English was not even a second language—the words seemed picked at random from a dictionary!

She finally abandoned them and put the house together herself. It was nearly eleven when the roof refused to sit correctly atop the assembly. By then she was frustrated, exhausted and feeling inexplicably emotional.

She should not have bought the dollhouse. It was a silly, sentimental reversion to a childhood she should forget, yet still clung to.

She propped the roof against the side of the house and slipped off her pants. She left her shirt on since she had a fresh one to wear in the morning, turned off all the lights except the one in the bathroom, and climbed into bed.

She did her best to quench her agitation. The last thing she wanted was for it to bring on the dream. This was a new life, she told herself firmly. And the dream was a part of the old one. She'd be fine. She just had to relax. She'd be asleep in minutes.

She was—but the dream came.

It was night, again. For the past three mornings she'd awakened, certain that this was the day her mother would come home. She'd have part of a sandwich, or a package of crackers, or a pop—something to end the gnawing hunger.

Veronica was five. She knew because she'd just had her birthday, although there'd been no cake and no presents.

She listened to the tenement noises: arguments, babies crying. Though the angry shouting next door usually frightened her, she'd have been willing to risk meeting the man that voice belonged to if he'd give her something to eat.

Her mother had been gone a long time. Days. She'd locked the door before she left and told Veronica to eat the crackers and the chips in the bottom cupboard. She'd done that the first day, but the second day there'd been a rat in the cupboard, and she'd been afraid to reach in for the bag. She closed the door instead.

She tried to put the lights on when it grew dark, but they didn't work, and neither did the phone.

She sat near the window, and, with the light from the street, looked at the numbers-and-letters book the woman in the blue suit had given her. She forced herself not to think about being hungry.

She fell asleep, and when she woke up it was dark again. The building was unusually quiet and she wondered if everyone had died. She went to the grimy window and looked out. The streetlights were still on, but there were no cars in the street, no people walking.

She was alone. She was alone all the time, but this was different. No one was coming—ever. She knew that with a certainty that changed her forever. She would always be alone.

And that was when she began to cry.

She'd been proud until then that every time she'd wanted to cry, she'd sat and looked at her book instead. But she couldn't swallow the tears back anymore. Her stomach hurt, her head felt funny, and everyone else was dead. Surely it was all right to cry now.

She heard herself sob. She didn't call for her mother because she certainly wasn't coming—and there was no one else....

CHAPTER EIGHT

MIKE WOKE WITH a start, heart racing for an instant before old training took over. Calm down. Take a breath. Assess.

And then he heard the sound that must have awakened him: sobs coming from Veronica's room. In the briefs and T-shirt he'd slept in, he burst through the door without knocking. The light from the bathroom lit a clear path on the side of the room nearest the window, and he followed it to the shadows that surrounded the bed.

"Vee?" He sat down on the edge of the bed and caught her arm, unsure if she was awake or asleep.

She was unaware of him and continued to thrash and sob; high, desperate sounds seemed to be ripping their way from deep inside her.

He pulled her into a sitting position, took hold of both her arms and shook her. "Veronica!" he said firmly.

"Here! I'm in here!" Her eyes were closed tightly, her forehead furrowed, her mouth contorted in anguish.

He shook her again as he shouted a second time, "Veronica!"

And then she opened her eyes. It took her a moment to focus on him, and when she did he saw such fear on her face that he felt it himself. Then she collapsed against him, still sobbing.

He wrapped his arms around her. Judging by the desperate strength with which she held him, that was what she needed.

His pulse slowed to normal and the fear she was ill receded with the knowledge that she was at least physically safe. But what in God's name had caused her distress?

"Okay. It's okay," he said over and over as he gently rubbed her spine. He finally felt her relax.

A moment later she raised her head to look into his eyes. Hers were still filled with tears. Her nose was red, and her hair stuck up in little spikes. "Do you have anything to eat?" she asked in a raspy voice.

The question didn't make sense, but he was eager to do anything that would wipe the terrified look from her face. "Ah, I've got the mint patties from the restaurant." They'd come with the bill, and Veronica had scooped them off the little tray and handed them to him on their way out of the restaurant.

"Can I have them?"

He brought them to her.

Her hands were shaking, so he peeled the foil off one for her. She wolfed it down. He removed the wrapper from the second one, and she ate it more slowly, taking deep breaths, as though trying hard to draw herself out of the remnants of the nightmare.

"In my dream," she explained, "it's been four days since I've eaten."

"Do you have this dream often?" he asked, then tried to lighten the grim mood surrounding them. "Like Scarlett O'Hara?"

He was relieved when she smiled, too. "Actually, it's a memory. So, it's always there, only some-times..." The smile vanished, and he sobered, too, at the sudden sadness he saw. "Sometimes I dream it. I'm five years old and it's happening again."

Her bottom lip trembled, and he reached out to run his thumb over her mouth to stop it. He was surprised by how much her anguish hurt him. "It's not happening again. You were just dreaming."

She leaned her cheek into his hand, and his heart melted. Then she took his hand in hers and drew it down to her lap. He noticed absently that her legs were bare.

"Do you want to tell me about it?" he asked. "So you can exorcise it once and for all?"

She looked skeptical. "Do you think we ever ex-orcise the past?"

He didn't, but they were talking about her past, not his, and he wanted her to feel that she could. "Sure," he said confidently. "Not the actual events, of course, because you can't erase what's happened. But you can banish what frightens you or debilitates you, or otherwise prevents you from getting on with your life."

She squeezed his hand a little more tightly. "It's never stopped me from going on. And though I know my worth shouldn't be affected by how little I meant to my mother, sometimes I can't help myself. When I look at children, I'm overwhelmed by their beauty and their cleverness and their ability to learn. And I'm not even connected to them by blood." She sniffed and ran a hand over her eyes. "I mean, *everyone* reacts that way to children. But my mother saw none of that in me. She felt none of that *for* me. So it's hard not to wonder if there's something missing in me."

He framed her face with his hands and looked into her eyes. "I'll let you get away with that because you've had a rough night, but *think,* Veronica. She spent all those years in and out of jail, living for drugs. You survived and dedicated your life to helping children. Where was the real problem?"

She nodded, and a big tear slid down her cheek. "It's just that what I know and what I feel get all tangled up, and I have trouble remembering what's right."

"I know." He pulled her to him again and wrapped his arms around her. "I've been there. Now, tell me about the dream."

Veronica relaxed into his solid warmth and told him about the terrible days she spent alone, locked in a sixth-floor tenement with the power and phone disconnected and nothing to eat.

"She'd been arrested during a drug bust," she said, concentrating on the stroke of his hand along her spine instead of the remembered fear trying to claim her attention. "And she failed to mention she'd left a five-year-old at home."

"God!"

"I was used to being left all day," she went on, "but nighttime was scary…. That's when the rats came out."

He held her more closely. "I've seen children of drugged-out parents. Most end up just as lost. How did you survive?"

"Caring foster homes. Teachers who understood and gave me special attention." She closed her eyes against his cotton T-shirt and smiled. "And the hope that I'd be okay once I had my house in the country."

She felt his lips against her temple. Then he pointed to the roofless dollhouse. "I see you were trying to put the house together."

"Yeah. The roof won't fit, though." She sat up wearily, hating to move out of his arms. "I had to give up on it. I was afraid I'd break it. I should pack it away so I don't hold you up in the morning."

"No," he replied, getting to his feet and gently pushing her back into the pillows. "You lie down, and I'll have a look at it."

Shaking her head, she followed him to the dollhouse. "The instructions were awful. I finally had to ignore them. Everything else sort of went together, but the roof's a little off on one side."

He knelt beside the house. "Let me have a look."

"It doesn't matter," she said, picking up the box

and propping it against the wall near the door. "It was silly."

Frowning, he studied the dollhouse, then removed the sides and switched them. He glanced at her as he worked. "Buying this was silly?"

She gathered up the plastic figures and dropped them into the plastic bag in which they'd been packaged. "No, wanting to have it was silly."

He reached for the roof.

"It won't fit," she warned.

"It will now," he said. "You just had the outside walls reversed."

He lined up the roof carefully, then pressed the edges one by one until everything snapped into place. A perfect fit.

Mike smiled at her, pleased he was able to do this small task for her. "There. Good as new."

"Thanks," she said. Her voice was high and tight. "I'm sorry about the fuss."

Almost before he knew what he was doing, he got to his feet, stepped over the dollhouse, took her in his arms and kissed her. It was chaste because what he felt was chaste—just the brief meeting of lips.

She responded in the same way, all sweetness and innocence—a friend grateful for another friend's comfort and help.

"You did scare the hell out of me. But I don't think that matters, considering what you've been through. Will you be able to sleep now?"

A shadow rose in her eyes, and he read her

thoughts easily. She didn't want to be alone, and she didn't want to ask him to stay.

"Sure," she said feebly.

He looked at the queen-size bed and made an instant, if somewhat reluctant, decision. "Which would you hate more?" he asked. "Being left alone in the room, or me in your bed? On my own side, of course."

She smiled brightly. "So this *is* going to turn out to be one of those scenarios where fate throws us into the same bed."

"Not too horrifying for an ex-nun?"

"Not if it means I don't have to be alone in here."

"Why didn't you just let me take you home?"

"Because I wanted the extra time with you."

He pointed a warning finger at her. "This is not the time to be talking like that."

She agreed with a nod and walked around the bed. "You asked. Good night, Mike. And—" she smiled at him as she climbed under the covers "—thanks for understanding."

"Anytime. You want the bathroom light on?"

"If you're staying, you can turn it off."

He did, then silently cursing himself, he got into bed. He understood, all right. He was a masochist.

VERONICA OPENED HER EYES to sun streaming through the window, and felt a curious peace. She was usually eager to start the new day and its challenges. But peace was different. She lay still a moment, trying to figure out where the feeling had come from.

Then she remembered. She'd told Mike about that awful night, and he'd stayed with her.

She turned her head to the left, and there he was, facing her, though still carefully on his side of the bed. She entertained the fanciful idea that he'd fallen asleep watching her.

"You're Step Four," she thought, affection swelling up in her. Affection, and something else. Something deeper that made her forget that she'd ever been anyplace else but right here. That peace again. "I know you don't want to be." She whispered softly. "And I'm not sure what to do, because I didn't expect to find you so soon, but I have to take what I'm offered or I'll lose out. So brace yourself, Delancey. You're being worked into the plan."

MIKE KEPT HIS EYES CLOSED. He'd spent a long and sleepless night and had reached a sound decision about...something.

He tried to explore the thought, but it was waking him up and he didn't want that. He fell onto his back, looking for the spot between the pillows that always made him feel hidden away.

But there was a slight pressure on his stomach that claimed his attention. Grilled onions. He'd had grilled onions with his steak last night. He should have known better.

The pressure moved up to his rib cage, and he realized drowsily that it was more external than internal. Then he felt a little puff of air against his face, like a breeze or a...breath.

Mike opened his eyes and remembered suddenly, clearly that his decision had involved the brown eyes now looking into his.

Veronica was on her side with an arm across his ribs. She was wearing her new yellow sweater over slacks, and a look he identified immediately as trouble.

But he was rather reluctant to fight it. In her eyes was a kind of adoration he'd never seen before. She smelled of soap and a floral shampoo. The spikes in her hair were missing, he noticed, replaced by a smooth, springy cap, glossy from the sun streaming in the window.

"Good morning," she said, leaning closer.

He didn't reply. He didn't think he could.

She brought herself even closer until her lips were only inches from his. "I'd like to kiss you," she whispered.

His decision came back to him, but he realized now that it had been stupid. "I seem to be at your mercy."

She seemed displeased by his answer. "I want you to *want* me to kiss you."

"Oh, I do," he replied quickly. "Believe me, I do."

"You have to understand that I've never done this before." Apparently she felt obliged to warn him. "I mean, well, last night you kissed *me*. It was really sweet, but I feel...something different this morning.''

Something different. Trouble multiplied astronomically. But he could hardly wait.

He put a hand to the back of her head and urged her closer. ''Then, by all means,'' he said softly. ''Express yourself.''

The first contact against his lips was tentative. Her soft, warm mouth seemed to be gauging how it fit against his, touching and retreating, exploring, opening.

He followed her lead, careful never to overtake her. Then she raised her head to look into his eyes, and she was smiling—glowing, even. A corner of his brain identified the look in her eyes for what it was, but refused to make it clear to the rest of him. *Later,* it told him. *Later.*

This time her mouth met his with a different purpose altogether. He felt the tip of her tongue against his lips and had to bank the instant flare rushing through him.

She traced the line of his mouth with a delicacy he found completely debilitating, then she kissed his cheek, his eyelids, the bridge of his nose, his other cheek. Then she was back to his mouth again.

He caught her to him and rolled her under him. He'd had about all he could take of quiet submission. And careful as he wanted to be about her sensibilities, she had to know that kissing was best with two participants.

He kissed her with all the desire she'd aroused in

him. His body was functioning without his brain—this was all heart, all emotion, all need.

Still, one little corner of his brain tried to flash the warning. *Danger. Danger. Danger.* But he was too distracted to listen. Her hands were in his hair, on his shoulders, running down his sides.

His fingertips found the hem of her sweater and her bare, silky skin. He turned so that they lay side by side, then closed a hand over her lace-covered breast.

She gasped and was absolutely still. He felt her shudder and saw the startled, even astonished, look in her eyes. He expected her to pull away, but she dropped her forehead to his chest instead.

He came quickly to his senses, confused though they were. "Did I scare you?" he asked.

She raised her head and propped her elbow on the pillow. She didn't look horrified, just surprised. "No," she answered, placing her fingertip on his chin. "No. I guess the power of what I'm feeling scares me. I've cautioned and counseled kids about sex for years based on books I've read and classes I've taken from other people. But I didn't really know...what a force attraction is. How much you can want it, and not just for the satisfaction, but for the connection it promises with the other person."

Danger! Danger! Danger! His brain was shouting again, only this time it provided detail. *She's in love with you! What are you doing to do now?*

Veronica saw his expression change slightly and knew what he must be thinking. "Please understand that I'm not sophisticated enough to have been teasing you. I wouldn't do that. I wanted to kiss you because I woke up feeling so...free.'' She smiled when she saw understanding in his eyes. ''And I know it's because you helped me so much last night. Not that I thought I could repay you with a kiss, but because I wanted to know...'' How on earth did she explain that she was falling in love with him, when she knew it was the last thing he wanted?

''What it was like to kiss a man,'' he finished, sitting up, swinging his feet to the carpet and standing in one graceful movement. ''I understand. You're experimenting.''

She leapt off the bed and followed him as he went through the open door to his room. She stopped in the doorway. ''I wasn't experimenting.'' She was offended that he thought so. ''I wanted to know what it was like to kiss *you*. You, specifically.''

He pulled on his jeans and zipped the fly. ''Isn't that an experiment?'' His manner was calm, even reasonable, but she knew he was upset about something. She guessed he was feeling like her test subject.

He bent to pull the new shirt he'd bought out of the bag on the chair.

''No, it's not an experiment,'' she persisted, now a little annoyed herself. ''I wanted the experience with you because you've become important to me. Because you're so determined to keep your distance, and I want to know more.''

He sat on the edge of the bed to pull on his socks

and shoes. "More isn't a good idea, Vee. You might find I have deeper passions, but my emotions only go so far. I thought I'd already made this clear. I'm not in the market."

She folded her arms. "There's a market?"

Shoes on, he got to his feet and stuffed his old shirt and socks into the bag, then collected his watch and keys from the bedside table. He had a mildly impatient expression on his face as he put the keys into his pocket and slid the watch onto his wrist. "You know what I mean. The marriage market."

"I don't remember proposing," she said as he glanced around the room, apparently checking to see if he'd forgotten anything.

He gave her a knowing look as he came toward her. "You didn't. But you think you can fit me into your plan." She stood in his path, determined to bridge the distance he insisted on keeping between them. It hadn't been there last night, but this morning it was back, as great and unbroachable.

"If you let me in," he said, pointing into her room, "I'll pack up your dollhouse."

She finally stepped aside to let him pass, thinking that if she was a weaker woman, that would be precisely what he'd be doing. Packing up her dollhouse. Packing up her dreams and putting them in a box.

But she could have sworn there'd been feeling at least as deep as the passion in the kiss they'd just shared.

"So, actually, *I've* scared *you*." Veronica yanked her bedspread into some semblance of order and gathered up her stack of books. "That's funny when you think of it. Mike Delancey, ex-cop and tough guy, is afraid of Veronica Callahan, virgin."

"For a virgin," he said, turning the box upside down so that the plastic bag of figures and furniture fell out, "you have a couple of worldly talents that show real promise."

All right. She had to admit she was flattered. But that wasn't what she was trying to get out of this conversation. "And you're going to pass on ever seeing how they develop because you're afraid?"

He put the disassembled walls into the box. "Veronica," he said with a chiding smile. "I've been baited by hostile crowds and angry felons. You don't really think your calling me a coward is going to make me agree to be Step Four, do you?"

She picked up her purse and slung it over her shoulder. "What will?" she asked.

He laughed as he pushed the roof into the box. "You, Sister Trouble, should have been a hostage negotiator instead of a teacher."

It was her turn to laugh. "My guess is the job descriptions aren't all that different."

He stood and tucked the box under his arm. Veronica, books in hand, opened the door and held it for him. "Ignore the situation all you want, Delancey. Last night changed everything between us."

He went into the hallway. "Come on. I've got a meeting at home this afternoon. We've got to get moving."

She closed the door and followed him down the corridor. "'Fraidy cat," she muttered.

CHAPTER NINE

VERONICA HAD TO HOLD three teddy bears in her lap during the ride home, while the other three sat on and around her feet. The back of the Blazer was packed with linens for the B-and-B and the restaurant, as well as with Veronica's dollhouse.

Mike put the radio on a blues station. While Veronica leaned back against the headrest and closed her eyes, he tried to decide if and how things had changed between them.

He didn't know, he realized finally. When he held her, he desperately wanted to have a relationship, not just a friendship. But was that a reaction to loneliness, or was it real feeling?

They had lunch in Portland and were home carly in the afternoon. Mike pulled the dollhouse from the back of the truck, and she balanced books and bears while opening the door of the barn.

She flipped on the light. The smell of paint had dissipated somewhat, and the bright colors of the play area lent the big space a cheerful atmosphere.

She set down her things on a sawhorse. "Put the box anywhere," she told Mike. "Thanks for all the meals and for taking me to the toy store."

"Sure." He propped the box against the wall. "It

was good to have company. Do you have something to eat besides cookies?''

She swatted his arm. ''Yes, I do. Don't worry. You won't have to rescue me from under the bathroom sink again.''

He didn't want to leave her. What was wrong with him? He was only going to be across the compound, but after twenty-four hours of being with her, it would be strange to turn around and *not* see her. Did that mean…?

''Okay,'' he said, heading for the open door. ''You know where I am if you need anything.''

She stayed in the middle of the room, but her smile reached him. ''And if *you* need anything,'' she said quietly, ''you know where *I* am.''

For a minute, he didn't understand. He was the one with all the resources. Then he realized she meant something else entirely.

With an abrupt nod, he turned and found his way blocked by a short, roundish, middle-age man in a black suit and a clerical collar. The man smiled. ''Good afternoon. I'm looking for Veronica Callahan?''

Before Mike could respond, he heard a squeal from behind him. He moved just in time to avoid being trampled by Veronica's headlong rush into the man's arms.

''Father Wolff!'' she exclaimed in obvious astonishment. ''What are you doing here?''

The priest wrapped her in his arms for a moment, then freed her so he could step back and study her.

"Sister Veronica!" he said, clearly as disbelieving as she was. "I can't believe it. I've just been assigned to French River, and I'm on a mission to find a new source for sacramental wine. The young man I met at the restaurant explained there wasn't any wine yet, but we got to talking, and eventually he told me about the new day care center being started by a ex-nun—"

Veronica hugged him again. Then, remembering Mike, she caught his arm and pulled him closer. "Father Paul Wolff, meet Mike Delancey. You were probably talking to his brother, Shea. Together with their older brother, Tate, they own the place."

The priest shook hands with Mike. "Glad to meet you, Mike. Yes, it was your brother I spoke to. He told me you and Veronica were away picking up supplies or something."

Veronica blushed slightly, but Mike didn't think the priest noticed.

"Father Wolff and I served in the same parish in Santa Margarita, California," she said quickly.

The priest nodded. "Yes. We were both part of a small but determined force who wanted to replace weekly bingo with Saturday night dances."

Mike laughed. "Did you win?"

Father Wolff feigned regret. "No. There were apparently more gamblers than dancers in the parish." He turned back to Veronica. "I can't believe my good fortune. I was just about to leave when I saw your vehicle arrive. I understand this is where your day care center will be."

"Yes. And I'll be living in the loft. I can't tell you how happy I am that you're here!"

"If you'll excuse me," Mike said, "I'll be on my way so you two can visit. I'm sure Shea would be happy to put another plate on for dinner, Father, if you'd like to stay."

Father Wolff shook his head. "I'd love to, but the president of the Altar Society has already invited me. But I'd be happy to take a rain check."

Mike nodded. "Set a date with Veronica. Welcome to French River, Father."

"Thank you, Mike. A pleasure to meet you."

As he left, Mike cast Veronica a parting glance. It reminded her of all that had happened between them in the last day and a half.

"Seems like a nice young man," Father Wolff said. "Is there a relationship there? Even I caught something in that look."

Veronica rolled her eyes at him. "Honestly, Father. I thought the Archdiocese was going to send you to classes on subtlety."

He seemed unrepentant. "They didn't work. I just wanted to know if you're happy."

She sobered and sighed. "The truth is, I'd like us to have a relationship, but he's not so sure."

"Finds you scary, does he?"

"Yes. And he doesn't want to have children." She explained briefly what Colette had told her about the hostage experience. "I don't know all the—"

Veronica stopped abruptly when she noticed Mike

standing in the doorway, a teddy bear in one hand. She knew by the anger in his eyes he'd heard her talking about his past.

"Excuse me," he said in a painfully cold voice. "I found this under your seat."

As Veronica took the bear from him, misery welled up in her. She'd ruined everything.

Father Wolff, never at loss for words, jumped right in. "She wasn't discussing you behind your back, Mike. I asked about you. She was only answering my question."

"I'm able to talk, Father," Mike replied. "You can ask me whatever you want to know."

The priest looked into the tight lines of Mike's face. "I don't think that would be smart right now. Instead, why don't you get in touch with me. Just come and see me at St. Jerome's." He gave Veronica a quick hug. "I've got to get back. I have boxes and junk everywhere. I'll call you about dinner." He turned to Mike. "I presume I'm still invited."

Mike drew a steadying breath. "Of course."

The priest patted his shoulder and left.

Mike also turned to leave, but Veronica caught his arm. "Mike, I'm sorry. I didn't mean to hurt you."

He tried to shake off her hands. "Just tell me how my past happened to come up in conversation. 'By the way, Father.'" He mimicked her voice. "'Step Four in my plan is in danger of death. Can you help me resurrect it, please?'"

Color rose in her face. That was a little closer to the truth than he probably wanted to know.

"It was nothing like that. He said he liked you and wondered if we were involved. I said you didn't want to be, but he'd noticed the way you—looked at me. So I couldn't explain why you didn't want a relationship without telling him why."

He studied her steadily, but said nothing.

"How can you believe after what you did for me last night, that I'd talk about your past indiscriminately?"

"I just don't like people discussing it," he retorted, "indiscriminately or otherwise. I'm not a case study."

"That's not what we were doing."

He seemed unconvinced.

"So now," she suggested with fatalistic calm, "I suppose I'm just annoying *without* being interesting."

"You," he said, "are now a major aggravation." He freed himself and headed for the door. He stopped to turn once he'd stepped outside. "But you can still call me if you need anything."

As MIKE STARTED to unload the truck, Shea appeared beside him.

"Classy," he said, looking at the napkins through the protective wrap. "Sorry you had to stay over in Longview." He pushed the restaurant linens aside and made himself a stack of bedsheets that he placed atop a thick bedspread.

Mike carried in two bedspreads and set them on the kitchen counter. He remembered the kiss he and

Veronica had shared, and for a moment that blotted out her conversation with the priest. "It wasn't a problem."

He looked up to find Shea watching him. "It wasn't, huh?" Shea's voice was speculative as he followed Mike back out to the truck. "So, what happened?"

Mike put another bedspread in Shea's arms. "Nothing."

Shea stood dutifully as Mike piled on sheets and pillowcases. "It looks like *something* happened."

"Nothing happened. We had dinner, I helped her put together a dollhouse..."

"A dollhouse?"

"It's a long story." Mike took another load of linens and they walked side by side up the B-and-B steps. "Anything happen while I was gone?"

"No. Everything was quiet. Armand and Rachel went out last night. Some church thing."

"It's about time he let her know how he feels. How'd it go?"

Shea stood aside to let him through the door. "Haven't heard. He's been in the vineyard all day, and she hasn't been out of the cottage. Oh, we got a postcard from Tate and his ladies. They're having a wonderful time, and they don't miss us a bit—and us so charming."

"I know. I don't understand it."

They made two more trips with the rest of the linens, then drove the short distance to the restaurant. The canthus-leaf wallpaper border had been applied around the top of the wall, and a gold-leafed molding created just beneath it. Mike stopped to admire the effect.

"I was afraid that might look pretentious," he said, doing a slow turn. "But it doesn't. It's just classy."

"Thanks." Shea nodded, looking satisfied. "Yeah. I like it, too. And it'll warm up when we get tables and chairs in and something on the walls. Veronica recovered from the other night, then?"

"Yes. She's fine." Mike returned to the Blazer, Shea behind him. "And leave me alone about it, will you? Nothing happened, and nothing's going to happen."

"That's a stupid thing to do to yourself."

Mike turned on his brother. They squared off the way they used to do when they were teenagers. He'd been four years older and several sizes larger, but that had never stopped Shea from trying to take him on. Even then he'd had trouble faulting him for it, because Mike had always reacted the same way to Tate.

"That seems to run in the family, then," Mike said, poking a finger at Shea's chest, "because I seem to recall you having your own problems with a woman."

Pain entered Shea's face. Then he blinked and it was gone. "She's not right for me. Veronica, though, seems to be just what you need."

"You hardly know her." Mike reached for another armful of linens. "Why isn't this San Francisco woman right for you? You must have thought so once.''

"A lot's changed since then.'' Shea put his arms out and accepted the burden. "But we're talking about you.''

"No, *you're* talking about me. I'm talking about *you*. And maybe we'll get this grunt work done quicker if we *stop* talking.''

"Okay. But I remember when you wanted something out of life—to make a difference, own a Harley and find a woman who'd share your life and give you kids. I think you're crazy to let a drugged-out idiot who'd have killed his family whether or not you were there ruin that.''

"I remember when you wanted the same thing,'' Mike retorted. "Except with a restaurant in an old neighborhood and a woman with a knack for pastry. If I'm crazy, so are you.''

"At least I don't think it's healthy to sound so proud of it!''

ARMAND CAME TO DINNER wearing a black eye and a smile.

"What happened?'' Mike asked as he closed the door behind him. Together they walked into the kitchen where Shea worked over a thick, rich stew.

"Jeez!'' Shea exclaimed, pushing Armand toward the nook. "You want an ice pack? Sit down.''

"Too late for treatment,'' Armand replied with a good-natured grin. "It happened last night.''

"I thought you were just going to dinner," Shea said in puzzlement.

Armand jabbed the air with both hands. "You forget with *whom* I went to dinner."

"Rachel," Shea said, failing to make the connection. "You went to dinner with Rachel."

But Mike got it. "Rachel gave you the black eye. My God, what did you do to deserve a shiner like that?"

Armand looked pleased with himself as he settled into a corner of the nook with a groan. "I helped myself to a kiss. She thought I should have asked first."

Shea went to the kitchen and returned with a bottle of wine and the stems of three glasses caught between his fingers.

"What now?" Shea asked.

Armand shrugged. "Hers was a passionate response. I believe she has more feeling for me than she thinks she has. I'm a patient man."

Mike was a little concerned for the older man's sanity—and his safety. "Then I'd brush up on my self-defense skills," he recommended.

Armand laughed. "I will win her over. She now has a freedom she does not want to compromise by promising herself to a man she thinks will prevent her from living her own life."

"But you wouldn't do that."

"Of course not. But she believes I might try." He shook his head. "Which is a difficult argument to battle. She's seen that I am guilty of it at times with my daughter."

Mike struggled to get a clear picture of what Armand was saying. He glanced at Shea and saw by the pleat on his brow that suggested he didn't understand, either. "So, you left her feeling you *are* the kind of man she's unwilling to get involved with?"

Armand nodded reluctantly and toasted them with his glass. Mike and Shea raised theirs.

"I imagine I did," Armand said.

Shea sipped his wine, then narrowed his eyes at Armand. "But that's not good, is it? I mean—why are you so cheerful?"

Armand leaned back with a broad smile. "Because, gentlemen, she is worth the battle."

DURING THE NEXT WEEK, delivery trucks came and went from the Delancey Vineyards compound. Five sets of bedroom furniture were delivered to the B-and-B, a different style for each room—a tall, pineapple topped four-poster, an intricate cast-iron one, a sleigh bed, and two ornate brass beds. Veronica imagined all the beautiful linens they'd brought home being smoothed and tucked and fluffed on them.

She watched enviously from her upstairs window as elegant armoires and several chests with padded seats were unloaded. Greed was an interesting thing, she thought. As a child she'd had almost nothing to call her own, and as a nun she'd willingly forsworn all physical possessions.

But after seven months out of the convent, she was just like everyone else: deeply attached to her things and devoted to the acquisition of more.

Tables and chairs arrived for the restaurant. The tables were oak with ball-and-claw feet, and the chairs were deep with high backs, upholstered in a dark blue and mauve tapestry.

But then Veronica noticed two deliverymen coming toward the barn with one of the tables.

Moments later, a loud knock on the door sent her running downstairs.

The man holding the left side of a table and consulting an invoice taped to the protective plastic asked, "Veronica Callahan?"

"Yes," she said, "but there must be some—"

Her protest was ignored as the men moved forward with the table, forcing her to step out of their way. But once inside, both men stopped to stare at the large open space, then the colorful walls of the playrooms.

"I'm opening a day care center in a couple of weeks," she explained, then tried to reclaim their attention. "I didn't order—"

The spokesman for the two, a paunchy man with a photo button of a baby on his cap, turned to her with new interest. "I'll have to tell my daughter. She's moving to French River next week to take over as manager of Northwest Bank." His already considerable chest puffed with pride. "She'll need a good place for Andy."

All right! Providence at work! Veronica pointed to the button on the man's cap. "Is that Andy?"

"No, that's the newest grandson. Elliot. Belongs to my son. Andy's six. You have a business card or something?"

That was still on her to-do list. "Not yet." She patted her overalls, searching for something to write on.

"You can put your number on the invoice," the man said. "Where do you want it?"

"You're sure it's mine?" she asked, finding a pen.

He pointed to the invoice again. "Clear as day. Twenty-four tables to Delancey's, one to Miss Veronica Callahan. Orders from Shea Delancey, himself. Ma'am, I could hold this all day, but Smitty, here—" he grinned at the much smaller man holding the other side of the table with interminable patience "—he only eats health foods, so he's gotta be getting tired."

Smitty smiled a wry smile. "Don't start with me, Francis. It is getting on to lunchtime, though, ma'am."

Veronica led them upstairs to her apartment, where she had them place the table in the kitchen. While she wrote her name and telephone number on the invoice, Smitty returned to the truck. In a few moments he reappeared with four ladder-back dining room chairs.

Veronica was delighted at both having possibly acquired a third client and knowing that even if the table had been delivered on "orders from Shea Delancey, himself,'' Mike Delancey was at the bottom of it. She hadn't completely alienated him.

She went to the house in search of him, but there was no one home. A calico kitten meowed at her from the windowsill; two others, a gray and a black, sprawled on the back of a sofa. The calico batted at her playfully through the window, and she poked back with her index finger, laughing at the young cat's antics.

Then she heard the sound of the winery's asthmatic truck bouncing up the slight incline from the compound. It appeared around the back of the house, the bed of it first, filled with odds and ends of furniture. Mike was at the wheel and stopped at the edge of the bottom step of the back porch. Armand climbed out of the passenger side and waved at her with a warm smile, then went to lower the truck's rickety tailgate.

She remembered hearing Tate talk about Armand moving out of the house he shared with Colette and into Tate's room here. Tate and Colette would eventually build their own home, then Armand would return to the house.

"Something wrong?" Mike asked as he got out of the truck, looking at her in concern over the hood. Not anger, she noticed happily, simply concern.

"No," she denied quickly. "I just came to thank you for the table and chairs."

"You're welcome." He headed to the back of the truck and so did she, maintaining eye contact over the battered length of the bed. "We were ordering all the others anyway."

He reached the back just in time to help Armand wrestle a large round mirror out of the truck. "It's all paid for by the company. Armand, I cannot believe you're this vain!"

Armand started walking backward with the mirror toward the house. "My wife and daughter looked into this mirror every day of their lives before leaving the house. When I look into it, I see them and not me. I must have it."

Veronica picked up a lamp and a small box and followed the men up the steps.

It took just under a hour to move Armand's things into the house. When they were finished, Mike produced molly bolts to hold the weight of the mirror, and Veronica stood by to supervise its placement. She was comforted by the knowledge that two people had once loved each other so much even death didn't end it.

Armand stepped back to nod his approval. "Perfect," he said. Then he hugged Veronica. "Thank you for helping. I know how hard you have been working on your own home."

"I was happy to. Someone's always helping me. It seemed only fair."

"Well, you go on back to your work now. I'm going to get these things put away—" he pointed to stack of boxes in corner "—then I have to get ready to spray tomorrow."

"Spray?"

"For powdery mildew. With soap. Friendly to the environment—it saves the good bugs, unlike pesticides, which kill everything."

"I've always heard that birds were a problem for grape growers, too."

Armand nodded. "Robins and starlings are a nuisance around here, and deer and yellowjackets, too. But not this early. Later, when the grapes are more mature, they'll come looking for a tasty meal, but we keep them away with distress signals broadcast from loudspeakers."

"And that does the job?"

"Somewhat." He laughed. "I've heard another vintner say that what we must breed is a robin that eats yellowjackets and migrates in August. Thank you, too, Mike. I appreciate your help."

"You're welcome, Armand." Mike shook the hand he was offered, then left the room with Veronica.

"So you let *him* thank you," she taunted as they walked side by side dow the stairs. "But whenever I try to, you silence me with some distraction."

"He's a venerable old man," Mike explained.

At the bottom of the stairs, she turned to him, feeling just a little bit as though she were becoming a part of this community. She'd lent a helping hand.

"And I'm a charming young woman," she replied tartly, the happy mood making her playful. "Isn't that worthy of some consideration."

"Charming?"

"Yes, charming," she insisted. "You remember.

I was sick all over everything, woke you up with screams, let you buy me large pieces of furniture…''

"That's *right*. How could I have forgotten?"

They had walked to the front door, and Mike was about to pull it open. A sharp knock sounded.

It was Rachel. In her hands were a box of chocolates and a beautiful bouquet of flowers.

"Where is he?" she demanded. "I see his truck is parked outside."

"He, uh…" Mike groped for an excuse, concerned about Armand's *right* eye.

"I'm here, Rachel." Armand came down the stairs and stopped in the middle of the room, hands in the pockets of his work pants. "No need to shout."

Rachel strode past Mike and Veronica. "Apparently, there is," she said, shoving the flowers and the chocolates at him and holding them against his chest when he didn't take them. "Because you didn't seem to hear me the first time."

He smiled. "The time you gave me the black eye?"

"That was an accident, and you know it. I simply meant to push you."

"In the eye?"

"You were leaning over me, trying to be more familiar than a lady of my breeding is accustomed to." Her voice rose a decibel. "Take these! And pay attention when I say there is no possibility of anything romantic between us, ever!"

Rachel dropped the flowers and the candy as tears

flowed. "I finally feel as if I've discovered who I am—competent, free, independent!"

"And you'd rather be free than in love?" Armand asked in quiet disbelief.

"Love is a lot of trouble."

"Ah." He patted her shoulder. "Grown lazy in your maturity."

She shook off his hand, looked for a moment as though she intended to "push" him again, then turned and stormed out the door.

Armand stared after her, shaking his head.

Mike had been with Armand when he'd put the flowers and candy in Rachel's mailbox. He'd admired the other man's determination in the face of such heated opposition.

"I can't believe she didn't want your gifts," Veronica said, picking up the battered bouquet and giving it a little shake to revive the flowers.

"I think she did." Armand accepted the bouquet she handed him, and stopped her when she would have knelt to gather up the scattered chocolates. "The problem is, she doesn't *like* the fact that she wanted them."

Veronica studied him worriedly. "Armand. Aren't you being a little…optimistic?"

He blinked at her. "Is there any other way to be?" Then he handed back the bouquet. "I'm afraid the chocolates are ruined, but why don't you take the flowers?"

Veronica dipped her head to smell a carnation.

"Thank you. They're beautiful. You're right. She'll come around eventually."

Armand groaned and got down on his knees to scoop up the chocolates and their brown crenellated paper cups. "I only hope I have that much time left."

CHAPTER TEN

VERONICA DIDN'T SEE Mike for several days. She wondered if he was avoiding her. Perhaps the fact they hadn't crossed paths was a natural result of the finishing touches going on at the B-and-B and the restaurant, and the sudden influx of parents looking for day care and claiming *her* attention.

Bob Burgess stopped by one afternoon with his children, five-year-old twins, Claudine and Spencer. Claudine was dressed in pink, and Spencer wore glasses and a Tigger T-shirt. They were sweet and well-behaved and became Veronica's first official clients.

"I'm not open until next Monday," she told Burgess. "My nap mats haven't arrived yet. Neither have the rest of my toys and playground equipment."

Burgess nodded. "I'll manage, but whether or not my sanity will be intact by then remains to be seen." He shook her hand and paid her a month in advance.

It was all she could do not to give him a hug.

The daughter of the man who'd delivered her table arrived the following morning. She was blond and slender and looked as if the weight of the world rested on her shoulders. Her son Andy was a soft-spoken child whose wide blue eyes studied every inch of the room while Veronica spoke to his mother.

The blonde introduced herself as Delia Moore.

"Your father told me you're taking over as manager of the bank," Veronica said. She'd brought her into the main play area where they sat in colorful, child-size chairs.

Delia laughed, her weary expression vanishing for a moment. "He didn't show you my school pictures, did he? He still carries them. Actually, I'm a loan officer, but he seems to think that's more important than manager, and therefore puts me in charge."

"How nice to have a doting father." A day never passed when Veronica didn't wonder what her father had been like—then, considering the choices her mother had made in other areas, decided she was probably better off *not* knowing. "It must make you feel very special."

Delia sobered again. "It does." She put an arm around her son. "Would it be all right if Andy played with that truck?" She pointed to a row of sturdy toys Veronica had placed on a low bookshelf.

"Of course. Go ahead, Andy."

Andy hurried to get the toy, then ran to the stairs where he settled cozily on one step and ran the truck along the one above it.

"Andy's father and I are divorcing," Delia said, lowering her voice as she kept an eye on her son. She had his soft blue gaze. "And I'm afraid Andy's not feeling special at all lately. It's been a bitter and sometimes very loud separation. Andy's pretty upset about it.''

Veronica put a hand to her arm. ''I'm sorry. I'll do my best to help.''

''Thank you. I'd appreciate that.'' Delia looked forlorn. ''His father used to be such a wonderful man, but he had a difficult childhood in an alcoholic family, and he takes any small failure personally. He lost his job six months ago and has been a horror to live with ever since.''

''Is he abusive?''

''No. But he's always angry and makes our life unpleasant. I—just don't know him anymore. It was like living with a stranger. He's had therapy, and I know he's tried...'' She sniffed and squared her shoulders. ''But I have to think of Andy. I have to protect him.''

''I promise I'll take good care of Andy for you,'' Veronica said. ''So, don't worry about that. Just start your new job and know your son will be safe and happy here. We open Monday morning at seven.''

Delia smiled. ''Perfect. I report to work on Monday, but I don't start until eight-thirty. So we'll be here about eight. Okay?''

''I'll be ready.''

THE LAST OF THE AWAITED supplies arrived a couple of days later. All the bigger toys she'd bought from the shop in Longview, and the colorful nap mats, pillows and cozy blankets she'd ordered from a catalog. The swing set, teeter-totter, monkey bars and slide came, along with wood chips that would cushion the ground beneath them so the inevitable falls would not result in serious injury.

She went out at sunset to try the swings, and found Mike checking the frames and chains.

"Hi," she said, letting herself imagine they'd just installed the equipment for their half-dozen children. The thought was pleasing and started a little ripple of hope, even though Mike continued to look at the swing set and not at her.

"Not bad." He walked behind a swing and placed his hands halfway up the chains. Then his eyes went to hers and held them. "Want to test it?"

"Sure." She went to sit in the swing. "How's everything at the restaurant? I thought about stopping by, but I didn't want to be in the way."

"Come over anytime. Shea's so excited, he's been dragging in delivery people to look at it. Lift your feet." When she did, he pulled back on the chains until he'd lifted her several feet off the ground. "His flatware comes tomorrow—then he's in business."

He let her go, and she raised her legs toward the sky. She swung back and felt Mike's hands on her shoulder blades. She pumped with her legs and looked eye to eye with the setting sun. She couldn't remember a freer moment.

It wasn't perfect, however.

Mike was determined not to be the man in her life—but then, that *was* freedom. She was just as likely to *not* get what she wanted. And she had to understand that, or she wasn't free at all.

"Not so high!" he shouted at her.

While thinking, she'd unconsciously ended up almost parallel to the ground. When she swung back, Mike caught the chains to slow her momentum.

She finally stopped, and he leaned over her to frown down at her. "You are going to be more mature than the children, aren't you? No sliding down banisters, no half gainers off the swings?"

"Don't worry. I'll be the epitome of caution and decorum." She stood and walked across the yard to the slide. "Bob Burgess brought his children by and registered them. Thanks again. He even paid a month in advance."

"Now that's the best kind of client."

Veronica climbed the ladder and sat down at the top of the slide. She waved Mike away from the bottom. "I'm coming down like a rocket. Watch yourself."

He stood in place and folded his arms. "I hate to rain on your parade, but rockets go *up*."

"Well, I'm coming down like a rocket that's been disarmed."

·He frowned. "Not a good image. I'll stay handy to catch the debris."

That was promising. Confusing, but promising.

His expression became decidedly predatory as he took a position about a foot from the base of the slide. "Are you coming or not?"

Now that was promising *and* hopeful. She pushed off.

The ride was over in two seconds. The instant her

feet touched the ground, her body was propelled into Mike's.

He opened his arms to catch her, and the collision of their bodies knocked the breath out of her. Then he lowered his mouth to hers, and she didn't have to breathe anyway. The contact itself was life-sustaining.

Please let this feel to him the way it feels to me. As right. As perfect. As inevitable.

Veronica clung to Mike, responding with the emotion she'd had to suppress for so long. It rose out of her eagerly as his lips roved the line of her throat. She kissed his jaw, nipped at his earlobe, kissed his temple.

He breathed her name, she whispered his. And she had that feeling of flight again—Veronica Callahan, eye to eye with the sun.

Mike pushed himself out of Veronica's arms and said gravely, "We have a major problem here."

Veronica accepted that she was new at this, but she didn't think those were the words *any* woman wanted to hear after such a wonderful kiss.

Now she was Veronica Callahan, eye to eye with the root system of a carrot.

She wanted to punch him—hard—but instead she asked patiently, "What's that?"

"I'm falling in love with you," he said.

"And who would that be a problem for?" Her patience was definitely thinning. "I like the idea."

"Veronica, don't. Trust me." He seemed edgy, grim. "Where do you see this going? Us. Together."

"You're the one with experience in these matters," she said, forcing herself to remain calm. "Where do these things usually go?"

He dropped his hands. "You want me to say the altar, but I can't." His voice and his manner softened slightly. "I can't marry you, Vee."

That hurt, but it wasn't as if she hadn't heard it before. "So you've told me on more than one occasion. But *you* kissed *me*."

He opened his mouth to reply, then turned away from her and walked toward the swings. "I know. You've got me."

She made a scornful sound. "Funny. It doesn't feel at all like that."

"Come here." He came back, caught her by the hand, and led her to the swings. She sat down in one, and he stood beside her, reaching a hand up to the top of the frame. The sadness that often darkened his eyes was back. She knew he was going to tell her about what happened in Dallas.

"Please," she said, and braced herself. "Tell me…"

"It's an ugly story," he warned.

She turned sideways to look at him directly. "You've heard mine. I can take it."

"Okay." He drew a breath and focused on the horizon, but it took him a moment to begin.

"On the ride to Longview," she encouraged, "you stopped at the point you became a hotshot negotiator."

"The trouble with early success," he said, "is that

you begin to feel invincible. You know better deep down, but negotiating is hard and complex, and I have to say, thrilling. And when you can do it—when you can make it turn out all right—it's an adrenaline rush.''

His voice fractured on the last word. He dropped his arm and put both hands in his pockets.

''What happened, Mike?'' Veronica asked gently.

He closed his eyes and let himself remember. It took only an instant for the cherubic little faces to take shape in his mind's eye.

''I was called to a ranch. Just outside of Dallas. The house was dilapidated. This guy, wild on drugs and alcohol, was holed up with his wife and two little girls. It was the classic domestic crisis. He was broke, unemployed, sick of himself, and wouldn't stop doing drugs. His wife was trying to leave him, and he was determined she wouldn't.''

Mike swallowed, his throat as dry as it had been that day. ''When I got there, he said he had his wife tied to a chair, and I could see his two daughters pressed up against the front window. He had a hand around the throat of the five-year-old and a—a Glock at the temple of a toddler about two.''

Mike felt the old horror rushing through him, to his fingertips, to his feet. It seemed to be gouging a crater in the middle of his stomach. He had to get control. He inhaled deeply and tried to remind himself why he had to make Veronica understand what he'd gone through.

''I could see the frightened blue eyes of the older

one. Flushed apple cheeks. Curly dark hair. The little one was crying for her mother.''

Veronica got to her feet and tucked her arm in one of his. ''I'm sorry,'' she whispered. ''I know it's going to be awful. But I need to know.''

''I talked to him for hours,'' he went on. ''I promised him everything he wanted, thinking if enough time passed, he might sober up, be more reasonable.''

Mike heard the shots in his head as he had every day of his life since. Two in rapid succession—the children. Then the wife. Then the man, himself.

''But the hotshot miscalculated,'' he said. ''When the guy did come down, I guess the only thing he saw was a lifetime of self-loathing—and he decided to spare his family and himself all of that and just...blew them away.''

''Oh, Mike.'' Crying, Veronica wrapped her arms around him. ''I'm sorry. I'm so sorry.''

''I see those little faces watching me,'' he said, his voice barely audible. ''Big blue eyes, the little one crying. Then...nobody.''

She reached up to frame his face in her hands. ''Mike. You can't blame yourself for that!''

''I understand that intellectually. But holding people accountable was my job. And I should have been able to do something.''

She shook him—or tried to. ''Listen to me. You were just a man in a job that sounds as if it required God, Himself. He can make miracles, Mike, but *you* can't.''

He took her hands in his and took a step back. "What I'm trying to make clear, is that while I'm falling in love with you, a relationship is never going to work. I'm not the hotshot anymore. I don't want to be responsible for anyone—especially a family. I can't handle it. Tate's worried all the time about his daughters, about Colette's daughters, about Colette."

"Wait a minute." Veronica's jaw firmed. "Nowadays, a woman looks out for herself, doesn't she? And children would be my responsibility every bit as much as yours."

He smiled thinly. "In theory. In practice, I'm a Delancey. We like to be in charge. And I was a cop. Cops feel responsible for everyone—always."

"That's—" She began to protest, but he cut her off with a shake of his head.

"And I don't believe anymore, Vee. I have no faith."

She abandoned her tough stance. "I don't believe you're without faith. I think it's just smothered under your anger. You just have to find new reasons for hope."

"You've been a reason to go on," he said, affection edging aside his sadness. "I'd like nothing more than to just let this be. But I can't give you anything permanent, and I can't ask you to accept anything less. So what's left?"

A little of the light seemed to go out of her. "I guess we're left with friendship." She shrugged, the gesture full of grace and regret. "Nice, but it falls a bit short of what we could have had. That's life, I guess.''

He hugged her to him, and when he drew away, he seemed resolved about something.

''I want you to find your Step Four,'' he said.

She chose not to remind him that she already had.

''We have some kind of chemistry that keeps drawing us together when you should be checking out other prospects.''

She shook her head. ''Chemistry? Prospects? You make love sound like commerce.''

''It's not love,'' he insisted. ''It's only love if we let it be. When I first came to Oregon, I didn't plan to stay. I was going to help get things started, then leave eventually for someplace tropical.''

She concentrated on her joined fingers so he wouldn't see how she hated *his* plan.

''Then we'll both be free,'' he went on, ''to find what we need. I have responsibilities here until after the harvest, but then—''

He was interrupted suddenly by the sound of a honking horn and the cheerful cries of young voices.

''Hi, Uncle Mike! We're home!''

''We brought you maple syrup!''

Mike turned, his hand still wrapped around Veronica's arm, and saw that Tate and Colette and the girls were indeed home.

Veronica pulled out of his hold as they all piled out of the van. The women embraced and the girls ran to Mike, jumping up and down in their excitement at being home again.

Tate came toward him and wrapped his arms around him. "It's good to see you! Everything looks great." He pointed toward the restaurant and the B-and-B. "How's everything inside?"

"Shea will be ready to open once the flatware gets here," Mike replied, forcing a smile and trying to evade his brother's perceptive gaze. It was already narrowing on him as though he'd detected something wrong. "And the furniture and bedding are all in the B-and-B. I'm just waiting on the sofas for the great room and the desk for my office."

Tate studied him another minute, then gestured in the direction of the barn. "The play yard looks good, Veronica," he said.

She smiled, but anyone who knew her would have recognized the gesture as phony. Her sparkle was missing. Mike knew he was responsible for its absence.

"I'll be ready to open Monday. I even have three clients already."

Colette moved from Veronica to Mike to give him a hug. "How's my dad?"

"He's good," Mike replied, arms around the girls who stood close to him. "He moved his stuff in to our place a few days ago. And he's been out cleaning barrels ever since. You'll probably find him in the winery."

"Good." Colette shooed the girls toward the van. "Let's find Grandpa and tell Uncle Shea we're home."

Tate followed his new family. "I'm inviting myself to breakfast tomorrow," he said to Mike over his shoulder. "You can fill me in on everything."

Mike waved. "All right. See you then."

The moment Tate drove his family across the compound, Mike turned to Veronica. "I'm sorry," he said. "I'd like to be different, but I can't promise I ever will be."

She hooked an arm around one of the swing set's supports and leaned her head against it. "No need to be sorry. It's good for me to know where you stand—even when that's on the outside." She straightened. "Well, see you around. I've got things to do."

Mike watched Veronica enter the barn, then got into the Blazer. He headed for town, then drove right on past it.

Shea and Armand were finishing a poker game when he got home just before midnight. Mike reached into a bowl of popcorn in the middle of the table and took a fistful.

"Who won?" he asked.

Shea pushed a pile of pennies toward Armand. "I'm into Armand for three dollars and a dinner of beef bourguignonne. Where you been?"

Mike went into the kitchen, pulled a cola out of the refrigerator, then returned to the living room and sat in a corner of the sofa. "I went to Lincoln City for dinner."

Shea glanced up from squaring the cards to stare at him. "Lincoln City? What's at the coast that I can't fix for you here?"

"Nothing. I just felt like a drive. It's a beautiful night."

"Something happen with Veronica?" Shea asked.

"I said I went for a drive."

"All right. I was just asking."

"At least he doesn't have a black eye." Armand tossed Shea the velvet-lined box that stored the cards. "So he has to be doing better than I am."

Mike took a long pull on the soft drink. "The truth is, I've decided not to 'do' at all."

The older man frowned at Mike. "But, it's life, my boy. You must 'do.'"

"Not me. I'm going to get this B-and-B on its feet, then I'm off for parts unknown."

Shea looked at Mike, startled and grim. "What do you mean? I thought we were all in this together."

"We are. Until everything is up and running. It's not like I'm leaving tomorrow—just...eventually."

"So, something did happen with Veronica."

Mike sighed impatiently, then remembered the promise he'd made to himself on the long drive back from the coast: Patience and neutrality until he left.

He'd made that promise when he'd first come to French River, but Veronica had made him forget it. He'd gotten drawn into the vortex she created around herself. For both their sakes, he had to break free.

"We don't want the same things from life. It's nobody's fault, but we've agreed just to be friends."

Armand gave him a pitying look. "A man is never friends with a woman. He is either her lover or her admirer. And in both cases, he is also her slave."

That was a grim pronouncement. Mike refused to believe there was any truth to it. "It's a different world now, my friend."

Armand accepted the comment with a Gallic shrug.

It was Shea who challenged Mike. "The world might have changed, but women are pretty much the same." Then he amended his statement, "Actually, they're not. Now they can do very well without us."

VERONICA WENT TO TOWN to buy clothes on Saturday afternoon. Her sweats were not appropriate for work, and although her jeans were respectable, she had very few tops.

She pulled on a pair of navy-blue slacks and realized what a difference it made to have clothes that actually fit. The slender cut of the pants clung flatteringly, emphasizing the length of her legs and her slim hips.

"I'd kill for a body like that." The fortyish clerk was well-groomed but plump. She smiled wryly. "Makes me want to hold you down and force-feed you milk shakes."

Veronica laughed. "You wouldn't have to hold me very hard."

"What about some shorts and T-shirts? If you're going to be working with kids, you'll need some clothes that can take on a little punishment."

"I know. But I'm on a budget and—"

The clerk dismissed that by waving an empty hanger in the air. "We'll open an account for you.

Did you see the lightweight denim jumper in the window? With a white or a colored cotton shirt, it'd be perfect.''

''I've never established credit,'' Veronica felt compelled to say, as the clerk led her toward a rack of denim skirts and jumpers.

''Oh, good heavens. If you can't trust an ex-nun, who can you trust? Don't look so surprised. It's a small town. No secrets here. And I own the shop, so there's no one else to answer to when I extend credit. I'm Margie McGowan, by the way.'' Veronica was about to offer her hand, but Margie was searching through hangers, rearranging as she went, and never looked up. Then she pulled out a sleeveless, round-necked jumper. ''Here we are. A six.'' She drew a white T-shirt off a shelf and handed it to her. ''If you like the jumper with that, we have every color imaginable. What are you going to do for shoes?''

Veronica looked down at her battered tennies. ''These will have to—''

''Those are great, but now we can give you fashion as well as comfort.'' She pushed Veronica toward the dressing room. ''See what you think of the jumper, and I'll find you some loafers and some sandals to try with it. Are you a seven-and-a-half? An eight?''

''Eight. But I really shouldn't—''

''You try that on and let me worry about the bill.''

The jumper looked very pretty, was wonderfully comfortable and would be durable. She tried to calculate her purchases so far and knew the jumper would put her over budget.

She changed into her own clothes and left the dressing room, prepared to decline the offer of a charge account—and walked right into Felicia Ferryman.

"Hi, Felicia," she said cheerfully, despite the uncomfortable memory of the day she and Mike let Felicia think they were a couple. "How are you?"

"I'm fine." Felicia studied Veronica's outfit—jeans and the gray waffle-weave shirt Mike had given her. "You should buy a *Vogue* magazine, honey," she said in a patronizing tone. "The baggy look is out."

Veronica had known women like her—even nuns—who'd boosted their own self-image by deriding others. But they'd never made her feel this angry rush of jealousy. Probably because there hadn't been men involved. Step Four—men.

"It's Mike's," she said, continuing to smile. She knew she should tell Felicia the truth, but allowed herself the little fantasy a while longer. "I always feel so good in it." She started toward the corner of the store where the shoes were.

"Then, you'll be with him at the Rotary barbecue?" Felicia called, the condescension still in her voice. "I called this morning to ask him how many tickets I should save, and he said eight. So there's Mike, Tate and his family, Shea and the two old folks, which—if my calculations are correct—" she smiled as though hoping they were "—leaves Mike without a date.'' She stared pointedly at Veronica's left hand. "Hasn't he bought you that ring yet?"

"What a rude question, Felicia.'' The clerk took Veronica by the arm. "Not everyone is supported by large trust funds, you know. Come on, Veronica. I've got some shoes for you to try on.''

Margie led Veronica to a chair surrounded by floor-to-ceiling shelves full of shoes, a rack of purses and the rich smell of leather.

"Do you believe her?'' she asked under her breath. She sat on a low stool, unceremoniously picked up Veronica's right shoe, pulled it off her foot and slipped on a bone-colored flat made of glove-soft leather. "That woman desperately needs a dose of real life. And since she couldn't get Tate, she wants Mike.''

"How do you know?'' Veronica asked as her other foot was slipped into the matching shoe.

"Because *I'm* in Rotary. And I know Felicia. She goes from man to man, looking for something she knows her trust fund will never buy her.''

Veronica stood and walked across the carpet. "That's sad,'' she said quietly. Particularly since she'd become convinced after her last discussion with Mike that Felicia would be perfect for him.

She put Mike and Felicia out of her mind and stopped in front of the low mirror. "These feel wonderful, Margie.''

"Good. Come on back, and we'll try these.'' She held up a pair of sandals.

Veronica decided against the sandals and settled

on two pairs of the loafers. As well as the jumper and T-shirts in white, red and bright turquoise—instead of the buttercup-yellow Mike would have preferred—she bought the blue slacks and several shirts with designs she thought would amuse the children: two hedgehogs in animated conversation, a teddy bear holding on to a colorful kite, and a tiger asleep on a tree limb.

"Could you use a few more little bodies at your day care center?" Margie asked as she bagged Veronica's purchases. "My sisters aren't happy with the sitter they're using. The kids are bored."

"Oh, I'd love to have them!" Veronica held the bag upright while Margie stuffed in a small catalog. "I'm open on Monday if they'd like to come by."

"Great. I'll pass the word."

She gave Margie the cash she'd brought, then signed her name to a charge slip for the rest. Life was moving on. She now had bills.

"I'M FIVE!" Alissa Baldrick said to Veronica at the top of her voice. They were in a small reception area she'd furnished with an old floral sofa and chair Colette had donated. Alissa had auburn braids, round, wire-rimmed glasses, and a perfect line of baby teeth.

"Darling, hush!" Denise Baldrick, a tall, elegant woman with the same color hair cut in a short, businesslike style, sat beside her. She smiled apologetically at Veronica. "I'm afraid she likes to be heard. I think it's partly our fault because Jim and I rush from appointment to appointment and really only have time with her for an hour in the morning when we're hurrying to get ready, and an hour at night when we're preparing for the next day.''

"You're absolutely right. Children do talk loudly to be heard. And I'll do my best to listen.''

"So, she can stay today?'' Denise glanced at her watch. "I have a house to show at eight-thirty. I'm sorry for showing up like this. I wasn't even sure you'd be open this early, but I just heard about you last night when I showed a house to Delia Moore. She said Andy's coming today.''

Good old word-of-mouth. "That's right. Of course she can stay.''

"Miss Callahan…''

"Veronica. My friends call me Vee.'' She liked the way that sounded, as if she had a lot of them. So far there was only Colette and Mike, and she wasn't sure she could count Mike.

"Vee.'' Denise sucked in a breath. "I feel I should tell you that we used to have a baby-sitter, but she terminated us because we were often late picking up Alissa. I'm afraid that's one of the perils of our work. Did I mention that Jim and I are in real estate? So we can't help last-minute emergencies. I'll try to give you some warning, of course, but will that be problem?''

"I don't think so. We'll deal with it as it happens.''

Denise seemed grateful. "Great. Well!'' She leaned down, kissed Alissa's cheek and smoothed her hair. "Be a good girl, sweetie, okay? This looks like a really neat place. I'll call at lunch to see how you're doing."

"Okay. Bye, Mommy." Alissa headed toward the back of the barn where Veronica had placed all the riding toys. The child was apparently not upset by the change in her daily routine.

Veronica let her go, and walked her mother to the door. "Don't worry about her, Mrs. Baldrick," she said. "I have your number if there's a problem of any kind."

"Good. If I'm out, it'll transfer to the cell phone, and if that's busy or off, it'll go to Jim's. We're never out of touch." She drove off in a silver BMW.

Alissa came racing at Veronica in a pedal-operated fire truck, making siren noises and shouting, "Fire! Fire!"

Veronica went to a low row of pegs she'd installed in the big playroom. It held a collection of hats she'd bought for dress-up from a toy catalog and the local thrift shop. She removed a firefighter's hat and put it on Alissa's head on her next pass by.

Andy arrived shortly after Alissa and watched her silently for some time. Veronica finally led him to the other pedal toys.

"Would you like to play police?" she asked, pointing to the black-and-white car. "Or with the dump truck?" She indicated the truck that was filled with a set of plastic bricks.

He looked at her shyly, but said nothing. Then Alissa stopped beside him and gazed at him from under the brim of her helmet. It had fallen to her eyebrows.

"Hey!" she shouted. "There's a fire, and we have to save everybody!" She pointed to the police car. "Get in your car or they'll all be burned up!"

Galvanized by her scenario, Andy ran to the car, climbed in and followed Alissa in her noisy circuit of the play area, making yet a different siren noise.

Veronica went back to the hat rack and retrieved the police officer's cap. Andy idled long enough to let her put it on him, his eyes as bright as if it was his coronation. He smiled at Veronica and pedaled off.

Claudine and Spencer Burgess arrived at eight-thirty, and a power struggle began immediately. Claudine, also five, had a saucy brown ponytail and a bright pink shorts outfit. Her manner was just as dictatorial as Alissa's, except that she saw herself as regal rather than executive.

Veronica handed her a crown, and Claudine had brought her own white towel, which she wore around her neck as her mantle. She climbed into the dump truck and started chasing the other children—a sort of royal sanitation engineer, Veronica guessed. Soon she cut Alissa off.

"Hey!" Alissa shouted. "People are getting burned up! We have to get to the fire."

"Where is it?" Claudine asked.

Alissa looked around, then pointed to the foot of the stairs. "There!"

"No!" Claudine declared. "It's there!" And she

pointed outside, leading the way toward the door. Andy traitorously followed, and Alissa was left alone with her fire truck, her arms folded, her expression outraged.

Spencer had become Veronica's shadow. He now took her hand and tugged her toward the door.

Veronica extended her hand to the abandoned firefighter. "Come on, Alissa," she said. "Let's go try the swings."

The boys took two of the three swings, and the girls fought for the third. Veronica leaned over them before they could come to blows. "One of the rules here," she said, "is that we have to share the toys and the playground equipment. We can all use them, but they belong to the day care, not to you, okay? So we have to take turns. Alissa, why don't you have a turn on the swing, and Claudine can try the slide. Then you can switch."

Having reestablished peace, Veronica stood at the bottom of the slide to catch Claudine. Predictably, because Claudine was getting that attention, the three other children moved to the slide.

By morning break, they were a high-pitched, noisy little group. Spencer had found a coonskin cap and was holding his own with the others.

Veronica had prepared fruit and yogurt for snack, and she sat everyone at a small round thrift store table, which she'd sanded and repainted blue.

Andy asked about the animals they'd seen next door, and Veronica promised they would visit them after lunch. She watched her little brood eating and planning the rest of the day's activities, and thought with pride that though her personal future held little promise, day one at the Green Acres Day Care was off to a good start.

CHAPTER ELEVEN

MIKE LOOKED OUT RACHEL'S kitchen window at Veronica and four small children. Rachel's dogs leapt around them playfully as they petted the llama. He'd just brought Rachel home from grocery shopping, and she left him quickly with the directive, "Thanks, Mike. Just leave everything there, and I'll take care of it in a minute. I want to meet the children." If that little group wasn't trouble, Mike didn't know what was. They all seemed to be about the same age—five or six—and were jumping up and down like pistons.

As Victoria, the llama, sidled away from them, Mike watched Veronica make a quieting gesture with her hands, apparently explaining that they were alarming the animal.

At that point, Rachel appeared. She seemed to give them some instructions, and then four little hands went to the llama's side to pet her.

Victoria nuzzled their heads, and Mike could see them start to giggle. Rachel led them out of sight, probably toward the deer and the raccoon at the back of the pen.

Mike opened the window and leaned forward to watch Veronica follow the children. The tension he'd felt since the evening he'd told her he intended to leave had increased.

She was very slender, but the formfitting pants revealed a rounded and decidedly sexy derriere that had been completely lost in her sweats and too-large jeans. She'd curled her hair or something, because it looked a little longer and fluffier.

She'd moved from view, but he could still hear her laughter—a cheerful ripple of sound that softened his mood.

But he didn't want to soften. Being seduced by her insidiously captivating little ways was what had gotten him into trouble in the first place. It had made him forget his promise to himself. Neutrality. Non-involvement.

He shook his head. Veronica certainly seemed to find it easy to greet him neutrally, even cheerfully, when they saw each other.

Rachel had told him to leave everything, but he knew that her canned goods were stored on a high shelf she had to use a step stool to reach, so he put those away for her: corn and green beans, asparagus, mandarin orange slices, and several different kinds of soup.

He was putting away three cans of tuna when a loud voice sounded behind him.

"I'm *five!*"

He juggled the cans, but managed to control them, then placed them on the counter. The owner of the voice, about two-and-a-half feet tall, now stood beside him. He was surprised to discover a little

girl, and not a burly linebacker. "I'm Alissa Marijane Baldrick!" she said. "532 Pasture Circle!
555-7211!"

"Hi," Mike said. He recognized the child from
Veronica's group. "Aren't you supposed to be outside with the others?"

"I have to go potty. The lady said I could. Do you
live here?"

"No. I'm putting away Rachel's groceries."

"That's the lady with Victoria."

"Right." He pointed toward the bathroom beyond
the kitchen. "The bathroom is in there."

She waddled off, but was back in a minute. "I
flushed!" she announced.

"That's good news." He picked up the now-
empty box to take it with him to the recycling bin.
"Thank you."

"I'm five."

"Yes, you said that."

"How old are you?"

"Six," he replied.

She giggled and shoved him. "No way! You have
to be *old*."

"What if I don't want to be old?"

She seemed perplexed by that. "You have to be a
grown-up 'cause you're big. Grown-ups are all big.
And old. What's your name?"

"Mike," he replied, admiring her little in-your-
face personality. He'd never said he didn't like
kids—just that he didn't want them around.

"What's your middle name?" she wanted to know.

"Anthony."

"Mine is Marijane."

"Yes, you told me that, too."

She discovered suddenly that she stood next to a drawer and pulled it open. Apparently not impressed by the simple flatware inside, she closed it again. "Do you know Veronica's middle name?"

"No."

"It's Violet. That's a flower."

The sound of the screen door slamming was followed by Veronica's voice. "Alissa?" She appeared in the doorway, looking relieved to see the child—and a little unsettled to find Mike there. "Alissa, are you finished?"

Alissa Marijane Baldrick nodded, then to Mike's complete surprise, took hold of his hand. "Do you know *his* middle name?" she asked Veronica.

Veronica noted their joined hands, then eyed him warily, as though expecting him to protest. She shook her head. "No, I don't."

"It's Anthony," Alissa reported. "What's Rachel's middle name?"

"I don't know," Mike replied.

Veronica held out her hand to her. "Why don't we go ask her?"

Alissa reached for it, retaining her hold on Mike's hand. "I want you to come, too," she ordered.

"Thank you." Mike squeezed her little fingers,

then let them go. "But I have some other things I have to do right now."

Alissa frowned.

"But I'll see you around," he said, for some reason wanting to reassure her. He pointed in the direction of the house. "I live over there."

The frown became a smile. "Okay." She waved, then started off with Veronica, who'd merely smiled politely at his words.

"Goodbye, Veronica Violet," he said, prodded by a wicked impulse to make neutrality harder for her. He was aware that made no sense, since he was the one who'd put the distance between them, but nothing had made sense since she'd walked into his life.

She glanced at him in surprise before Alissa's forward propulsion pulled her out of sight.

He looked around the kitchen, satisfied that he'd put away everything Rachel might have had difficulty with, then headed for the front door and home, his spirits lifted.

Because he'd seen Veronica? Or because he'd gotten to her?

THE DAY CARE'S ENROLLMENT had doubled by the following Monday, and grown to ten by the Monday after that. Veronica's new clients included three stairstep brothers, aged nine, eight and seven, who were absolute hellions. She'd managed to control them—somewhat—the first afternoon they stayed with her by withholding dessert at lunch. Rachel had made chocolate chip cookies, large chunks of chocolate pebbling the golden brown domes. It was an archaic method of child-rearing, but Veronica found it usually worked.

Ross, Ricky and Ronnie fell into line immediately.

Her other three clients were girls, keeping the sexes well-balanced. Two sisters, Jill and Lucy, and their cousin Brianne. Their enrollment was thanks to Margie at the dress shop, who was their aunt. Jill was seven, and Lucy and Brianne were both six.

Veronica carefully organized their days. Playground in the morning and right after lunch, stories mid-morning, then art projects and reading later in the afternoon, which allowed them some time on their own and put them in a mellow mood before their parents picked them up.

She planned to have some field trips and special projects, such as cookie- or candy-making or talent shows, for when they needed a change in routine.

At the end of her first month of business, she had enough money to pay her rent. It wasn't required because Tate had traded her work on the inside for two months' rent, but she wanted to know that she'd have it, and put the money in a bank account for a month when she might not.

She bought some of the food for the day care for the following month. And she purchased one more pair of slacks—because she was discovering that her clothes took a terrible beating thanks to the constant tugging of sticky fingers, and there was no motherhouse to replace her habit.

She still had enough money left to buy several

board games and to support herself in relative comfort for the next month. She couldn't believe her
good fortune—as long as she dismissed matters of
the heart.

Delancey's Restaurant and Delancey's Bed-and-
Breakfast were both open now, and the compound
was as busy in the evening as it was during the day.
The restaurant was closed on Mondays, but the
B-and-B was open every night.

Still, the clientele drawn by the country setting
were generally quiet and well-mannered and caused
little disruption to the comfort of those living on the
compound.

Veronica caught occasional glimpses of Mike as
he walked from the B-and-B to the winery, but that
never satisfied her. It had been more than a week
since they'd actually spoken to each other, and that
had only been because Shea had asked him to get
her order for supplies so that he could put it in with
his own.

Tate, Colette and Armand walked the vineyard
every day, watching the growth and counting clusters
on the vine to estimate the crop. According to Rachel, they said the grapes looked healthy, and growth
was on schedule for their cool climate.

Colette, Katie and Megan spent every weekend at
the farmer's market, and sometimes conscripted Veronica to help. She enjoyed it enormously and came
home every time with a fresh bouquet from the
neighboring booth.

Her apartment was beginning to look like a home.

In the thrift shop, she'd found a sofa that was in fairly good condition, and Rachel had given her a colorful throw with which to cover a bald spot on the middle cushion. She'd made gingham draperies and had found a delicate, leggy white wildflower— or maybe it was a weed—behind the barn that she planted in a tall pot, also from the thrift shop.

The older children were back to school now, and came to day care only in the afternoons, making her day a little less hectic.

Early one Friday evening in the middle of September, she went out to the playground to make sure the children had left no litter or personal belongings. With restaurant patrons coming and going all the time as well as the winery's regular tourists, she tried to be even more vigilant.

As she surveyed the area, an old motorcycle raced through the archway past her, chrome polished to perfection, motor roaring.

Her heart flipped with excitement. When she'd been assigned to St. Anthony's outside Geyserville, the convent hadn't had a car, but the pastor had allowed the sisters the use of his vintage Harley.

Veronica had been the youngest sister there by about twenty years, so the duties of shopping and running errands on the bike had fallen to her, and she'd loved it. She felt as though she could shake off all her burdens when she rode it.

The bike pulled up in front of Delancey's and a tall man climbed off, removing his helmet to reveal a very blond brush cut. He hung the helmet on the handgrip and strode into the restaurant.

Veronica walked across the compound and did a slow circuit of the motorcycle. It had custom-painted yellow-and-cream fenders, a white leather seat and pillion, and fishtail pipes on each side. She closed her eyes and imagined what a ride on the bike would feel like coupled with her new freedom.

"Are you thinking of absconding with my bike?"

Veronica started, guilt and surprise on her face. The blond man was back and she recognized him as the man who owned the station where she bought gas for her car.

"Not at all," she assured him with a nervous laugh. "But I used to ride an old Harley. Watching you ride in brought back some good memories, and I had to get a closer look."

The young man smiled at her. "You're the '82 blue compact with the broken gas cap."

She laughed again. "That's me."

"The Softail's not a real antique, just made to look that way."

"Well, it's beautiful anyway." She sighed wistfully. "A bike is so much more fun than a car."

He dug into his pocket and held up a single key on a gold ring. "Here. Help yourself. The maitre d' had a message from my girl. She's going to be late, so why don't you take it for a spin?"

She stared at him in disbelief. "I...shouldn't."

"Why not? I'm I insured."

Suddenly, she couldn't think of one solid objection.

MIKE STEPPED onto the B-and-B's porch, ready for a quiet dinner at home with Armand, followed by their customary poker game. He had a small fortune to recoup and a serious craving for pizza.

He paused on the top step, doing a diagnostic scan of the compound—a habit he'd developed when Tate was on his honeymoon. His attention was immediately arrested by the sight of Veronica in earnest conversation with a guy with platinum hair.

Mike had two thoughts simultaneously: one, that his hair wasn't at all natural; and two, that Veronica should have more sense than to talk to a stranger with a motorcycle.

But the stranger wasn't on the motorcycle, Veronica *was!* He watched in alarm as she walked the bike backward. He started down the stairs when the motor came to life, then stopped in shock, a surge of jealousy flashing through him, when blondie put the helmet on her head.

She took off down the road in a cloud of dust, and roared into the vineyard.

Mike strode angrily across the compound. "Why in the hell did you let her do that?" he demanded. "She'll kill herself."

The blond guy turned to him, green eyes questioning. It was Jay Morrow from the gas station.

"She's going to splatter herself all over the vineyard."

"I don't think so. She seems to know what she's doing. She told me she used to ride a classic Harley," Morrow explained. He indicated the top of the vineyard road as the roar of the bike's motor preceded Veronica's arrival. She lifted her feet out to the sides as she ran through a puddle, maintaining perfect balance. She turned, leaning with the bike, and headed down the road again. "She's pretty good."

Mike was amazed by her skill and easy control. He shook his head slowly, still watching the spot where she'd appeared, then disappeared again. "I can't believe it."

Morrow laughed softly. "You know how many motorcycle junkies would kill to have a girl who loved to ride as much as they do?"

Mike knew one. "I had a '77 Cafe Racer," he said.

Morrow whistled. "You'd get a fortune for that baby now. It's gone from ugly duckling to collectible. What happened to it?"

"Sold it to a friend when I moved here."

"Too bad. This one's for sale if you ever decide you want to ride one again."

The roar grew louder again. Veronica was coming toward them. She pulled to a stop beside them and took off the helmet. Her cheeks were pink, her smile wide. Mike expected it to fade when she saw him, but it didn't.

"I can't tell you how great that was!" she told Morrow.

Morrow turned to Mike. "You want a turn?"

"You ride?" Veronica asked Mike in surprise, handing him the helmet.

"Yeah." He took the helmet from her and put it on her head. "Back up. You can ride behind me."

She scooted backward and lifted herself onto the pillion as he climbed on in front of her. He made himself ignore the feel of her thighs around his hips and her hands on his body.

He turned the key in the ignition and they shot forward, doing a wide turn in front of the B-and-B and heading for the vineyard road.

The old thrill was on him as the vines closed in, narrowing the road to a shady, private world. The bike rushed forward through the wind and every sensation seemed to be intensified—the smells of the fruit and flowers, the heat of the sun breaking through arching canes, the touch of Veronica's hands.

The lane curved along the hill and Veronica's hands tightened, anticipating the bike's lean to the right. They rode into it, each of them moving perfectly.

Mike forgot that anything bad had ever happened to him—or to anyone he'd ever tried to protect. He knew only that he was racing through a beautiful world, the woman he loved riding behind him. Could this be?

Of course not. He was leaving French River. He concentrated on enjoying the ride and tried to forget Veronica.

But he couldn't. He could feel every one of her fingertips on his body as though his torso were bare.

He pulled to a stop where the lane met the road into the winery, and climbed off the bike.

"What—?" she began.

"You drive back," he said. He grinned when she moved forward without having to be told twice. "So, you're a motorcycle mama."

"'Fraid so. The sisters were given one when I was in Geyserville, and I fell in love with it. Can't afford my own. How wonderful this has been!"

"Yeah." He climbed on behind her, resting his hands on her waist. "I sold mine when I came here. Morrow says this one's for sale."

She had flipped down the helmet's visor, and now pushed it up again and looked at him over her shoulder. "What's he want for it?"

"I didn't ask. You thinking of buying it?"

"It runs beautifully, but I've got to watch my pennies. Why don't you buy it? Oh, that's right." Her smile dimmed. "What good is a motorcycle in the tropics? You'll get a boat, I suppose."

He changed the subject. What he wanted right now was an excuse to spend time with her—one that couldn't be construed as personal.

"You coming to the Rotary barbecue?" he asked. "I've got your ticket."

"I met Felicia while I was shopping a while ago," she replied. "She said you hadn't bought me a ticket."

"I did. Armand's not coming, but I still bought eight. One for you."

She seemed to be thinking about it. "Strange behavior," she said finally, "for a man who wants to stop seeing me."

"It's a barbecue. How intimate can that be?" Less intimate, he was sure, than sitting behind her on a bike.

"Father Wolff's coming," he coaxed.

"How do you know?"

"He's joined Rotary, too, and we're on the set-up committee together. Nice guy. I like him."

"I don't know," she said. "We don't want the attraction kicking in again. Somehow that always turns out to be my fault."

"You said we'd be friends," he reminded her. "And you'll have Colette and the girls mad at me if you stay home because of me. Come on. We have to learn to do this. I have to be there early, but I'll come back and pick you up at eleven."

She nodded, her expression doubtful. "Okay, but one grumpy glance in my direction and I'm out of there."

"Deal."

Just to show him she meant business, Veronica hit all the bumps on the way back to the compound.

CHAPTER TWELVE

MIKE PARKED THE BLAZER in front of the rectory beside St. Jerome's Catholic Church. It was a small, four-square Victorian, painted yellow with white trim. He was about to open his door when the priest hurried out, his movements light and quick for a man Mike guessed to be about thirty pounds overweight and in his early fifties. He had a volleyball under one arm and a backpack in his other hand. He got in the passenger side and tossed his things into the rear seat.

"Good morning, Father," Mike said as the priest settled in beside him.

"Hey, Mike." Father Wolff snapped his seat belt into place. "I called the market when you pulled up and told them we're on our way."

"Great."

The priest peered at him with a raised eyebrow. "I thought Veronica was coming with you."

"I'm going back for her after we've set up."

"How's that going?" Father Wolff asked as Mike drove toward the far side of town.

Mike glanced at him in puzzlement.

"The romance," the priest clarified. "I like to think of myself as a sort of Cupid in a collar to some of the special members of my flock. Veronica's been a favorite of mine for a long time. I'd like her to have everything she deserves.''

Mike frowned. ''I'm not sure that's me, Father.''

''Because of that experience you haven't come to see me about yet?''

Mike had grown used to the priest's candor in committee meetings. ''Because I can't forget that experience,'' he replied. ''Because she's trying to build a new life, and I'm sort of stuck reliving the old one.''

Mike stopped at French River's only traffic light. He left one hand on the wheel and leaned his elbow on the open window. ''The hard thing is that my heart insists on operating despite my brain. I want to be with her, but I know that just means trouble for her, so I'm getting ready to leave. But I hate the thought.''

The light turned green, and Mike drove on.

''It seems to me,'' the priest said after a moment, ''that you're getting a message from your heart. It's telling you to stop trying so hard to avoid dealing with this. You don't have to leave and you don't have to deprive yourself of Veronica. Let yourself love her.''

Mike couldn't quite believe he was discussing romance with a priest.

''Father, she loves children,'' he said patiently, ''and I don't want children. I'd only end up hurting her.''

''Or maybe she would help you. You seem to be thinking only of what you can give to love, not what it can give to you. It's very selfless, but in this case, shortsighted. And also proves that you have more to give her than you think. Generosity, to start.'' He swept a hand toward the blue sky and green countryside. ''And you don't really want to leave this wonderful place, do you? I'm in love with it already.''

Mike was saved from answering because they'd arrived at the supermarket. The moment he and Father Wolff cleared the front door, they were met by the manager and a box boy, each pushing a flatbed cart with the products the store was providing at cost.

Mike thanked the store manager and the boy for their swift assistance, and the priest wished them blessings on their day.

Mike smiled at Father Wolff as they climbed back into the Blazer. ''You're out to save everybody, aren't you?''

''No.'' He returned the smile. ''I'm out to make sure everyone knows it's within their power to save themselves. But nothing's going to save you when I get you on the volleyball court this afternoon.''

''Volleyball? My game's basketball.''

''Then you might want to start praying.''

THE FRENCH RIVER CITY PARK was a twenty-acre patch of green at the far end of the little town. It straddled a slow-moving creek and was surrounded by oak and ash trees planted by the founding fathers.

There was playground equipment for the children, a volleyball net for the adults, and park benches in both sunny and shady spots for old folks and parents with sleepy children.

On that afternoon there were picnic tables and benches everywhere, and many families had brought blankets to spread on the grass. Children played, dogs barked, birds sang, and the sun shone from a bright blue sky, warming Veronica's arms and making her feel languid and lazy as she rested her chin on her hand and watched the scene.

Rachel and the Delanceys were gathered around her under the wide branches of a mountain ash, its whitish berries just beginning to turn red. Katie and Megan had run off to play.

Rachel assumed hostess duties and seemed forcedly cheerful today. Veronica wondered if she was trying to prove to everyone that Armand's absence didn't matter to her.

At the other end of the table, Tate had partially unrolled his plans for the new house he was building for his family. Colette had told Veronica it was to be situated in a grove of cedar trees a small distance from Armand's house.

Shea and Mike leaned across the table to look, and Rachel stopped pouring iced tea to follow Tate's pointing finger.

Mike reached out to pull Veronica closer so that she could see, too. She guessed it was an instinctive gesture. But he seemed lighthearted and relaxed today, as he'd been when they'd ridden the bike.

"This is the great room," Tate said, pointing to a large rectangle. "It'll have windows looking out on the vineyard, a fireplace that also provides an oven and a cooking grate in the kitchen. The kitchen will open into a family room that goes out onto a patio where there'll be a hot tub.''

"Wow." Shea peered closely at the plans. "Where are Mike's and my rooms?''

Tate a waved hand off the paper. ''Way off here, somewhere, back at Jack's old house.''

Shea turned to Mike in mock dismay. ''He meets a beautiful woman, is charmed by two little girls, and you and I are just forgotten.''

Mike nodded. ''Awful, isn't it? Whatever happened to 'blood is thicker than water'?''

Tate put an arm around Colette's shoulders and pulled her close for kiss. ''It was superceded by 'all for love,''' he said.

"Apparently. So, where's the master bedroom?''

Everyone continued to ooh and aah over the plans until a loud voice from the barbecues announced that the food was ready. People swarmed toward it from all over the park, children in the vanguard.

Veronica followed her companions as they fell into line a good two-thirds of the way back from the food. Megan and Katie waved to them from the head of the line.

''Doesn't being their stepfather allow me cuts in line?'' Tate asked plaintively.

Colette patted his arm. ''Sorry. You're just the man who pays the bills. No cuts.''

''Not fair. If there's nothing left when we get there, I'm going to be upset.''

"There's always plenty of food," Rachel assured Tate from her place in front of Colette. "And I have three kinds of salad and a chocolate cake in my cooler."

Tate leaned over Colette's shoulder and said in a theatrical whisper, "Maybe we should think about inviting *her* to live with us."

"We can't," Colette replied. "My father will be over all the time, and she doesn't like him anymore."

Rachel stiffened and ignored the other woman's teasing, much to everyone's disappointment.

"Hi, all." Felicia appeared beside the line, a white bib apron covering her chambray shirt and jeans. Her blond hair had been braided and tied with rawhide bows. Veronica thought she looked like a very cunning Annie Oakley.

She smiled at Mike and Veronica, standing side by side. "I thought you two would be engaged by now," she said with forced sweetness.

Mike put an arm around Veronica's shoulders and squeezed her to him. "We're working on it."

Felicia appeared demoralized for a moment, then she shifted her attention to Shea. "Sweetie, can you help us? There's a crisis in the kitchen."

Shea frowned. "There is no kitchen."

"You know what I mean. At the barbecues."

"What kind of crisis?"

"It's hard to explain." She became all dewy-eyed and innocent. "Will you come with me? Please?"

It was clear Shea had become Felicia's next target.

"Sure." He looked at his brothers as she led him off. "One of you guys fix me a plate?"

Mike retained his hold on Veronica when she tried to move away. She gazed at him in puzzlement. "This pretense," she said quietly, "is costing you the attentions of the one woman who might be perfect for you."

He frowned at her in exasperation, but removed his arm.

"Hey, you two!" The priest strode into view, trailed by a group of children. He stopped to hug Veronica and shake Mike's hand.

Mike introduced him to Tate and Colette and Rachel. Veronica explained how she and the priest knew one another.

The children danced around him, trying to drag him away, but he stood his ground.

"Then I run into her in French River, of all places!" he said with a shake of his head. "Isn't life amazing?"

Tate nodded. "That it is. Father, I wonder if we could impose upon you to bless the harvest? Around the end of the month or early September."

"I'd be happy to. Mike tells me you haven't actually bottled wine yet, but when you do, perhaps we could talk about the church using it as our sacramental wine."

Tate shook his hand. "That would make you our first contract."

"Excellent. Call me when the harvest is ready.

Mike and I are meeting up later for volleyball. Did he tell you? Would you care to join us?''

"Uh, no, he didn't." Tate sent Mike a glance full of laughter. "He might have been hoping to avoid witnesses. We'll meet you at the court. What time?"

"After lunch I have to judge a race and some games," the priest explained. "You can get started without me. I left the ball in your car, Mike."

Mike groaned. "Thanks, Father. I haven't played volleyball since the police academy."

"That's good. We'll have to put money on the game."

Mike raised an eyebrow. "That's gambling. Aren't you supposed to be opposed to that?"

"In some forms, yes. But haven't you ever heard of bingo?"

The children pulled on the priest until he was forced to follow them. He waved as they dragged him away.

Shea reappeared as they sat down to eat. Tate hid the plate they'd filled for him on the seat.

"Well, you hadn't shown up," he explained when Shea asked where it was. "I was sure you were eating with Felicia and your plate would go to waste."

Shea looked at the long line waiting to be served, many people already on their seconds. "Tell me you're kidding."

Veronica couldn't stand it. "He's kidding," she said. "Tate's hiding your plate."

"Hey." Mike pretended disapproval. "You shouldn't interfere. Shea expects us to torture him.

It's a tradition first forged when he was nine months old, and Tate and I thought it'd be interesting to see if cryogenics really worked.''

Colette put a hand over her eyes. ''You didn't put him in the freezer?''

''We would have,'' Tate answered, ''but Mom caught us.'' He sighed. ''She had absolutely no respect for scientific research.''

Mike, too, sighed. ''Stunted our scholarly inclinations. Well, mine, anyway. Tate did go on to be brilliant.''

Tate spread both arms, as though prepared to take more praise.

''Could I have my plate, please?!'' Shea demanded. ''And I suggest you don't mess with me. I've spent the past half hour with Felicia Ferryman attached to my right side. The woman's not big on subtlety.''

''What was the 'problem in the kitchen'?'' Colette asked with a grin. ''She couldn't tell the flour from the salt?''

''Not nice,'' Veronica put in. ''Neither can I.''

Everyone laughed, but Shea ignored them, apparently anxious to share his grievances. He sat across from Veronica on the end of the bench.

''One of the gas grills wasn't working,'' he said. ''The propane tank was empty. And of course I tried everything else because I was sure she'd have checked that first. Then she insisted I go to the store for another one because she wouldn't know what to buy, and when Bob Burgess volunteered to go, she said I'd be happy to do it. And I would have been, to get away from her, but she came with me.'' He looked at Mike pleadingly. ''Come on. You're trained in self-defense. *You* be the Delancey brother she wants.''

''Sorry. We've all had to cope with Felicia. Now it's your turn.''

They played volleyball after lunch, with Tate, Colette, Megan and Katie against Mike, Veronica and Shea. When Tate's team beat them, Mike blamed Shea.

''All I asked,'' he said, ''is that you be better than two little girls.''

''I was good!'' Shea declared modestly. ''You're the one who can't play the net for beans. You're looking for placement there, not for distance. You hit the ball out of bounds so many times—''

''Uncles!'' Megan shouted, taking each man by an arm. ''It's not your fault.''

''It isn't?'' Mike asked.

She shook her head. ''Katie and me are just better than you. We play all the time at school, and you're, you know, old.''

''Would you like to be sold to another family?'' Shea asked, picking her up while she giggled. ''I could arrange that, you know.''

Veronica rescued her. ''Gentlemen, the truth hurts, but you have to suck it up. Let's try men against women and see if you do any better in large groups.''

They didn't. Shea blamed it on being outnumbered. "There are four of them," he complained. "And only three of us."

"Well, let's see if I can even things up." Father Wolff appeared on the sidelines. "I'm known for saving scores as well as souls," he said, taking his place in the serving position. "May I?"

Tate threw him the ball. "Maybe you'd better lead us in prayer first."

The priest laughed. "I have a power serve that will allow us to win without divine assistance. You ladies ready?" He turned to the other members of his team. "Do we want to place a bet of some kind on this game before we start?"

"Losers owe the winners dinner one night next week!" Veronica called. She started doing exaggerated knee bends and flexes. "Shall we place our order now?"

Colette and the girls crowded around her. "What are you doing?" Colette asked anxiously. "Father Wolff acts like some master athlete. I do *not* have time to cook, and you'd be no help! You live on cookies and canned goods."

Veronica gave her a playful shove that made the girls laugh. "First of all, your daughters are the master athletes here, and I've played with the good Father before. He's a weekend warrior with power but poor aim. Trust me. The men will be cooking."

"How long's that huddle going to last?" Tate heckled.

"As if you've got a strategy!" Mike contributed.

"What you need is a recipe for dinner!" Shea shouted.

"Gentlemen," the priest scolded. "Compassion in victory, please."

"COMPASSION IN VICTORY," Shea muttered. The family was gathered around tables drawn close to a square of the park that had been cordoned off for dancing. A small, local band played slow, nostalgic music under Japanese lanterns strung among the trees. Rachel had pleaded weariness and taken Megan and Katie home with her so that their parents could continue to enjoy the evening.

It was after eight on the warm September night. The aroma of barbecue was gone, and a fragrant breeze drifted across the park. "You not only boasted, Father Wolff. You lied! You must have learned to serve the same place Mike learned to play the net. The white lines on the side are there for a reason, you know. You play *inside* them."

Father Wolff shook his head, clearly unaffected by Shea's comments as he poured coffee into paper cups and distributed them. "Criticism is an unattractive quality in a man, Shea. Particularly one for whom preparing a dinner should not be a problem."

Shea rested his hands on the edge of the table, his quivering lip betraying his desire to laugh. "Aren't you supposed to set a moral example for us?"

"I am," the priest claimed, pressing his hand to his heart. "I'm offering you the opportunity to forgive me for having more enthusiasm than athletic prowess. And you might remember that *you* scored a measly four points.''

Tate did laugh. ''You're sure you don't have a Delancey in your background, Father? You shift the blame like one.''

Father Wolff shook his head. ''Nope. The Wolffs are shifty enough in their own right.''

Tate got to his feet. ''I'm sure we've at least been a bad influence.'' He offered his hand to Colette. ''Let's go see if we know how to behave on a dance floor without kids watching us.'' He winked at their companions as he led her toward the lantern-lit square. ''Don't wait up.''

Father Wolff shooed Mike and Veronica toward the music. ''Why don't you two go enjoy the band while Shea and I plan the payoff dinner?''

Veronica sent Mike a worried glance and began to offer an excuse, but Mike took her arm and drew her to her feet. ''Come on,'' he said in a stage whisper. ''He likes to think of himself as a Cupid with a collar. We have to humor him.''

Not that Mike had needed the priest's encouragement. He'd been looking for an excuse to hold her all day.

Veronica reluctantly followed Mike to the little crowd of couples. ''I think we should just walk through to the other side,'' she suggested as she glanced over her shoulder to where Shea and Father Wolff were talking earnestly. ''He'll never know we didn't actually dance.''

He stopped her in the middle of the dance floor and took her into his arms.

"Remember Tate's and Colette's wedding? You couldn't wait to *stop* dancing with me," she said in desperation.

"That was because I didn't want to get involved." He pulled her closer, putting one hand on her hip, the other between her shoulder blades. "That doesn't apply anymore."

She rested her hands on his chest for steadiness. "Why? What's changed?"

"Nothing that I can control," he replied. "I've been trying to think about leaving, but then I realize that if I go, I won't be able to walk out into the compound and see you playing with the kids or petting Victoria—and I can't imagine surviving."

Her pulse quickened and she looped her arms around his neck, needing to embrace him.

"Father Wolff told me I should think about what love could do *for* me, rather than worry about what I can't give to it. That I should just let myself love you. Except I'm torn. I can't stop worrying about what you might miss, but the feelings I have for you are there despite all my efforts to stop them."

"That's because love is a living thing." She smiled into his eyes as she held him closer. "It's strong, hearty stuff that can even survive starvation. No one knows that better than I. But I think if you feed it, it becomes…" She spread her arms wide and knocked the baseball cap off Henry Warren's head. He was swaying to the music with Felicia Ferryman.

Henry laughed over Veronica's apology, but Felicia rolled her eyes.

"It becomes…?" Mike prodded, catching Veronica's hands.

"The blob!" she said. "Spreading into every little corner, absorbing every object in its path."

He winced. "Now there's a romantic metaphor."

"Well, I was after a powerful reference, not a romantic one."

"So now I can look forward to having limbs consumed one after the other?"

She nuzzled his cheek. "Maybe just an ear nibbled."

"Can we just spend some time together?" Mike put a hand out to prevent a collision with another couple, then turned Veronica in the other direction. "You know—dinner, movies." He put his lips to her ear. "Clandestine meetings under the stars?"

Anticipation made her shiver. "That sounds wonderful."

"All I can promise you is that I'll try to reclaim the person I used to be."

"No." She frowned at him. "No one can ask that of you. Everything that happens affects and changes us. I'm in love with the Mike Delancey I know."

"I used to be more fun."

"Fun's important," she said, "but it isn't everything. Let's just relax and accept who we are."

The band began to play something romantic with a lot of brass and violin. Mike gathered her closer, and she leaned into him, abandoning herself whole-heartedly to the mellow moment and the music.

He put his cheek on her hair. "Then we're in agreement," he said. "We're approaching Step Four."

"Yes, we are." She lifted her face to him, happy that he was finally ready to believe. "We should mark this milestone."

Mike lowered his mouth to hers and committed himself to her plan.

CHAPTER THIRTEEN

THE TELEPHONE CALL from Mike's friend and former partner on the Dallas P.D. who'd become a private detective came on Sunday afternoon. Since Tate and Colette and the girls had returned from their honeymoon, Sunday afternoon had become a traditional family time. Everyone gathered around the dining table at the old house, with Veronica in attendance, as well as Armand and Rachel—who managed to be civil in the interest of peace in the family, though they seldom spoke to each other.

Mike excused himself to take the call in the kitchen.

"You asked for the goods on Robert or Theresa Mullins," Vince Rushford said.

Mike could hear the quiet clicks of a computer keyboard. "Right. You found something?"

"She died in a train accident in '92. You already knew that."

"Yes."

"Did you know Robert's still alive and collecting Disability and Social Security?"

Mike leaned a hip against the edge of the counter. "No, I didn't. You have an address?" He pulled a pen out of a cup on the counter and looked around for something to write on. He found a paper towel as Vince began to rattle off the information.

"Found something else, too," Vince said. Mike heard more clicking of the keyboard. "Here it is. The purchase of a yellow Cadillac from an auto parts shop in Seattle. Had the same plates you gave me. Some guy named...Al Girdling, who sold it to a party in eastern Washington."

"You have that name and address?"

"No," Vince replied dryly. "I thought I'd just take your money and let you work out the details for yourself."

Mike laughed. "Money? You're expecting money for this?"

"You don't think I'm doing this for old times' sake? It's not like you ever took a bullet for me or anything."

"No, but I bought enough raffle tickets and sweatshirts for your boys' club. How's that going, by the way?"

"Good. You'll have to come down here and talk to them. Show them how even a hopeless loser with everything against him can still end up with smart brothers willing to support him."

"Aren't we hilarious? Can I have that eastern Washington address now? And the Girdle guy's address?"

"Gird*ling,*" Vince corrected. "And I couldn't find him anywhere. I don't know how to explain that. Unless he just made himself up. But here's the next buyer. Chester Doyle. 121 Biddle Road, Twin Deer, Washington.''

''Where is that?''

''South of Spokane on I-95. You guys got a fax? I'll send you copies of the bills of sale and some other stuff.''

''Yeah.'' Mike gave him the number. ''Thanks, Vince. Guess I'll have to pay you, after all.''

''Appreciate that. We're taking the boys camping at the end of the month and I'm short a few sleeping bags.''

The men had moved from the table to the living room when Mike rejoined them. The women were clearing away and cleaning up, working like some beautiful and efficient machine that functioned on laughter.

Tate muted a baseball game on television to listen to what Mike had learned.

''Girdling?'' Tate repeated.

Mike checked his notes. ''Yeah. He bought the car from a salvage yard, but Vince couldn't find anything else on him. Why? Sound familiar to you?''

Tate turned off the TV. ''No. But *girdling*'s a term I came across when I was learning about vineyards. When you make an incision around a vine trunk or cane to improve the fruit set, that's called girdling.''

''So we've got a name that would be familiar to someone who knows about grapes,'' Shea said thoughtfully, ''used to identify a man for whom there are no other records.''

"You think Al Girdling is Jack," Armand asked, sitting up.

Tate shrugged. "Or it's all just a weird coincidence." He smiled suddenly, looking around the room. "I, personally, prefer to think it's Uncle Jack, and he's still alive."

"But why disappear?" Shea asked. "Why assume a phony name? Why buy his own car back from a junkyard?"

Mike sank onto an arm of the sofa. "Love?" he suggested, thinking that before Veronica had sailed off a banister and into his life he wouldn't have considered it as a reason. But now he knew love could make you sacrifice everything, take outrageous chances, or do things no one else would ever understand. "Maybe Tess is still alive, too."

His brothers and Armand stared at him, waiting for him to explain. "If he'd just been grief-stricken by the loss of the woman he loved, I don't think he'd have killed himself. He wouldn't have left everyone in his life to just wonder what had happened to him. But if Tess hadn't died in the train wreck—if she'd escaped, although she was thought to be dead, and then got in touch with him, I think he'd have moved heaven and earth to get to her, then taken every precaution to see her deception wasn't discovered."

"Why?" Shea asked again.

"Because she left her husband once," Tate replied, frowning in thought. "She wasn't happy. And if Robert Mullins is still collecting Disability, he's still around. Maybe she just saw an opportunity to be happy with Jack—and took it.''

They all considered that silently.

Finally, Shea broke the quiet. ''So, do we mess that up for them by checking it out?''

''We can look into it without messing anything up,'' Mike said. ''We see what the guy who bought the Caddy from 'Al Girdling' can tell us about him. And we make our decision then. If we think Girdling is Jack and he's just hiding out, maybe we should let him be. But even if it wasn't Jack who sold the car, we still owe a share of this place to his son— agreed?''

''Agreed,'' Tate and Shea said in unison.

''Then we *have* to pursue this.''

Tate leaned toward Armand. ''Do we have time to be gone for a couple of days before harvest?''

Armand nodded. ''I think so—if you go right away. I'm counting on another week's ripening. The weather report seems to be in our favor. You should go.''

''YOU'RE GOING TO BE GONE how long?'' Colette asked mournfully after Tate explained. The girls had gone outside to play.

''Depends on how long it takes us. Probably just two or three days.'' She sat on the arm of his chair, and he pulled her backward into his lap. ''Mike and Shea can't afford to be gone much longer. You'll have to oversee their staffs for us and make sure everything goes well. You won't have time to miss me.''

She wrapped her arms around his neck and kissed him, disputing his theory.

Mike walked Veronica to the barn in the twilight. The B-and-B was full, and patrons were arriving for dinner at the restaurant. The compound was a lively place.

"It was a nice day," she said as they stopped at the barn door. She looked up at him worriedly. "Promise me you'll be careful. The whole thing's kind of iffy, and you don't know what's behind it— so watch yourself.''

He loved her concern. "I was a cop. I'm trained for this kind of thing.''

"That doesn't make you impervious to injury.''

"What injury? We're just going to ask questions. It's nothing to worry about.''

She hugged him to her, clearly unconvinced.

He held her close, rubbing a hand gently up and down her spine. "What's the real problem here?" he asked.

"Selfishness, I guess," she answered, holding him tightly. "This was a wonderful afternoon. I've never spent Sunday around the dinner table before. Even though you're all different from one another and each do your own thing, you can join hands and hold good things in and bad things out.''

He'd never thought about it in quite that way, but knew her observation to be true. Particularly now that he and his brothers were working and living together.

"I don't want to see any breaks in the circle," she said, her voice a little strained. "Not that I can claim to be part of it, but everyone's welcomed me and I feel—"

He silenced her with a deep and thorough kiss. "I promise you there'll be no breaks," he said when he raised his head. "And you *are* part of it—so hold your place until I get back."

TWIN DEER, WASHINGTON, was almost on the Idaho border, twelve miles south of Spokane. Mike, Tate and Shea arrived late Monday, spent the night in a spartan but clean motel, then went in search of Chester Doyle the following morning.

The town was small, with lawns dry from the hot summer, and trees just beginning to turn color. The faint smell of woodsmoke drifted on the crisp, clean air.

Doyle lived in a stone-and-frame house bordered by fading flowers on the top of a knoll. He appeared to be in his late fifties.

Mike assumed the role of spokesman since he had the papers Vince had faxed. He explained to Doyle about the search for Jack Delancey and their suspicion that he might be masquerading as Al Girdling.

"Can't be," Doyle said. He'd invited them to sit on the wooden glider and the molded plastic chairs on his deep front porch. A bleached-blond woman wearing false eyelashes and a leopard-patterned le-

otard and leggings brought out a tray of lemonade.
The leopard, Mike imagined, had probably had considerably more room in his skin than she had. "Girdling was my neighbor for years," Doyle continued.
He pointed to a prefabricated house at the bottom of
the slope. "He was the real thing, all right. Worked
in the feed store, and she was an aide at the conva-
lescent home."

"He was married?" Tate asked.

"Oh, yes." Mrs. Doyle passed around mono-
grammed napkins. "Pretty woman. Not much sense
of style, though. She could have done a lot with those
looks, but she never tried. She was just happy being
gray and plump."

Gray. The woman in the photograph had been
blond and slender, but the passage of time could easily have altered that.

"What did Al Girdling look like?" Mike asked.

Doyle shrugged. "Like anybody. Bald in the
back—black hair going gray. Tall, rangy. Quiet. Nice
guy, though. Woulda given you the shirt off his back.
He was a good neighbor. Sold me his car for two
hundred bucks before he left."

"Do you still have it?"

Doyle shook his head regretfully. "Drove it for
over a year, then it conked out on me near Sunnyside.
Sold it for junk."

Mike glanced at Tate, then at Shea. They'd hoped
a look at the car might have provided some clue as
to whether it had been Jack's.

"Do you know where they moved to?"

"Seattle, I think. She was excited."

Mrs. Doyle waved a beringed hand. "She was excited about everything. Happy all the time. Made me tired."

Doyle smiled, his eyes unfocused. "Jane sure loved him. And he treated her like she was glass."

The ice clinked as Mrs. Doyle brought her iced tea to her lips. "Unnatural for people who'd been married that long." She took a long sip and missed Doyle's frowning look in her direction.

"Do you know why they moved away?" Shea asked.

Doyle nodded. "Al's health was getting delicate. Had some kind of heart problem they couldn't quite pinpoint, and Jane thought it'd be smarter to be closer to doctors and a good hospital. He collapsed a couple of times right here in the backyard."

Mike showed Doyle the old photo they'd found of Tess and her son. "This is about forty years old," he said, "but do you think it could be Jane?"

Mrs. Doyle leaned closer, studied it, then shook her head. "I'm not sure. Like I said, when they lived here, she was gray and plump. If this was her, it was a lifetime ago."

Doyle took the photo from him and studied it closely. Then he held it a little closer to his face and finally smiled. "It's her," he declared. He pointed to her face with his little finger. "See that irregular tooth? Just to the left of her front teeth. Always flashed when she smiled—and she smiled all the time. That's her."

Mrs. Doyle snorted.

The brothers drove back toward Spokane, then onto the highway that would take them west. "What now?" Shea asked. "Your detective friend couldn't find any information about Al Girdling, so we're not going to trace them that way."

"If Uncle Jack's in poor health," Tate said, "maybe he had to go back to his real name. He doesn't have health benefits or Social Security under Al Girdling."

"But he's been declared dead."

"Let's find a library and look for a Seattle phone book," Mike suggested. "We'll look under both names."

"Wouldn't your friend have tried that?"

"He was looking for public records. You can have a phone listed under your name without proof of identification. It's worth a try. Who's got the map?"

"I do." Shea opened the road atlas. "Why don't we just drive to Seattle?"

"Because it's a wasted trip if we have nothing to go on."

"Okay. Looks like Yakima's the only city of any size around us. We turn off 90 and take 82 South."

Mike followed Shea's directions.

Neither the Seattle phone book nor any of those for outlying communities had a listing for Jack or John Delancey, or Al or Jane Girdling.

"What was Uncle Jack's middle name?" Mike asked Tate.

Tate winced as he thought. "It was mentioned in the will. Ah…Harvey! Or try the initial *H*."

Mike looked up J. H. Delancey. Still nothing.

"What about Tess Mullins?" Shea suggested.

Still nothing.

Seated at the library's round oak table, phone books littering the surface, Mike, Tate and Shea exchanged dispirited looks.

"If he's in delicate health," Mike said, "I hate to say it, but we could—lose him before we find him."

"Maybe he just made that up as an explanation for why he was leaving." Tate fiddled with the pages of the Bellevue book. "Maybe they were just moving to Seattle to be with their son. Isn't that where he's supposed to be?"

Shea slouched in his chair. "He's gone to great lengths to hide. Maybe he wouldn't appreciate our finding him."

"That could be." Tate ran his fingers down page of the phone book. "But if we find him and can see what he's doing without revealing ourselves, we'll know for sure he's all right and that this is what he wants— Hey, look at this."

"What?" Shea and Mike leaned forward simultaneously.

"Daniel Mullins on Eaglet Circle in Bellevue."

Mike took a pen out of his pocket and noted the address and the phone number on the pages Vince had faxed. "His son?"

"Could be," Shea said, then added cautiously,

"but we still can't be sure that he knows Jack's his father, or even if Jack would want him to know."

"We could call," Mike suggested, "and say we're looking for his mother. If we find her, we should find Jack. Maybe."

"What if he wants to know who we are and why we're asking?"

Tate closed the book and dug in his pocket for a quarter. "I'm the current owner of a store in Cave Beach, and I'm doing an historical pamphlet for its anniversary. I want to know what she remembers." He looked from Mike to Shea. "Okay?"

Mike thought Shea appeared to be as reluctant as he felt. The whole thing seemed fraught with pitfalls. But they had to know, and there seemed no other way to find out.

They crowded around the public telephone near the library's back door while Tate made the call.

"Hi," he said after moment. "Is your dad there?" A pause. "Thank you." He covered the mouthpiece. "A little girl answered. She's getting him." Then he pressed the receiver to his ear again. "Hello!" he said, smiling cheerfully as if he were there in person. "Daniel Mullins? Oh, good. I'm—Joe Sterling from Cave Beach. I've just bought the Coast Grocery Store, and I'm putting together a pamphlet outlining the history of the place for our seventy-fifth anniversary. I'm trying to locate Tess Mullins, who used to work here. I understand she also lived above the store with her son Daniel. I wondered if that was you, and if you could help me find her."

Tate listened for a short time, then nodded. "I see. Well, I'm sorry I bothered you. Thank you, Mr. Mullins." He hung up the phone and shook his head. "He said his mother's name is Judy, and she's from Canton, Ohio. He never lived in Cave Beach. So, either that was another Daniel Mullins…"

"Or he's covering for her," Mike speculated. "If we had unlimited time, we could go stake out his house and see who comes and goes."

Shea pushed open the library door, and they walked into the sunny parking lot. "But we don't. We shouldn't even have been gone this long. And it wouldn't be right to hire a detective to spy on him. Isn't that illegal? I mean, if he's not guilty of anything?"

Mike shrugged. "Depends on how it's done. We can trust Vince to do it right, but I'm not sure he'd be available. Or that we could afford him, if he was."

"Talk to him about it when we get home," Tate said. "We can afford him if he can do it."

They were five hours from home, which meant it was almost midnight when Mike dropped Tate off.

Mike pulled the Blazer in behind the main house, and Armand opened the kitchen door for him and Shea. "Any luck?" he asked without preamble.

Mike explained while Shea made decaf cappuccinos.

"How'd everything go here?" Mike asked once they were all settled at the table.

"No problems. I think if the weather holds, we're going to have a beautiful harvest."

"When?"

"We'll start in about two days."

"You can really be that specific?"

Armand smiled with the confidence of experience. "It's just an educated guess. And I'm putting my trust in providence and the weatherman."

Shea changed the subject. "How are things with Rachel?"

The elder man's confidence seemed to slip a little. "Very well. She found a mouse in the feed cupboard yesterday, though she made it clear she called me only because you three were gone and Veronica went screaming in the other direction."

The brothers laughed.

"Did you catch the mouse?" Shea asked.

"I did. But he was just a baby—probably part of a litter somewhere behind the cottage. Rachel may be visited again."

"Was she grateful?"

"Ha! She tried to give me a bag of cookies, but I told her I'd prefer a polite 'thank you.' She said I would take what she was willing to give. And I told her she was stingy woman."

Shea winced.

"Let me guess," Mike said. "She hit you with the cookies and threw you out."

"Close enough."

"Armand." Mike put an arm around his shoulders. "You may have to give a bit here. The cookies were really a nice gesture."

Armand sighed with dissatisfaction. "They were

in place of a sincere expression of gratitude. She believes that if she acknowledges she owes me anything, it will somehow diminish her—which is foolish! Worse, it makes it impossible for me to get close to her.''

"But is your attitude getting you any closer to her?''

Armand thought that over, then finally admitted with a sigh, "No. We are behaving like two old fools.''

"Old people,'' Mike said, "don't have the market cornered on foolishness.'' He excused himself and went upstairs to bed.

He'd thought about Veronica all the time he was gone. He'd been able to smell her fragrance, feel her in his arms. Time to accept he was doing more than approaching Step Four—he *was* Step Four. And he was even starting to think about Step Five.

That would be more difficult. Even as he framed the thought, his brain formed the image of the children in the window. He made himself think about it, allowed it to hurt, then closed his eyes. There. It hadn't killed him. He was living with it. That was probably the best he was ever going to be able to do. And maybe he wouldn't have to live with it alone.

He would talk to Veronica in the morning.

VERONICA SUPERVISED a full complement of children on the playground the last Friday in September. There was an all-day teachers' meeting at school, so the older children were back for the whole day.

The law only required one adult for every ten children over the age of five, but she asked Rachel to help later that afternoon. She had a baking project in mind for after naptime, and previous experience had shown that an extra pair of eyes might avert chaos when the cookie cutters and the sugar sprinkles started flying.

Now that harvest was only days away, the taped sounds of birds in distress and shotgun blasts drifted to the playground from the vineyard. Keeping the grapes safe was now a full-time job.

After a particularly loud blast, Ricky James hung by one knee from the monkey bars and shouted to Veronica, "It sounds like pirates!"

Veronica had explained earlier the noise was nothing to be alarmed about. That it was being made to protect the grapes. "It's just Mr. Beauchamp in the vineyard," she reassured him again.

Ricky and his brothers—affectionately known in the compound as the James Boys because of their outlaw tendencies—were charming and funny, but hard on the nerves. They terrified her with their antics on the monkey bars, but their mother wanted them watched but not stifled. "Knocks and bruises are all part of growing up," she insisted when Veronica spoke to her about it.

So Veronica watched them closely, and prayed about them a lot. Andy kept up with them very well, but little Spencer was usually left in their dust and preferred to play with the girls.

Mid-morning, Veronica caught a glimpse of Mike

as he spoke with one of the roofers working on Rachel's cottage. The men had brought a power-operated scaffold, and the boys—along with Rachel's animals—had stared in fascination as it was moved into position on the far side of her house.

Mike had been on his way to the winery, but when he finished with the roofer, he detoured to speak to Veronica.

"What are you doing for dinner?" he asked.

She'd frowned regretfully. "Making weenies, and macaroni-and-cheese. I'm going to have Alissa until about eight. Her parents are working late."

"Weenies and mac-and-cheese happen to be my favorite things," he'd said with a smile. "What if I bring the wine?"

"Uh…"

"The chocolate milk?"

"Okay." Her pulse raced as his gaze roved over her face, studied her mouth for several seconds, then returned to her eyes. She loved contemplating what that meant. "What's the news on your uncle?"

"We're on his trail," he said. "But it's complicated. I'll explain tonight."

She nodded and glanced back to check on the children. Ross was perched atop the monkey bars; Ricky hung from the uppermost crosspiece and moved across it, hand over hand; and Ronnie swung upside down from his knees, swaying back and forth. The other children happily played on the swings and the teeter-totter.

She turned back to Mike and found that he, too, was watching them.

"They remind me of a living Rube Goldberg sculpture," he said, shaking his head at their antics. "Things turning and spinning in all directions."

She laughed lightly. "That's an apt description. They're the force that moves the world."

His eyes came back to hers, filled with an easy affection she absorbed like a balm.

"I have other things to talk to you about tonight, as well." There was an element of promise in his voice.

She wanted to ask what that would be, but she didn't want to push him.

"Then I'll see you at six o'clock with a bottle of Moo-ton Lait au Chocolat, 1999?"

He laughed, and she knew he wanted to touch her. But because of the children, he just winked at her and walked away.

CHAPTER FOURTEEN

"THERE!" RACHEL STOOD back to admire her test pan of pumpkin-shaped cookies. "With cooking oil spritzed on the cookie cutters, they come out very easily. The children should have no trouble."

"Good." The children had been napping for an hour—just long enough for Veronica and Rachel to get ingredients measured and distributed into three areas on the counter so the children could work in groups. "Did you bring the orange sprinkles?"

Rachel had insisted they'd be the perfect touch and had volunteered to pick them up with her groceries.

She groaned. "I swear my brain has slowed to half speed. I probably put them away with my herbs and spices." She held up floured hands. "Would you mind getting them? I'll watch the children. The jar is probably in the cupboard to the left of the sink on the turntable."

"Okay. I'll just be a minute." Veronica hurried next door to Rachel's and found spices on the turntable, but no sprinkles. She spent several minutes trying the other cupboards and was about to give up when she spotted the bottle way back on the counter between the blender and a bowl of fruit.

She snatched it up and was letting herself out the

door when she heard giggles—suspicious and youthful giggles—coming from around the side of the house. There were no tourists in the compound at the moment, so she concluded her charges had somehow escaped Rachel.

Guessing that the animals had attracted them, she started toward the pen, then remembered the animals had been sent to the Ledbetters until the work on the cottage was complete.

Dread struck her even before she rounded the corner of the house. The scaffolding! She ran to it and saw her worst fears realized. The workmen were gone. They often took a late lunch and drove to the shade of the cottonwoods on the riverbank to eat what they'd brought.

Afraid of what she might see, she hesitated before looking up. Her heart thudded against her ribs as she saw Andy and Ronnie perched on the roof like little mountain goats, and Ross and Ricky on the platform, playing with the controls and making the scaffolding go up and down. They laughed hysterically as it jerked to a stop somewhere between the first and second floor.

"Ross!" Veronica shouted to the older boy who held the control. "Bring that thing down this instant!" The she reconsidered. "Andy! Ronnie! Can you get back on the scaffold?"

She held her breath while both boys moved carefully down the slope to the gutter.

Ross worked the controls, presumably to take the platform up, but it suddenly tilted at an awkward angle. The boys screamed and scrambled to hold on to the sides.

Veronica's heart rose into her throat and lodged there as she tried to shout instructions. "Hold on! Don't fall!"

She didn't dare leave them to go for help, but turned toward the compound and shouted as loudly as she could, "Help! Somebody!" But the compound was deserted.

She noticed the platform was level with Rachel's upstairs window and ran into the house and up the stairs. She took a moment to find the right room, then threw the window open.

Ross and Ricky were holding tightly to the side of the scaffolding, their faces white. Ricky reached toward her, she caught him and pulled him in. She did the same with Ross, then told them to go for help.

Veronica leaned out the window as far as she dared. "Andy? Ronnie?"

"I want to come down *now!*" Andy cried.

"I'm going to get you down," she promised, staring in dismay at the control box hanging from a wire way beyond her reach.

She hurried to the closet and found a wire hanger. She leaned out the window again and tried to snag the control box with it, but she still couldn't reach.

She unwound the hanger, then reached out again...and caught the control box. She hauled it in as far as the cord would allow.

Leaning forward with her stomach on the windowsill, she tried to make sense of the buttons. *On. Off. Up. Down. Forward. Tilt.*

Tilt! She pushed the button one way and the scaffolding tilted even farther. She pushed the other way, and the edge of the platform rose slowly and clicked into place.

Oh, God. Oh, God. Oh, God! Veronica stepped out of the window and onto the platform.

MIKE LISTENED to the blessed silence of the Delancey Bed-and-Breakfast. The guests in the three occupied rooms were all out this afternoon and had their own keys.

All was well. He could go home for half an hour, put his feet up, and think about how he was going to explain to Veronica that he wanted to turn their friendship into something more.

As he stepped onto the porch, movement by Rachel's cottage made him turn his head. He gasped as he caught sight of Veronica on the scaffolding looking toward the roof—where two little boys lay facedown. He could hear their soft, childish sobs.

He didn't take time to think. Images of the two little girls in the farmhouse tried to form, but he refused to let them. He raced across the compound toward the scaffolding, absently aware of two little boys running toward him, pointing toward the roof and shouting for help.

He'd known something like this would happen, but would anyone listen to him? Of course not. He was just an ex-cop with twelve years' experience saving children from themselves or others who meant them harm.

As he ran, he saw Veronica climb onto the waist-high metal barrier of the platform in an attempt to reach the little boy closest to her.

He opened his mouth to shout at her, then thought better of it. He continued to run, through Rachel's house and up the stairs.

Without bothering to warn Veronica, afraid he might overbalance her, he straddled the windowsill, caught her around the thighs and pulled her down onto the platform.

"What're you—?" she demanded, struggling against him.

He pushed her back through the window, shouted, "Stay there!" and climbed out onto the platform. He grabbed the belt of the boy nearest him and plucked him off the roof and into his arms. He handed him through the window to Veronica.

The second boy was out of reach, flattened against the roof. Mike moved toward the middle of the platform so that he was in line with him.

"Okay, let go, buddy. You're going to slip right into my arms."

"I'll fall!" the boy protested tearfully.

"No, you won't," Mike promised. "I'm here. I'll catch you."

"I want Veronica!"

"She's waiting for you. All you have to do is let go."

There was a moment's pause. "Okay," the boy

said, as though it was the last thing in the world he wanted to do.

"Great. Let go."

The boy didn't move. "You're sure it's all right?" he asked, voice trembling.

"I'm sure."

The boy screamed and his little body slid downward. First his feet, then his ankles, then his knees cleared the roof—then Mike was able to catch him.

The child relaxed against Mike for a second before twisting around to hold him in a deathgrip.

Mike gave him a brief hug, then urged him through the open window into Veronica's arms. The other boy clutched her waist.

Veronica, eyes closed, held the two boys to her. Mike imagined she was saying a prayer of gratitude. Needing a minute to collect himself, he hit the Down button and rode the scaffolding to the ground. It was only then that he noticed the crowd gathered in Rachel's yard: Tate and Armand, Shea and two little boys, and one of the couples staying at the B-and-B.

Mike accepted their congratulations with a perfunctory nod, then pushed past them, heading for Rachel's front door.

Tate and Shea fell into step on either side of him. "Calm down," Tate said. "I know you're upset, but so is everyone else."

Mike turned to him, the anger he'd controlled suddenly claiming his full attention. "I told you this would happen! Didn't I?"

Tate was giving him that diagnostic look he hated.

"Yes. And apparently you were right. But presumably, part of your concern was *your* not being able to function if it did. An unnecessary concern, it turns out."

"That's not the point!"

Shea caught his arm. "A potentially dangerous situation ending well is not the point?"

Mike yanked free. "The point is that it happened."

"Veronica's dealing with ten children," Tate said reasonably. "Obviously we have to discuss what happened. But let her deal with the kids before you try to deal with her."

That made sense, but Mike was unwilling to be reasoned out of his anger. "This is my business and not yours."

Tate raised both hands. "You're absolutely right. She's our tenant, but you're the one involved with her."

Mike would have liked to punch his brother for that—not because it *wasn't* true, but because it was.

Veronica and the children came out of the cottage and were joined at the steps by the other two, just as Father Wolff pulled to a stop beside Mike and Tate. He stepped out of the car and smiled at them over the roof. "Hi!" he said cheerfully. "I was just coming to talk to you about reserving some rooms. I have some church dignitaries coming to visit in October and very little room in the rectory." His smile faded a little as he noticed the tense expressions on their faces. "Is something wrong? Should I come back tomorrow?"

"Of course not." Mike pointed in Tate's direction. "My brother will take you into the great room and give you a cup of coffee. I have a couple of things to talk over with Veronica. Can you give me a few minutes?"

Father Wolff nodded. "It's my afternoon to golf. Take your time."

Mike followed Veronica and the boys to the barn. She stopped them at the door. "They have something to say to you."

The first boy he'd pulled off the roof had a fist inside the hem of his G.I. Joe T-shirt and was stretching it nervously. "Thank you for helping us," he said.

"Yeah." The smaller one leaned against Veronica, partially hiding behind the skirt of her jumper. "I was really scared. But you caught me."

The oldest boy took a step forward and looked up at Mike with a reluctant honesty Mike had to admire. "I wanted to try the scaffolding. It's all my fault. I'm sorry."

The fourth boy moved up to stand beside him and made a face. "Me, too. Thanks for helping Ronnie and Andy."

Mike braced his hands on his knees and leaned down to look into four little faces chastened by their experience.

"I'm glad nobody got hurt," he said gravely, "but it's pretty amazing that nobody did. All the equipment around here can hurt you if you don't use it properly. That's why only adults are allowed to operate it.''

"It's cool the way it goes up and—" The G.I. Joe fan stopped mid-sentence when Mike turned to him.

"It is, but it's working machinery, not a toy. Do you understand that?''

He got a unanimous "yes."

"Good," he said. "Because anybody who touches anything other than the toys in the barn and the stuff on the playground is in big trouble with me. Do you understand that, too?''

Another unanimous and even more enthusiastic "yes."

"Good." Mike straightened and focused on Veronica, anger flaring anew at the memory of her climbing onto the side of the scaffold's basket to try to reach the boys. "I'd like to speak with you," he said calmly, "when you have a moment."

She was still pale as paper, but there was a pugnacious set to her mouth.

"How about now?" she suggested a little sharply, reaching for the barn's open door. Rachel and the other children were gathered in front of it, eyes wide.

"Uh..." She looked from Mike to Veronica, then beckoned the four boys inside. "Veronica," she began, partially closing the door, "I didn't—"

"I'll just be a couple of minutes." Veronica interrupted. "Why don't you get them started on the cookies?"

Before the other woman could say another word, Veronica walked away.

Veronica was in no mood for this discussion. She wasn't quite over being absolutely terrified and was hardly eager to deal with Mike's I-told-you-so. But it didn't look as if she was going to be able to escape. The gentle man she'd come to love had turned back into the man who didn't want her or her children anywhere around.

"What in the hell happened?" he asked.

Hands in the pockets of her jumper, she replied calmly, "The boys tell me they got out the window in the nap room, then closed it again. They've been fascinated by that scaffolding since it arrived. I took them by this morning so they could see it in action, thinking maybe that would satisfy some of their questions. One of the roofers even came down to talk to them for a couple of minutes. But…children just like to see things for themselves."

"You're pretty philosophical about curiosity that almost cost them bodily damage," he said, hating her reasonableness when his own nerves had yet to settle down.

"Am I?" She removed her hands from her pockets and held them up. They were shaking. She shoved them back in again and angled her chin defensively. "Just because I'm not shouting doesn't mean I'm not upset. I apologize for having brought your worst fears to life. I accept the blame. Does that make you feel better?" Her final question was shouted.

"Keep your voice down," he said, looking around

the empty compound. Then he added on a quiet but dangerous-sounding note, "I'm less concerned about my own comfort level than I am that four little boys almost fell two stories!"

"I know!" she retorted loudly. "It's my fault. I try to second-guess them, but those little guys are particularly wily." Tears rose in her throat, but she swallowed them, determined they wouldn't fall. "So, I guess I've just proven that no matter how hard you try, you can't guarantee a child's safety!"

He seemed to grow about six inches, spine stiffening and shoulders squaring. "I simply asked what happened. I'm one of your landlords. When four children almost fall from a building I own, I think I have a right to ask a few questions. Why in the hell didn't you call for help?"

"I did, but I was afraid to leave them to go looking for you! I sent Ricky and Ross for help and then decided I didn't have time to wait."

"So you climbed onto a two-inch-wide bar on top of an unstable platform two stories up? *That* showed clear thinking!"

Knowing she couldn't shout louder than he, Veronica consciously lowered her voice, trying to show superiority by exercising control. "You have no right to shout at me," she said with dignity. "I wa—"

"Excuse me, but I have every right. There's something between us, which means you have to explain yourself to me. That's how it works."

"What's between us?" she demanded, dignity instantly lost. "Approaching Step Four isn't *being* there! I don't have to answer to anyone!"

This was no longer about the boys and the scaffolding.

"I don't know how it works in the convent," he said, "but out here, you can't bend everyone to your will. You don't think that freedom from your vows means you can suddenly get everything you want just because you want it, do you?"

"You've disabused me of that notion, haven't you?"

"I had intended to tell you I've missed you the past couple of days and that I realized I'm not just me anymore. I'm part of us. And I know I've got to accept that I don't control everything and never will. Maybe that's a truth *you* should come to terms with, too."

He waited for a response, but Veronica's throat was too tight to allow one. She simply looked away from him, her eyes brimming with tears.

"Excuse me," he said finally. "Father Wolff's waiting for me."

MIKE WALKED into the B-and-B, fifty-percent temper, fifty-percent nerves. Tate gave him his annoying big brother look. When Mike silently threatened to ram it down his throat, Tate left him alone with Father Wolff.

"Tate told me about the kids on the scaffolding," the priest said. "That's why they have guardian angels. Nothing mortal could survive the shock of all the trouble they get into." He looked Mike in the eye. "He also told me more about your children."

Mike wasn't interested in discussing it. "I have no children, Father."

The priest nodded and pointed to Mike's heart. "You do. Right there. Priest, doctor, cop—we're all the same. Everyone we lose lives with us for the rest of our days. It's almost as though because we couldn't save theirs, we want to give them our lives to make up for it. That doesn't work, of course." He fidgeted, then said with a sudden, unfocused look, "I lost a man when I was a young priest. He'd felt like a loser all his life. He worked minimum wage jobs and had no luck with women, and though I counseled him for more than a year, I was never able to make him understand that God judges us by a different standard. And in the end, I just didn't have the words to make him want to live. I know your situation was different—and it's so much harder to lose children— but if I had destroyed myself over that loss, then I wouldn't have been there for the other people I've helped since. You can't win them all, Mike."

Mike opened the reservations book, hoping to end the conversation. "About your guests. When are they—?"

"But you have to keep fighting," the priest went on, determined to make his point. "And you have to put up with friends who care and don't want to see you do yourself harm. While Tate was pouring our coffee, I looked out the window and saw you and Veronica arguing."

Mike gave him a dry smile. "Don't worry about Veronica. She's hardly the humble little nun. She had a lot to say."

The priest made a sympathetic face. "That's the way women usually run arguments—or so the men I counsel tell me. She's the warmest and most giving woman I've ever known. And in a profession where those qualities are required, that's saying something. She always behaved as if she was in charge, but in her eyes I could always see this very lonely child." Father Wolff grew even more serious. "That was gone from her face that day I first met you. I wonder if you even realize how important you are to her. She's always needed to belong somewhere. With you, apparently." He smiled again. "It's thanks to me, you know, that she came your way. I've prayed for her since the day she walked into the rectory in Santa Margarita to introduce herself."

Mike tried to imagine her in a plain blue dress and veil, but the woman he knew was too stubborn, too nonconformist to fit the picture.

He also tried to imagine himself being everything she needed—and couldn't quite picture that, either.

So he tried to imagine life without her—and that was even darker than his memories of Dallas.

"Well, don't stop praying now," he advised the priest.

"Lovers' quarrel?"

"Big time."

"Not to worry. I've got a novena for everything."

CHAPTER FIFTEEN

VERONICA DIDN'T LEAVE her apartment the next day, vacillating between guilt and anger.

Colette arrived Saturday afternoon with some soup.

"Thank you." Veronica invited her inside, mystified by the gift.

"Rachel was feeling a little down," Colette explained as she sat on the reception area sofa. "I know you've reassured her over and over that it wasn't her fault, but she still feels badly—particularly since it's caused a problem with you and Mike. So I brought her some chicken rice. I thought you might be needing a little TLC yourself."

Veronica guessed Tate had told Colette what had happened Friday afternoon. Veronica put the soup on the coffee table and sat down beside Colette. "Mike was awful."

Colette smiled at her apologetically. "From what I hear, you were both a little overwrought. Understandable under the circumstances."

"Maybe. But he was completely unreasonable."

"I've been a mother too long not to know what escape artists children are." Colette made a self-deprecating face. "I even lost my kids once. But you have to understand—men react differently to fear than women do, and I think that was part of the problem yesterday.''

"The problem was he was angry at me for trying to get the boys off the roof myself. But there was no one around, and I couldn't just leave them.''

Colette shook her head. "That's what you don't understand. And since you haven't spent much time around men, it's not surprising you don't. He was angry because you and the boys were in danger, and that frightened him. Anger's acceptable to a man, fear isn't. They get loud to convince themselves they're bigger than whatever they're afraid of.''

Veronica tried to make sense of that in view of what had happened. But even if Colette was right, she still had a few grievances. Colette went on before she could voice them.

"And I know *you* were frightened. Rachel and Tate say you did a lot of yelling yourself.''

Veronica sank a little farther into her corner of the couch. "He accused me of wanting everything my way.''

"Well, don't you?'' Colette smiled in amusement. "I do. When Tate and I fell in love, I wanted to protect my daughters from a disruption in their lives. I wanted to protect myself from the changes Tate would bring to my world. And I wanted to protect Tate from me.''

"From you? Why?''

"I was, well—'' Colette waved away the past "—my point is, I was so busy trying to do what I was sure was right for all of us, that I forgot Tate was involved, too, and might have had better solutions than I did.''

''Mike's solution is to not have children around.''

Colette reached over to pat her knee. ''We're all tempted to find the easiest way out. Considering his past, I think you should try to understand.'' Then she pushed herself to her feet. ''Got to go. I have a pot roast in the oven.''

Veronica followed her to the door. ''Should I look in on Rachel?''

''No. She was going to have a nap. I think she's overdone it—what with helping out at the tasting room and cooking for the B-and-B. The trouble with my dad has to have upset her, too. They were always such good friends, but now that Dad wants more than just companionship, she's in a flap.'' Colette smiled fondly. ''But, isn't that wonderful?''

''It is. I wish she'd come to think so.''

''My father remains hopeful.'' Colette gave her a quick hug. ''You should, too. I know all you want to do is love Mike, but love requires a lot of faith and trust, not only in each other, but in the world you're going to live in. And I imagine that's pretty much destroyed when you watch little children die.''

On Sunday, Veronica considered what Colette had said, while she made templates of leaves for a fall project for the children. It was true: her fear for the children had somehow become fear for what they would mean to her relationship with Mike once the danger had passed.

And she'd begun to shout.

She finally called Mike to apologize, but reached Armand instead. He told her the brothers were working on a plumbing problem in the restaurant kitchen. She went back to her leaves—and her guilt.

THE FOLLOWING MORNING Veronica was surprised to find her enrollment holding steady at ten children. Considering the scaffolding incident, which she'd dutifully explained to the parents involved, she'd half expected Andy and the James boys to be withdrawn.

But as she'd discovered while teaching school, parents were often more—and regrettably sometimes less—understanding than she expected.

Delia Moore had listened with a frown to Veronica's explanation, but once she'd looked her son over and seen for herself that he was fine, she'd sent him off to the car and smiled.

"I'll have to punish him for sneaking away from you like that," she said in a low voice because other children played nearby. Then her smile widened. "But he's been so timid that I'm thrilled to see him doing things other little boys do. Am I insane?"

Maybe. But Veronica hadn't told her that.

Eden James had a similar reaction, but a considerably different approach. "I told Jet° that rock-climbing lessons were not a good idea, considering the level of enthusiasm the boys have, but…" She shook her head with more fondness than disapproval. She wore fatigues with a jeweled pink flamingo pin on the right lapel. "But he thinks nothing should stop them—including mountains.'' She put an arm around Veronica. ''Don't beat yourself up, honey. They get away from Jet all the time, and he led a Special Forces platoon. We have to paint the house next summer. Knowing about their interest in scaffolding could come in handy.''

MIKE WAS UP EARLY Monday morning, wondering if Veronica was even speaking to him. It was late yesterday, after spending hours on his back under the sink in the restaurant, before he'd calmed down sufficiently to think about what had happened. But he hadn't been able to sort it out.

Everyone was a little annoyed at him because of his argument with Veronica, and since the staff had Mondays off, he'd been prepared to put breakfast together for his guests without Rachel's help. One of the couples now spending a week with them was two avid explorers of anything and everything, and always up and ready for breakfast at six.

But Rachel arrived at 5:30 a.m. with the large box she carried over every morning filled with specially prepared meals she'd begun at home. However she greeted him a little stiffly.

''Are you angry with me, too?'' he asked, as he peeled and sliced fruit while she poured the contents of a covered plastic bowl of batter into a layer cake pan and placed it in the oven. He identified it as coffee cake, always a favorite among their guests.

''Not angry,'' she replied. ''You just made me grateful I'm not the one in love with you. You reminded me of my husband. You shouldn't have shouted at her. It was partially my fault.''

''She was shouting at me.''

''She was scared!''

''So was I!''

''Well, then maybe you should explain that to her. Unless you have too much pride.'' As she delivered her dare, she collided with him for the third time as they moved about the kitchen.

''You sure you should be here this morning, Rachel?'' he asked. ''You look a little...''

She glared at him stubbornly. ''I'm fine. One day you'll know what it's like when old age creeps up. Everything hurts. Shoulders, knees, back. And you haven't been very good for my nerves lately.'' Then she put a hand to the left side of her chest and frowned, rubbing absently.

Mike wondered what the gesture meant. Armand had made coffee by the time Mike had come downstairs and had taken off with a cheerful wave for the vineyard.

''Did you see Armand on your way in this morning?'' he asked casually, pouring her a glass of juice.

''No,'' she replied as she put a quiche in the oven. Chores done, she took the glass and sank into a dining room chair. ''Veronica was up, though, raking the wood chips on the playground to keep it soft. That girl really knows what she's doing. You had no right—''

Mike turned away from his bowl of fruit. ''I did not blame her. I just asked her what happened, and she got indignant. I guess when you're used to answering to God, you don't think you should have to answer to anybody else. Or—'' he put half an orange on a plate and carried it to her ''—maybe when you're *old* enough that you can do as you please, you resent the thought of ever having to consult with or compromise for anyone else.''

She made a face at him as she accepted the plate. ''Thank you. So I'm too old to change, and you're too foolish. We're a great pair.''

Mike sat down in the chair beside her. ''All you have to do is admit you love Armand. Come on, Rachel. You know he'd never bully you.''

She startled him with a sudden, wicked smile. ''He'd try. And why would I want to fight him for my independence, when I already have it now?''

''But you have it without him. Wouldn't it make life more exciting to have him and then work a little harder at your independence?''

She leaned her chin in her hand and sighed, her bright eyes focused on the dinnerware in the china cabinet. ''I don't know. I was just beginning to think so. But then I started having this…'' She put her hand to her chest again and rubbed just above her left breast.

''Good morning!'' The explorers arrived in khaki shorts and matching red polo shirts. The man was tall and slender with a young-Jimmy-Stewart look, and his wife was petite and dark. Mike thought of Dave and Suzi Berger as the poster couple for life in the burbs. But they were cheerful and friendly, and seemed very much in love. Appreciating how difficult maintaining a relationship could be, Mike admired them.

Rachel got right to her feet despite Mike's insistence that he had the Bergers' fruit bowl just about ready. He watched her worriedly as she set their places at the table and poured coffee.

Mike talked with the couple about their day's trip to the microbreweries in McMinnville, while Rachel layered the fruit with yogurt in a compote and topped it with a dollop of whipped cream.

"Mmm!" Suzi dipped her spoon into the cream. "It'll be tough going back to breakfast bars after this."

The Bergers were cutting into the quiche when Rachel asked Mike if he'd mind if she left before the other guests came down. "Everything's ready," she said. "You don't have to do anything but serve."

"No. Go ahead." He took the box from her as she started to collect her bowls and utensils. "Don't worry about that. I'll bring it over later. But, what's bothering you? You started to tell me about—"

And then, like a teaser in a soap opera, the matter was pushed aside again as the front door burst open and Armand stood in the foyer, his old woolen slacks, torn sweater and cap somehow appropriate to the restored-Victorian setting.

Seeing the guests at the table, he whipped off his hat and smiled widely from Mike to Rachel. "Harvest!" he exclaimed.

"Harvest!"

The word echoed throughout the house as the other guests coming down the stairs heard the news and collected in an excited little knot in the hallway.

"Tate's gone to town to get the processing crew and tell the pickers," Armand said. "He told me to let you know he'll be in the vineyard with us, so you're in charge of the compound. He also wants you to call Father Wolff. He said he'd bless the first truckload of grapes."

"Got it." Mike felt Armand's excitement. He turned to reach for the phone book—

Rachel clutched her chest and crumpled to the floor.

Armand pushed Mike aside to reach her first. Mike stepped over her feet, but was pushed away again, this time by Dave Berger.

Armand had braced Rachel against his knee, and Berger leaned over her to lift her eyelids, then feel for a pulse at her throat. He looked as though he knew what he was doing. "Call 9-1-1," he said.

Suzi Berger already had the phone in hand.

"What is it?" Armand and Mike asked together.

"Could be a couple of things." He touched Rachel's cheek, then her arm. "Is there pain in your arm? Difficulty breathing?"

She shook her head, her face devoid of color.

"I'd say myocardial infarction." At their blank looks, Berger rephrased. "Heart attack. Or angina, or maybe gallbladder. Do you still have your gallbladder?"

Rachel smiled thinly. "No. Lost it…after an orgy

of steak and ice cream in '85. You're a doctor? I took you for a professor.''

''Well, I am always lecturing someone. We'll hope it's angina. That can be treated fairly easily with medication. But we won't really know what we're dealing with till we get you to the ER.''

''But isn't angina the same as a heart attack?'' Armand asked worriedly.

Berger shook his head. ''No. It's an interruption of oxygen to the heart. Hurts like hell, but it's treatable.''

When Rachel tried to sit up, Armand and Berger held her down.

''Armand,'' she said, trying to push him away. ''You have to see to the harvest!''

''Hush,'' Armand warned gruffly, though Mike noticed that his hand stroking Rachel's crown of braids was shaking. ''The harvest can wait. You're more important.''

She frowned at him. ''But I—''

''Rachel, be quiet.''

Rachel looked for Mike's face in the circle of people. She jabbed a thumb in Armand's direction. ''See what I mean? Why would I want to spend my life with a man who—who…?'' She stopped, seeming to realize for the first time that she was cradled in Armand's arms while he stroked her hair.

The distant sound of a siren penetrated the air.

''They can't start the harvest without you, Armand!'' Rachel insisted. ''You know where to start picking, you have to—''

He put a hand lightly over her mouth for quiet, and said to Mike, "You must tell Colette what's happened. She's in the vineyard already, marking the rows where we will start the Pinot Noir. She must take charge of the harvest until I return. We've done it together for two years. She knows what she's doing."

"No." Rachel tried to sit up again.

Armand pointed finger at her. "You stop that. I'm coming with you, and that is final."

The siren grew louder, closer.

"I'll see the other guests get breakfast, Mike," Suzi Berger said. "And if anyone calls about reservations, I'll take messages. Don't worry about a thing."

The arrival of the ambulance brought Veronica and Shea running to the Bed-and-Breakfast.

Mike intercepted both of them as Rachel was carried into the back of the ambulance.

"Some kind of heart problem," he explained as they watched Dave Berger climb in after the gurney. "Turns out, one of our guests is a doctor."

"Shouldn't someone go with her?" Veronica asked.

Mike pointed to the passenger side of the ambulance, where an attendant was helping Armand climb in.

"Good." Shea raised a puzzled eyebrow. "But what was he doing at the B-and-B at this hour?"

"He came to tell us it's harvest time. Tate's gone to town to get the crew rounded up."

The old Jeep suddenly turned into the compound, raced in their direction, then screeched to a stop several feet from them. Colette leapt out, her red hair like a shout in the compound's grim atmosphere.

She ran for the still-open doors at the back of the ambulance, her eyes wide with worry.

Mike understood instantly what was on her mind. "Your father's fine," he said, shielding her from collision as an attendant came around to close the doors. "It's Rachel. Some kind of heart problem. We don't know how serious it is yet." He drew her back to the others and explained again what happened. "Your father's going with her."

She held on to Mike's forearms as the ambulance turned in a wide circle. "Is she going to be all right?"

"Your dad will keep us posted. Meanwhile..." He shook her lightly to get her attention as the ambulance took off, sirens blaring. "He said you're supposed to get the harvest under way."

She looked stunned. "Me?"

"He said you know what you're doing."

She rolled her eyes. "That's what I get for trying to give that impression." The she drew a deep breath and gave him a tremulous smile that revealed her usually well-hidden vulnerability. "In the past few years, we've harvested and sold the grapes to other labels. But this one's yours."

"Yours, too, now that you're a Delancey. So..." He grinned. "No pressure, but do a good job. Our livelihoods depend on you."

She gave his arm a playful punch. "Thanks. That'll help my tension headache." She gave Veronica a quick hug. "Pray for us. And pray for Rachel."

Veronica patted her back. "I'm praying for all of us. She's going to be fine, and the harvest will go well. I know it."

"Speaking of praying," Mike said to Veronica as Colette left in the Jeep, "We're supposed to call Father Wolff to come and bless the first truckload. Would you do that?"

"Sure."

There was no animosity between them. They were simply two friends sharing the load in a crisis. Then he noticed the pale purple under her eyes. She must not have slept well, either. A rush of words came to the tip of his tongue. *I'm sorry. I'm stupid. I'm yours.*

He almost said them aloud because she seemed to be watching his lips, as though expecting him to speak. But he bit down on them instead. He had to say the right words, or not speak at all. And he didn't know yet what they were.

She looked at her watch. "I've got Alissa coming in five minutes. I'll call Father Wolff right away." She turned to leave, then turned back again. "You'll let me know when you hear about Rachel?"

"I will."

She headed for the barn at a graceful run.

He watched her, his heart beating fast, until she disappeared inside the building. Rachel wasn't the only one with a heart condition that could go either way.

VERONICA TOOK THE CHILDREN to watch the harvest begin. She wasn't sure what she'd expected, but she was a little surprised to see that in this age of automation, all the picking was done by hand.

Up and down the rows, vines literally shook with the vigor of the workers' knives. The six-inch serrated blades looked lethally sharp. Some workers tied them to their wrists with a string so they would dangle between cuts, and some taped the handles—she guessed that was for comfort.

Veronica redirected the children's attention to the flats where the boxes of grapes were collected. The flats were hitched to every vehicle on the property that could pull one, and to the tractor they'd borrowed from the Ledbetters.

Colette had told her that a good worker harvested about fifty lugs, or boxes, a day, and each lug held seven thousand clusters.

The workers were deft and swift, some of them young men and women from town, others migrants who worked in families. Most of these people, she'd heard, picked strawberries in the spring and apples up north as well.

Like them, Veronica had always considered herself something of a nomad, traveling from place to place with her mother as a child, from one foster home to another as a teenager, then from school to school after she'd become a nun. Though she'd never gotten used to the loneliness, she'd accepted it. She thought it wonderful that these workers weren't alone. Their entire family traveled with them.

Everyone followed the first load, which Colette took to the winery—and Veronica and the children fell in with the small crowd watching Father Wolff bless the first fruits.

THERE'D BEEN A TIME when Mike had doubted he and his brothers would ever get the Delancey Winery to this point. They weren't home free by any means, but they'd raised their first crop.

He looked at his brothers and saw the same happy satisfaction on their faces that he was feeling. How far they'd come in less than a year.

He turned instinctively to share his happiness with Veronica—only to discover she and the children were walking toward the barn. Father Wolff had finished his blessing, and the workers were hurrying back to the vineyard.

He wondered if he should take that as a metaphor for their future. She heading one way with the children she would always have around her, and he going another. It would certainly be easier.

But even in his fiercest self-preservation mode, he knew he couldn't let that happen.

He was about to head back to the B-and-B when Tate's cell phone rang. He stopped in anticipation of Armand's call.

Veronica was just out of earshot, but brought her little group to a halt.

"Hi, Armand," Tate said. Mike tensed, and he could see that everyone else was worried, too. Then Tate smiled and covered the mouthpiece. "Not a heart attack,'' he said. "It was angina, and she's responding well to the medication.''

Everyone started to talk at once, and he had to shush them to hear what else Armand had to say. "Tomorrow morning? Are you sure?'' He listened a little longer, then nodded. "No, that's fine. You stay right there. Colette's being brilliant. We'll pick up both of you in the morning.'' He closed the phone and explained, "The hospital wants to observe her overnight. Armand's going to stay, and if all goes as well as the doctor expects, they'll be home tomorrow.''

Veronica smiled hesitantly from her place near Rachel's empty pen, and Mike went to her to relay Armand's message. She looked up at the sky and said with sincerity, "Thank you. Thank you!''

Then she turned to the children, whom she'd apparently told about Rachel's trip to the hospital. "Let's go make a Welcome Home sign to put on her door,'' she suggested.

"Hi, Father Wolff!'' Alissa shouted across the compound at the priest, who looked up from a conversation with Tate and Shea, and returned her eager wave.

Mike saw an opportunity and took it as the children began to wander toward the barn.

He caught Veronica's arm and held her back. "Kiss me,'' he said. "Father's watching. He'll be worried about his Cupid skills if you don't—''

She kissed him before he'd even finished explaining. It was brief and unsatisfyingly chaste, but he felt her soul was in it. She rubbed a hand gently over his heart. "I'm sorry about yesterday."

He put his hand over hers, relieved to know they were, at least, still friends. "Me, too. I didn't handle that very well. We have to talk."

She smiled in the direction of the vineyard. "You're all going to be working day and night for weeks."

"I'm picking you up at seven o'clock tonight," he said. "Wear jeans."

"Why?"

"Just be ready."

"But—"

"Seven." He walked away, leaving her looking uncertain.

CHAPTER SIXTEEN

"I DON'T GET IT!" Shea grumped from the passenger seat of the Blazer as Mike pulled up in front of the service station just after five p.m. "We're in the middle of harvesting, and you have to take a break to buy a motorcycle? I mean, I know how much you loved the bike you sold—but why right now?"

"I've already test-driven it," Mike replied. "I won't be long. All you have to do is drive the Blazer home for me."

Shea gave him a knowing look as he came around the vehicle. "You bit the dust, didn't you? Brother number two bitten by the love bug. I heard about your romantic bike ride thorough the vineyard with Vee. You've found the woman of your dreams."

Mike couldn't deny it, but was a little afraid to admit it. Considering what else he'd come to town for, that seemed ridiculous. "Yeah, I have."

"And you apologized for what happened Friday?"

"I'm going to do that tonight."

Shea looked worried. "You're sure she's willing?"

Mike sighed. "Not at all. But I guess that's when you know you're in love. You're willing to risk everything."

Shea studied him moment, then smiled and shook his hand. "Well, good luck. We all think she's pretty special, and we'd like to see you happy. We'd also like to see you less ugly, but it doesn't look as if that's going to happen."

Mike gave him a hug, then pushed him into the car. "Get out of here. And thanks for coming with me."

As Shea drove away, Mike headed for the small square building that served as the station's office.

AT GREEN ACRES DAY CARE, Veronica tidied up the play area. Eden James was unusually late picking up her boys. That morning she'd explained to Veronica she was taking her husband to the airport in Portland, but expected to be home in time to get the boys. But Portland traffic was thick and slow, Veronica remembered, and construction at the airport probably contributed to Eden's delay.

Ross, Ricky and Ronnie contentedly watched an animated film on video. It was after six and all the other children—even Alissa—were gone.

Veronica had a feeling that her date with Mike wasn't going to happen.

She deemed herself psychic a moment later when the phone rang. It was Eden.

"I'm in a service station just outside Portland," she said. "Veronica, I'm so sorry, but the car's thermostat died and they don't have the part! It's being overnighted here, but that's the best they can do." She sounded on the brink of tears—or profanity. "I called my neighbor to see if she could pick up the boys, but she isn't home. I'm trying to find a rental car, but it's not looking good.''

Veronica heard the desperation in her voice and accepted the inevitable. She suspected this would prove to Mike yet again that the care of children was troublesome and unpredictable, and having them should be avoided at all costs.

''That's okay, Eden,'' she said. ''Just find a motel room, buy yourself dinner, and the boys will be fine with me. I can put two of them in the bed and one in my sleeping bag.''

''But there's school in the morning.''

''I'll get them there. Don't worry about a thing. Call me when you get in just so I know you made it all right.''

''Oh, Veronica...''

''Have no fear.'' She laughed. ''This will cost you.''

''I'll see that there's a large bonus in your monthly check!''

''Now you're talking. Seriously, Eden, don't give us another thought. We'll be fine.''

Veronica explained the situation to the boys, who were thrilled by the thought of staying the night.

She had opened the cupboard and was searching for something to prepare for dinner, when the roar of a powerful motor drew all the boys toward the window. Veronica recognized the sound: the Harley Softail.

''Wowww!'' Ross exclaimed, racing for the door.

Veronica and Ricky and Ronnie were right behind him.

Mike had pulled to a stop right in front of the barn. He braced his feet to balance the bike, removed his helmet and grinned at her as she approached him in disbelief.

"Did you buy it?" she demanded.

"I did," he replied. "And I was going to take you for a *ride*." He emphasized the last word, suggesting the ride would have been very special. On this bike, she thought, how could it not be? He indicated the boys with a jut of his chin and a smile. "But you're still working?"

She explained about Eden James's car trouble. "I'm afraid our date's off," she said regretfully, waiting for his frown of disapproval. "Unless I can interest you in a tuna salad sandwich? I was just about to make some."

"This is so cool!" Ross said before Mike could reply. He ran a hand over the shiny cream paint. "Is this an old one? It looks different."

"It's just made to look old," Mike said.

"Can I have a ride?"

"Sorry." Mike held up his helmet. "I only have one, and the law says you have to wear one. But what if I take you for a ride in the Blazer?"

The boys jumped up and down at the suggestion without even a clue as to where Mike intended to take them.

He smiled at Veronica. "How about if I take you

and the boys to dinner at the French River Café? They have good home cooking.''

"Burgers and curly fries!" Ricky said. "Mom and Dad take us there sometimes. Can we, Veronica? Please?''

Mike pulled his bike inside the barn, then he and Veronica followed the boys to the house where Shea had left the Blazer.

It was hardly the romantic evening under the stars Mike had planned, he thought, but he was still getting to spend it with Veronica.

The boys asked him a million questions when they learned he'd been a cop. They spilled one glass of water, one glass of milk, and ate everything in sight—plus a couple of things for which they had to send the waitress back to the kitchen.

Veronica seemed to be having a great time. She was all smiles and good humor. He was beginning to believe they were going to have a happy ending, after all.

He'd thought long and hard while he'd been helping haul in grapes that afternoon, and he finally felt he had the right words. He was hoping he'd have the chance to say them after the boys went to bed.

He was wiping catsup off Ronnie's nose when he saw Felicia leave the restaurant in the company of a man he'd never seen before. She glanced their way as the man paid the bill.

"That's the mayor!" Ronnie said loudly, pointing in her direction. "Mommy works at City Hall, too! Hi, Mayor!" He waved enthusiastically.

Mike saw the first vulnerable expression he'd seen on Felicia's face since he'd known her. She returned the boy's wave and smiled. That seemingly sincere expression of friendship was also a first. He'd only known her smiles to be greedy, or calculating, or self-satisfied. But this one was...sweet.

"He's the new swimming instructor," Ross said. "He swims good, but he's kinda crabby."

"I thought crabs were found in oceans," Mike said seriously, "not in swimming pools."

"No, I meant—" Ross began, then realized he was being teased. He elbowed Mike. "You're nutty."

The boys pleaded for a second dessert. Mike would have accommodated them, but Veronica stood firm. "You've eaten enough to feed a small country. Do you have homework?"

The boys made faces at one another.

"I don't!" Ronnie said proudly.

"That's 'cause you're the baby!" Ricky taunted. "First graders don't get homework!"

Ronnie reached across Mike to get his brother, but Mike caught him. "Hey, hey!" he said, sitting him down again. "No bloodshed. It makes me throw up."

"Cool!" Ross said. "Liver makes *me* throw up. Chunky, oozy—"

Mike put a hand over his mouth. "We get the picture."

Veronica waved to the waitress for the check and shooed the boys out of the booth before the conversation could deteriorate further. Mike snatched the check from her.

Ronnie held Mike's hand as they walked to the parking lot, and the other two boys walked backward in front of him, asking him yet more questions.

He'd opened the back door and the boys were scrambling in when a loud voice split the evening. *"No!"* a woman said firmly. "I can't go! I have work—" Then she screamed, and there were sounds of a tussle.

"I think that's Felicia!" Veronica exclaimed.

Mike closed the door on the boys, then gave Veronica the keys and pushed her into the front seat. "Lock the doors. I'll be right back."

"Mike—" she began, but he was already running toward the sound.

Veronica locked the doors, then turned on the headlights, illuminating the scuffle between Felicia and the swimming instructor. The boys hung over the front seat. It was clear the man had amorous intentions, and that Felicia was resisting.

Mike approached, saying something to the man that made him turn around, his expression angry. Felicia went to Mike's side. The man reached for her, but Mike held him away. Then he threw a punch. Mike dodged it and flattened the other man against the side of the car.

More words were exchanged. Mike seemed to be arguing with Felicia. Then he opened the car door and shoved the man inside. The car drove away with a squeal of tires, and Mike took Felicia's arm and led her toward the Blazer.

"Wowww!" Ross said with admiration in his voice. "Did you see that?"

"He was a cop," Ricky reminded him. "Cops know how to do that stuff."

Ronnie gleefully made explosive punching sounds.

Great, Veronica thought. *First I let them get stranded on a roof, then I take them to a brawl.*

Mike opened the back door to help Felicia in, but Veronica realized there would be too few seat belts.

"I'll sit in the back," she said. She jumped out.

Felicia looked stunned. "No. I can sit…"

Veronica touched a finger to a reddening bruise on Felicia's throat. "Are you all right?" she asked as Mike opened the back.

"I'm okay." Her voice was thin and shaky. "Just a little upset. But I can sit here."

The boys hung over their seat, watching. "Mike slammed that guy up against the car!" Ross said as if everyone else had missed it. "Pow!"

"Yes, he did." Felicia trembled, not at all the condescending woman she usually was. "I'm lucky you guys were there."

Veronica pulled her away when she would have climbed into the back. "Please take my seat," she said, climbing in to prevent further discussion.

Mike closed the tailgate and gave her an affectionate wink. "Most interesting luggage I've ever had," he teased. Then he walked Felicia around to the passenger side.

"Boys, sit down, please," Veronica said. But they weren't listening.

"He was cop, you know!" Ricky told Felicia. "That's why he can fight like that."

Mike climbed in behind the wheel. "Everybody sit down and buckle up," he said, and got instant cooperation. He looked in the rearview mirror. "You okay back there, Veronica?"

"I'm fine."

He turned to Felicia. "I still think you should file charges," he said. "You've got the bruise to prove battery."

She shook her head. "I'll just find better dinner company next time. Thanks, though."

"Nobody should hurt the mayor," Ronnie said staunchly. "The mayor's important."

Felicia startled everyone by bursting into tears. The boys turned to Veronica in horror. She handed Ross a tissue, which he passed to Felicia.

In a few minutes, Felicia was composed enough to give Mike instructions to her home, a large Craftsman-style house across the street from the park.

"Hey! You can play in the park anytime you want," Ronnie said.

Mike unlocked the back of the Blazer, helped Veronica out, then walked Felicia to her door and waited while she unlocked it. Moving to the passenger seat, Veronica watched Felicia hug Mike for a long moment. Then Felicia went inside, and Mike returned.

The boys were overcome with hero worship. Veronica tried to put them to bed, but when they heard Mike intended to stay for a cup of coffee, they refused to go.

Veronica would have been more firm about getting them to bed, but Mike was being so patient she didn't have the heart. Besides, he seemed to be enjoying himself as well.

So she brought blankets to the sofa where they were crowded around him, and went to make a pot of coffee.

BY THE TIME the boys finished interrogating Mike and had drifted off to sleep, Veronica looked exhausted. He carried the two younger boys to her bed, then helped Ross, who was half-awake, into the sleeping bag on the floor.

"Where are you going to sleep?" Mike asked her.

She pointed toward the old sofa. "I'll be fine." She smiled sleepily. "Thanks. I really enjoyed tonight. But I'm sorry about Felicia. I called her while you and the boys were talking, just to make sure she was all right. She said to thank you again."

"She was lucky," he said. "That could have ended badly."

"The boys were very impressed."

"Cute kids." He took her face in his hands. "You want to try this again tomorrow night?"

She looked surprised. "You're not completely put off by having kids all over you?"

He shook his head. "I'm hoping that won't happen two nights in a row."

"Around here, you never know. But I'd love to try again."

"Good." He kissed her quickly, because the last thing he wanted to do was leave her. "I'll see you tomorrow."

Veronica walked him to the door, a little worried by his perfunctory kiss. Maybe he *had* been upset about the boys.

COLETTE, SHEA, VERONICA and her younger charges lined the walk to Rachel's cottage as the Blazer arrived.

The children held up a Welcome Home banner, and Colette waved a bouquet of flowers. Veronica knew Shea made his own get-well gift, preparing several days' worth of meals and putting them in Rachel's freezer. There was a fresh sparkle to Rachel, Veronica noted, and, apparently, a change in the way she viewed Armand. The older woman seemed to have difficulty taking her eyes off him.

Mike and Armand supported Rachel on either side as she walked up the steps to her cottage, but it was Armand who eased her into a chair and brought her the afghan from the back of the sofa.

She accepted his ministrations with a new docility. Veronica couldn't decide whether to be pleased or alarmed. Though she was sure Rachel and Armand would be happy together, she couldn't help but wonder if Rachel's health scare had made her feel vulnerable and unwilling to fight for herself.

Armand stood over Rachel's chair. "Remember

what the doctor said. Only mild exercise. No running
up and down the stairs. No making twelve dozen
cookies and standing for hours in front of the stove.
No getting up at five a.m. to cook for the B-and-B.
You have to take it easy for a couple of days.''

Rachel sighed patiently. "You act as though I
wasn't there. I heard everything he said.''

"But will you listen? That's the question.''

"I'll listen. Now, you'd better be on your way to
the vineyard. I'm sure you and Colette have lots to
do.''

Armand smiled at his daughter. "Already she's
tiring of me." He turned back to Rachel. "Is there
anything I can get you before I go?''

"No, thank you." Then she raised her arms, and
he bent down, and they kissed—a sweet but long kiss
that made the adults look at each other in surprise
and the children giggle. "Oh, yes there is!" Rachel
reconsidered when the kiss ended. "Can someone get
my animals from the Ledbetters?''

"Mike and I'll do that," Shea promised. "Tate's
sorry he couldn't be here, by the way. He's supervising things in the vineyard this morning.''

"Of course." She made shooing motions toward
everyone. "Thank you all for welcoming me home.
I missed you terribly. Now go about your business
and stop worrying about me. I've got my medicine
now, and I'll be fine.''

Armand leaned on the back of her chair. "Isn't
there something else you'd like to tell them?" he
asked.

She smiled with shy embarrassment. "I'm sure they're all anxious to get back to—"

"We are getting married," Armand interrupted. "As soon as she's gotten a little rest."

Before anyone could say a word of congratulations, Rachel said, "We're getting married because I realized in the hospital—when Armand held my hand for twenty-four hours—that it wasn't that I didn't want my independence challenged by a man. Instead, I'd settled into a somewhat lackluster but comfortable life without having to be there for someone."

Shea took issue with her. "You're always there for us."

She smiled. "That's a pleasure. But for a husband, a woman has to be there virtually every moment, and I remembered how difficult and demanding that could be." She reached for Armand's hand and held it to her cheek. "What I'd never had a chance to see in my first marriage was how much that effort is reduced when someone is always there for *you*."

"Amen," Mike said, squeezing Veronica to him.

MIKE WALKED VERONICA and the children back to the day care center.

"I'm happy for Rachel and Armand," she said on the way. "They're going to be so happy."

"I'm sure they will," he agreed, stopping abruptly as Alissa squatted in front of him to pluck a dandelion.

The child held it up toward him. "Smell!" she commanded.

He leaned down to comply. "Smells like dirt."

She frowned and sniffed it herself. "How come it doesn't smell pretty?" She was clearly disappointed. "Flowers are supposed to."

"This one's a weed," he explained. "But it's pretty neat because when it dries, it gets all this fuzzy stuff you can make a wish on."

She nodded, then handed it to him. "It should still smell good." And she scampered off toward the playground where the other children had gathered.

Mike laughed, then tucked the dandelion behind Veronica's ear. "Seven o'clock tonight?"

"I'll be ready," she promised.

CHAPTER SEVENTEEN

BY MID-AFTERNOON, construction paper leaves were in full production, and paper, crayons and markers were strewn the length and breadth of the day care's play area. They planned Halloween costumes while they worked, and talked about Indians and pilgrims.

"Ross is gonna get a motorcycle!" Ronnie cut out an oak leaf with blunt-edged scissors. "I forget what kind."

"A Harley like Mike's," Ross shouted from the nap room. "Only a big black one!"

Ross and Ricky were having a time-out for putting crayon shavings into the milk during snack. Ross's explanation had been simple. "White is so boring."

"It won't kill ya." Ricky defended his brother's actions and his own collusion. "I eat crayons all the time."

Veronica was about to tell the boys they could come out, when the barn door opened and a man, wearing a blue jacket over work pants and a chambray shirt walked in.

Veronica looked up from supervising Ronnie's coloring, and mistook the man for a worker from the vineyard who'd found himself in the wrong building.

"Can I help you?" she asked, walking toward

him. As she drew closer, she noticed beautiful but troubled green eyes and a nervous manner, which made her instantly uncomfortable.

Then she heard a small gasp from Andy. He sat back on his heels in front of the coffee table, pencil in hand. He looked both pleased and worried.

Her heart beat double-time as she realized who this man must be.

His eyes went to the boy, and his face split with a bright smile at odds with the troubled eyes. "Andy," he whispered, and started toward him.

Veronica stepped quickly between them and offered her hand. She hoped he wouldn't notice it was shaking. "Mr. Moore," she said with a smile. "I'm Veronica Callahan."

The man looked at her hand, then into her face, his expression unreadable. He turned abruptly and walked back toward the door.

As he did, she grabbed Andy's arm and pulled him to her.

"That's my dad," Andy said in a small voice. "But I'm not ever supposed to go with him."

"I know."

Andy's father pushed the door closed and locked it. Then he turned to Veronica.

She felt everything inside her go cold as he came toward her and Andy. As calmly as she could, she pushed Andy toward the other children. They were all watching her, their lively intuitions detecting trouble.

"I'd like you all to go into the nap room," she said firmly.

"No!" the man shouted. The children jumped.

Veronica faced him, trying to look fierce. She found it difficult, with everything inside her trembling. "You're intruding on this class, Mr. Moore," she said. Then, without breaking eye contact, she repeated, "Children, go into the nap room."

"No!"

Spencer and Claudine began to cry. Moore seemed to regret that.

"The other children can go," he said more quietly. "I just want my son."

Veronica shook her head. "I'm sorry, Mr. Moore, but I can't let you have him."

"I'm his *father!*"

She managed not to flinch. "I know. But I can't let anyone except his mother pick him up. It's one of the rules."

"His mother doesn't understand."

"What doesn't she understand?"

He swallowed and said in a strained voice, "That he's all I have left. I have no job, no wife, no friends…" He stopped and cleared his throat. "I can live without them, but not without my son. Now, let me have him."

"I can't, Mr. Moore," she insisted, backing up with Andy as the man came threateningly closer.

He pulled a gun out of his jacket pocket, aimed it directly at her face, and said softly, "Oh, I think you can."

Of course. She should have seen this coming. It was a pattern in her life. Wrong mother. Wrong path. Wrong man.

And even when it looked as if the wrong man had decided he might be the right one, she ended up being in the wrong place at the wrong time.

She drew a ragged breath and thought that while that was all true, it wasn't important. All she could worry about was Andy's safety. She was all that stood between the boy and his dangerously troubled father.

"I'm sorry, but you're wrong," she said. "Because I care about him, too. And I'm not going to give him to someone carrying a gun, even if you are his father. You might not like it, but that's the way it is."

Big talk. Especially since he seemed to be thinking about calling her bluff.

"I CAN'T SAY FOR CERTAIN what the harvest will be," Tate said. He stood in a corner of the B-and-B's kitchen, refusing a chair at the table where Mike and Shea sat; he was dirty from the vineyard. "We reevaluate with every load that comes in. But it looks pretty big." He toasted Shea with his coffee cup. "And thanks to our brilliant little brother, the restaurant's exceeding everyone's expectations. We should think about adding on a banquet room somewhere. We get requests for banquets all the time."

"We were going to use the upstairs for extra

rooms for the B-and-B," Shea said. "Maybe we should put a banquet room up there."

"I don't know. The B-and-B's full most of the time, too. We'll have to—"

"Mike? *Mike!*"

Mike got up from the table when he saw Ross James burst through the door. "Ross! What is it?" he asked, hurrying toward the boy.

"There's a—a m-man at the d-day care…with a—with a gun!"

"*What?*"

"Andy's dad, I think." He paused to gulp in air. "He wants to take Andy and—and Veronica won't let him. I got out the window in the nap room."

Mike swore his blood froze. "Are all the other children still inside?"

Ross nodded.

Shea was already at the phone, and Tate was running for the door.

"Tate!" Mike's command stopped his brother. He pointed Ross toward a kitchen chair. "You stay right here until someone comes for you."

"Okay."

Mike passed Tate on his way outside. "You let me handle this," he said as they ran toward the barn. "We can't do this wrong. You get the kids out of the nap room. I'll handle Andy's father."

Mike expected an argument, but Tate only said, "Be careful."

Mike tried the doorknob carefully, though he knew

it would be locked. He inserted his key and opened the door.

The sight that greeted him was enough to liquify his bones. Andy sat quietly on the sofa, skinny legs sticking stiffly out, eyes wide and frightened. Facing him was a tall man who stood behind Veronica, one hand clutching a fistful of her jumper, the other holding a 9mm Smith & Wesson to her right temple.

Mike saw the desperation and the plea in her eyes as he approached.

He couldn't look at her and think at the same time. He fixed his eyes on Andy's father and pretended ignorance. "What's going on?" he asked mildly, holding his arms out to indicate harmlessness. "I'm here to see Veronica. What're you doing?"

The man pointed the gun toward the sofa. "I just came for Andy. Sit down!"

"You came for Andy with a gun? Why don't you put it away before you hurt him?"

"He's mine. I'd never hurt him!"

Mike gestured toward Veronica. "Well, she's mine. Put the gun away before you hurt her."

"She won't let me have him!"

"Well, I don't understand how she can stop you when you have the gun." He glimpsed the look of confusion on Veronica's face, but ignored it, concentrating on the man. "Oh, I see," he said after a moment. "It's because you won't shoot her to get him, isn't it? Because you're not a killer. You're just a guy who wants his kid. What's your name, anyway?"

As he talked, Mike tried to figure out whether Tate had had enough time to get all the children out yet.

The man shook his head. "I'm not looking for a buddy, okay. I came for my kid. My wife has a restraining order against me, and I can't even *see* him. So, I'm going to take him. Now, get over there against the wall and stay out of my way!"

Mike took several small, slow steps in that direction. "Why don't you have Andy wait for you outside? The door's unlocked."

Moore considered the suggestion, then looked suspicious. "Why?" he demanded. "Who's out there?"

Mike calmly shook his head. "No one. Everybody's working in the vineyard. Let Andy go outside."

He sensed Veronica watching him, probably trying to figure out what he was up to.

A slight thump came from the direction of the nap room.

"What was that?" Moore backed up nervously, dragging Veronica with him, but he kept a careful eye on Mike.

"Only the children," Veronica said quickly. "They're probably playing."

He waved the gun at Mike. "Open the door."

Mike shook his head. "Do you want to scare them? Just like you're scaring your son?"

The man's breathing was growing shallow. He turned to Andy. "He's not afraid of me. Are you, son?"

"No," Andy replied hesitantly.

The man turned to Mike triumphantly. "See?"

"But I'm afraid of the gun," Andy added. Then he stood up and went to his father. "Don't point it at Veronica. I really like her. I'll come with you, Daddy."

Moore was visibly shaken by Andy's plea. "Will you?" He pushed Veronica gently away from him. "There. I won't hurt her. I promise."

Mike pointed her to the nap room. "Go check on the children."

But Veronica had plans of her own. She tried to catch Andy's hand to take him with her, but Moore leveled the gun at her again.

Mike stepped between them, just as Moore cocked the pistol. Veronica screamed.

"No, Daddy!" Andy begged. "I was stuck on the roof before, and he helped me down. I like him, too."

"Why don't you give me the gun?" Mike's heart beat like a drum. He was amazed his brain continued to function. "Let's put it away so you don't keep scaring Andy. Then maybe we can work on a legal way for you to get to see him."

Moore was shaking, and his bottom lip was beginning to quiver. Mike pressed his advantage. "Come on. If the court found out you came for Andy with a gun, you'd never get to see him."

Over Moore's shoulder, Mike saw the nap room door opening slowly, Tate moving into the doorway, Shea behind him.

"Daddy," Andy pleaded, beginning to cry. "Please don't hurt anybody, Daddy."

Mike put a tentative hand to Moore's shoulder, and with his index finger surreptitiously pointed his brothers to a stop.

"I just want to see you, Andy," Moore said, his own face crumpling. "That's all. Just see you."

With his free hand, Mike took the gun from Moore's unresisting grip.

"All I wanted was to see him." He began to sob. "She moved away. She wouldn't let me visit. She said I scared her."

Mike handed the gun to Tate and heard sirens in the distance. Moore sagged against him, and Mike held him, completely able to relate to a loss that made a man crazy.

ONCE IT WAS OVER, Mike wanted to talk to Veronica. But she was busy trying to calm a hysterical Delia Moore. And when the police had finally taken away all three Moores, Veronica had to deal with the panicking parents who arrived to find ambulances on the playground.

After the children were gone, he and Veronica talked to the police. He watched as she answered questions and saw no sign of delayed shock. Still, he wished everyone would go away so he could just take her in his arms.

Darkness had fallen when Father Wolff drove into the compound, passing the last police car on its way out.

"Is everyone all right?" he asked as he hurried to join the Delanceys in front of the barn. "I just heard what happened."

Tate put an arm around Mike's shoulders. "Thankfully Mike was here. Pays to have a hostage negotiator in the family."

"Veronica's the one who wouldn't give Andy up," Mike said, turning, only to find that she was nowhere to be seen. She'd been doing that to him for the past two hours—beside him one minute, gone the next.

He didn't know what that meant, but before his family could start to interfere, he pointed to the other side of the compound. "Pizza at the house! Shea, can you order? Or do you have to be at the restaurant?"

Shea shook his head. "It's Charlie's night. I'll take care of it."

"Okay. I'll round up Veronica and be right there." Mike watched as his large—safe—family headed off. They'd been so lucky.

Once again, he remembered the crisis at the farmhouse, and then he closed his eyes and it was gone, relegated to a place where he kept things he couldn't fix and couldn't change.

He strode to the barn and was about to go in when he heard a low sound from the playground. He turned and saw Veronica sitting at the top of the slide, barely gilded by the outside light.

He went to stand at the bottom of the slide, knowing, somehow, that there was more wrong than what had happened this afternoon. Yet, he felt a curious inner peace when he realized he loved her too much to let anything keep them apart any longer.

"You coming down?" he asked. "Shea's ordering pizza."

"I was thinking," she said quietly. Her voice wobbled, as though she was holding back tears. "That—that you'll want to reconsider."

"No," he said. "I really want pizza."

"No," she said. "I mean reconsider us."

"No," he said. "I really want us, too."

And then she did cry, deep gulping sobs that made him feel helpless—and frustrated when he couldn't reach her. He finally climbed the ladder and wrapped his arms around her from behind.

"What?" he asked. "What is it? I know how scary that was. But it's okay. Andy's okay. All the other kids are okay. Even Moore will probably be okay."

That only made her cry harder. He held her more tightly. "Vee, I don't understand. You're going to have to tell me what's wrong."

"Everything's wrong! It happened again! Just like the roof, only worse. Like—like the farmhouse. When you're with me, everything you don't want happens to you!" She sobbed so hard she couldn't talk, and all he could do was hold her. "I kept telling you to put the past behind you, that it was over, that you had to get on with your life. But I didn't know what it was *like!* To be so helpless. I was so stupid!

I can't imagine what it must have been like for you. I can't stop thinking about it.''

"First of all—" he turned her slightly so she had to face him "—you weren't helpless. You were strong and you did all the right things. You wouldn't let him have Andy. You put yourself in danger to protect him.''

"But, I forced you to relive—"

"Yeah, but I've finally come to terms with it, I think. Up to now, I'd been defined by something terrible, something painful. but that changed the day I met you. You make me happy and hopeful and eager to see what tomorrow brings.''

She seemed pleased by that, but mystified as well. "I do?''

"You do. In fact...'' He delved into his pants pocket and produced the small square jeweler's box he'd been carrying around since last night.

She took it in the palm of her hand, stared at it for a moment, then covered it with her other hand until it was no longer visible. Mike decided that was not very promising body language.

When she began to cry anew, he felt a stab of fear worse than anything he'd felt inside the barn.

"Now I'm worried about what you used to worry about. If we have children...'' In a quick aside, she asked, "Would you even *want* children?''

"Most definitely.''

"Then...how will we keep them safe? When I was a counselor, we had all kinds of people who could intervene if there was a problem of abuse or neglect—but this..."

He struggled to think of a reasonable reply. "We'll teach them to be smart and to be careful. Sometimes we'll just have to be brave and let them out into the world to experience it. And other times, we'll lock them in and watch them like hawks. We'll just do the best we can."

"That seems so—flimsy."

He nodded. "I know. But maybe with your goodness and my skepticism, we'll be able to make it work."

She looked into his eyes, and he watched hers soften and melt. "You were wonderful this afternoon," she said, making him feel humble and shamelessly proud all at once. "I had no idea what to do, and you just kept talking until you made him see he really didn't want to hurt anyone. I hated for you to be in danger, but I was never so glad to see anyone in my life."

"I only did what had to be done. I'm happy I still can."

She looked a little concerned. "Do you want to go back to police work, now that you know you can?"

He drew in a deep breath of the delicious air and thought about what he and Tate and Shea had created in the past nine months. He shook his head.

"No. This is home for me now. But you haven't answered me. Is this home for you, too?"

"Yes," she replied, wrapping her arms around his

neck. "this is where I want to be! You're sure, though? You really want to get married and have children?"

He held her close. "I'm sure. And I'll be delirious when I can finally help you with Step Five."

AS FOUR LARGE PIZZAS steamed aromatically in the center of the table, Father Wolff reached for Armand's hand on his left and Megan's hand on his right to offer grace. Everyone joined hands to form a circle.

He blessed the food and said a prayer of thanks for Rachel's recovery, and for keeping everyone safe during the afternoon's crisis.

But before they began to eat, the telephone rang. Colette went to the kitchen as Shea started to serve. She was back in a minute, a questioning smile on her face. "Shea, it's for you," she said. "Samantha Haskell from San Francisco."

Conversation came to a halt around the table. Shea stiffened, then took Katie's plate and made a production of giving her a slice of sausage-and-pepperoni pizza. "Would you tell her I'm not here, please?" he asked.

Katie accepted her plate with a frown. "But that's a lie, Uncle Shea." Then she whispered loudly, "And Father Wolff's here!"

Shea looked at Colette. "Then please tell her I won't come to the phone."

"And what reason would I give?" Colette was clearly displeased.

"She knows the reason."

Colette spun on her heel and went back into the kitchen.

Mike leaned toward Shea, who sat on the other side of Veronica. "I'm here to tell you, brother, that you have to deal with unfinished business. You can go away—but it won't."

Shea looked as if he would react angrily to Mike's interference. But he smiled instead and toasted him with his glass of cola. "It's a night for celebration, not philosophy. To the Delanceys, and all who ride with them."

Everyone's glass went up.

Colette returned from the kitchen and lifted her glass belatedly. "And to Samantha Haskell, whoever she is," she said, "because she's apparently going to have to ride alone."

HARLEQUIN®
SUPERROMANCE®

From July to September 1999—three special
Superromance® novels about people whose
New Millennium resolution is

By the Year 2000: CELEBRATE!

JULY 1999—*A Cop's Good Name* by Linda Markowiak
Joe Latham's only hope of saving his badge and his reputation is
to persuade lawyer Maggie Hannan to take his case. Only Maggie—
his ex-wife—knows him well enough to believe him.

AUGUST 1999—*Mr. Miracle* by Carolyn McSparren
Scotsman Jamey McLachlan's come to Tennessee to keep the
promise he made to his stepfather. But Victoria Jamerson stands
between him and his goal, and hurting Vic is the last thing he wants
to do.

SEPTEMBER 1999—*Talk to Me* by Jan Freed
To save her grandmother's business, Kara Taylor has to co-host a
TV show with her ex about the differing points of view between men
and women. A topic Kara and Travis know plenty about.

**By the end of the year,
everyone will have something to celebrate!**

HARLEQUIN®
Makes any time special ™

HARLEQUIN®

SUPERROMANCE

Welcome to Hope Springs, Virginia, a town where you can leave your doors and your hearts open, where people are friendly and children play safely. The kind of place you'd be proud to call home.

June 1999—ALL-AMERICAN BABY (#845)
by Peg Sutherland

Heiress Melina Somerset is pregnant and on the run. Hope Springs, Virginia, looks like an ideal place to make a life for herself and her unborn child. The townspeople are friendly and don't ask too many questions. So her secret's safe—unless Ash Thorndyke stays around long enough to find out she's going to have his child.

The newest title in the **Hope Springs** series by popular author Peg Sutherland.

Look for the next installment in the **Hope Springs** series in early 2000.

HARLEQUIN®
Makes any time special ™

HARLEQUIN®
SUPERROMANCE

IN UNIFORM

THERE'S SOMETHING SPECIAL ABOUT A *WOMAN* IN UNIFORM!

WINTER SOLDIER #841
by Marisa Carroll

When Lieutenant Leah Gentry—soldier and nurse—went overseas as part of a team that provided medical care for those in need, she expected long days and hard work. What she *didn't* expect was to fall for Dr. Adam Sauder—*or* to become pregnant with his child.

Watch for *Winter Soldier* in June 1999 wherever Harlequin books are sold.

HARLEQUIN®
Makes any time special ™